Tempted

Qiana Rae

Princess of Erotica Books

Princess of Erotica Books

Cover Design: SelfPubBookCovers.com/Lori

ISBN: 978-0-9916187-4-3

Dedication

I dedicate this book to all of my family, teachers, and true friends who realized my talent even before I did. You inspired me to pursue my dreams.

Love,
Qiana Rae

Table of Contents

V

Acknowledgments

First and foremost, I must thank my Lord and Savior Jesus Christ for giving me the strength and endurance to work a full-time nine-to-five job, go home and tend to my duties as a wife and mother of two, and still find time to put my heart and soul into my passion for writing. Without HIM, my talent would be non-existent, therefore, this first novel that HE has given me the courage to publish, would also not exist. I praise HIM on a daily basis for all past, present, and future blessings because I know this is only the beginning.

I definitely can't forget about my wonderful husband, Devon, whom I love to pieces! You have been awesome during this exciting, yet sometimes, nerve wrecking time in my life. You put up with me through it all, even way before this new venture of mine. I personally feel sorry for you sometimes, but you're a lucky man! (*Smile*) To know me is to love me! I appreciate you for being there when I pulled those all-nighters, when we both still had to get up bright and early to go to our "regular" jobs. I also love you for being there to calm me down during those frustrating moments. You are absolutely correct when you say that I am my worst critic!

My two loving children, Darryon and Ariana, inspire me to work hard and strive for nothing but the best, so that I can continue to be a positive role model for them and instill in them those same important values. Thank you both for loving me so much, and no, Darryon, you still can't read Mommy's book, but I'll give you a copy of just this page! I am so blessed and thankful to have two smart, intelligent, thoughtful, and handsome (Darryon) / beautiful (Ariana) children. I don't have any doubts that both of you will make me very proud. Love you always!

My big sis, Teuwuna, has always been supportive of me and my dreams, no matter how big. You and Granny G (RIH) were both always firm believers in the saying, "You can do anything you put your mind to". Thanks for the constant reminder. I love you!

I thank my parents, Pat and Michael for coming together to help create me, if nothing else good came out of the situation! Just consider me your constant reminder that you both learned a lot from each other! You both helped mold me into the God-fearing, independent, intelligent, humble, and sometimes sassy, young Black woman I am today. You ought to be proud!

My step-dad, Greg has also been a part of my life for over half my life, so of course, he also had some positive influence over my life. I know it wasn't easy early on having a stepdaughter like me, but we made it through!

Everyone else, friends, family, frenemies, enemies, or whatever else you may be to me, I am and will forever be thankful for you as well. I am a firm believer that everyone comes into your life for a reason, a season, or a lifetime. Whether we had a good or bad experience, it was just that . . . An experience that we should grow and learn from. So just know, if you are, or have ever been a part of my life, you have been a positive influence in one way or another.

To all my readers, thank you, thank you, and thank you for supporting me, and I'm looking forward to being your new favorite author.

Peace and Many Blessings,
Qiana Rae

Chapter 1: July 21, 2012

I was in my last hours of being Kelicia Armstrong. The day I had been waiting for for what seemed to be forever had finally approached. I had been engaged once and almost engaged countless times. Let me stress the fact that I'm only twenty-three. But shit, what else does a twenty-three-year-old have to do besides look for that special brother she'll spend the rest of her life with? My ex-fiancé, Jaleel, who was my first love, broke my heart. I found out he was engaged to somebody else at the same time he was supposed to be engaged to me. I thought I'd never get over that one, but life goes on. I'm living proof of that. I finally found the man of my dreams. The man who made me forget all about my drama with Jaleel and made made me feel like the bad ass woman that I am. His name was Terrance. I could see the envy in all the women's faces when they watched us walk side by side.He had everything goin' for him. He was six feet four and two hundred twenty pounds of chocolate indulgence. He also had a head on his shoulders, unlike a lot of men around here who just went around looking for a woman to take care of their broke asses. For the moment, he was just working part time at the bank to get by until he finished law school in the fall. I was a hairstylist at Hair Haven beauty salon, which was near the bank where he worked, so we would go to lunch together on the regular. I didn't think that we would ever get this serious, for the simple fact that we met at a club when I was just out lookin' to have a good time with my girls. I met plenty of men in clubs who were cool to chill with but just not marriage material. We would chill together, talk, and get to know each other . . . Just when you think you're feeling the dude, then comes that uncomfortable moment when he tells you he has six kids with three baby mamas! I definitely didn't go for that! I didn't have any kids, so why in the hell would I take care of somebody else's?!?! I especially didn't want to have to deal with these crazy-ass baby mamas out there today!

Well, Terrance stopped me in my tracks. Sometimes I think it was for the good because there ain't no tellin' what I'd be doin' right now if somebody wouldn't have stopped me. Especially with the friends that I have! I was pretty wild, but who isn't at that age? I know it's time for me to get married before someone else snatches up my goods! All my friends keep tellin' me not to do it. That's because they like to run the streets and get fucked by every man that gives them a little compliment. That may sound harsh, but sometimes the truth hurts. They're a lot wilder than I was, but that's another story.

Bam! Bam! Bam!

"Who the hell is banging at my door? I just went to sleep!"

"Kellie! Open up this door! You do not have all day to get ready for this thing!"

This thing? Shit, the wedding! It was my momma at the door, taking charge as always. It was already eleven o'clock, and I hadn't even gotten my hair done yet. I slowly opened the door, unprepared to hear her shit.

"Why didn't you come earlier? You know I needed to get my black butt up!"

"Well, baby doll, if you didn't know, most women are too excited to sleep the night before their wedding. Let alone, on their wedding day, but yo fast tail was probably out in them streets with them heifas that ain't never gonna have no man!" my momma said sarcastically with her finger pointing and head bobbing from side to side.

My mother never did really like any of my friends. Maybe I shouldn't say she didn't like them. She just didn't trust them. Every friend that I ever had, she claimed, was jealous of me because of my good looks that she said I got from her. Imagine that! If they were jealous, I couldn't blame 'em, but not every friend I had was like that. I was a pretty good judge of character, and upon first meeting a person, I would closely watch and listen to everything they did and said so I could read what type of person they really were. If I wasn't feelin' their vibe, they could forget about, in any way, being a part of my minute circle. My momma always told me how I always needed to keep my guards up when it came to these "scandalous-ass women." She never believed in having female friends, only associates.

"Ma, I didn't even go out last night, but I did stay up late because I was so excited. By the time I did go to sleep, it was time to wake up."

"Good, well, you need to get those girls together to make sure they don't come walking down the aisle lookin' like some damn fools, 'cause you know they will. Call them and tell them to bring over all their stuff so we can take it down to the church. Y'all can get ready there. I DO NOT want them to have those dresses on before they get to the church!"

My momma always had to run stuff, but everything always got done as long as she was in charge, so I wasn't complaining. Just as I was pickin' up the phone, it rang.

"If that ain't part of your wedding party, you tell them you gotta call them back after your honeymoon 'cause you do not have time to be messin' around."

"Hello?"

"Hey, girl," Tasha said in a solemn tone.

"Tasha? What's wrong?" I asked worriedly.

Tasha was my maid of honor. We had been best friends for about ten years. She was pretty far out there, but she was still my girl. We were the type of friends that would cuss each other out, and five minutes later be huggin', and cryin' on each other's shoulders.

"I was just about to call you," I said.

"Today is not my day. I was takin' that big-ass ugly dress you picked out for me to my car, and it slid out the plastic and fell right in the damn water. You know it rained last night!"

I took a deep breath and said, "First of all, the dress ain't ugly, and second of all, what the hell are you gonna do? The wedding is in a few hours and you don't have a dress!"

"Who is that, girl? Who don't got no dress?" my momma asked, looking like she was ready to grab the phone away from my ear.

"Wait a minute, Ma. Now, Tasha . . ."

"Tasha! How the hell that heifa ain't got no dress!"

"Ma, wait!" I shouted, walking in the opposite direction of my momma, knowing she'd slap me any minute!

"Kel, do you think they'll take it back at the store and give me another one?" Tasha asked naively.

"How slow are you? You had alterations done on that dress! Do you think they gon' take it back? Hell naw! You need to get a blow-dryer and make that dress look as good as you can! Then get yo ass over here so we can go to this church before something else happens. I'll see you in an hour."

"Whateva, girl," Tasha said, as if she was the one with an attitude.

I slammed down the phone.

"Ahhhhhh!"

"Now don't you tell me to wait no more. What happened to that girl's dress?"

"She dropped it outside in the water."

"In the water? Yeah right. She probably did it on purpose just to irritate you on your day. She probably tryin' to sabotage your wedding. You know all your so-called girls are jealous of you anyway. Don't even let that bother you."

"Whatever, Ma. Now I need to call Tiffany and Briana."

They were my bridesmaids. I shouldn't have had to worry about Tiffany, because she had her shit together most of the time, but she had been acting unusually disturbed and careless lately. Almost like she didn't have much respect for herself anymore. I just took it as she was going through some things, like we all do at different times in our lives. Briana, on the other hand, was a little irresponsible when it came to anything outside of runnin' the streets. I had to go with her to make sure she bought her dress and shoes because if I hadn't, my day would've been here, and she wouldn't have had shit.

She was very immature. In my opinion, her immaturity came from her being the only the child. I was the only child too, but my momma taught me to be independent and very responsible. I called Tif first. Her voice mail came on.

"Hey, Tif. Call me as soon as you get this message. I need to make sure everyone's on the same page. I'll try your cell."

I called her cell phone, and Tif answered the phone, sounding like she was still asleep.

"Tif, where are you?"

"Kellie? Oh, I'm over Bruce's house."

"Who? Who is Bruce?"

"This real cool dude I met up at the Escalade last night."

"Are you stupid? You went home with some dude you met at a club? Please tell me you don't have a hangover. Please!"

"Just a little one. I only had a few shots of Patron and a vodka and cranberry."

"Look, I have to be at the beauty shop at twelve-thirty. Have . . . what's his name take you home and I'll be there to pick you up around eleven-forty-five and bring you over my house with my momma."

"OK. I'll see if he'll take me."

What else can possibly go wrong? Is this a sign? By the time I get everyone else together, I'm not gonna feel like having a wedding. I thought this was the reason I went through all those months of preparation, but I guess that shit didn't matter. I was about to throw some clothes on when I heard Beyoncé's "Ego." It was my phone ringing.

"Hello?"

"Hey, Kel. I was just callin' to let you know I'm on my way."

"All right, Bri. Make sure you have everything."

While I was on the phone with Bri, I decided to ask her to help me out. "Oh, can you do me a favor?"

"What's up?"

"Can you go pick up Tif for me from her house?"

"What's wrong wit her car?"

"She got a hangover. The last thing I need is for one of my bridesmaids to be in an accident."

"That girl is crazy. OK. I'll see you in a few."

"Thanks, girl."

The person who I thought wouldn't come through for me was the only person who was acting like they had some damn sense. I found something to put on real quick. Just some sweats and a T-shirt. It really didn't matter cuz I knew I would be the shit in a few hours and nobody would be able to tell me nothin'. I walked around my apartment, looking for my momma so that I could tell her I was about to leave.

"Ma. Momma!"

"What, girl? Did you get those girls together?"

"Yeah. They should be here in a little while, but I gotta go get my hair done."

"What kind of beautician . . . I mean hairstylist don't do their own hair? That just don't make no kind of sense to me. If I knew how to do hair, my hair would be sharp every time somebody saw me!"

I snickered at my momma for correcting herself when she called me a beautician. I preferred people to call me a hairstylist because it sounded much more professional, and hey, it is my profession!

"Ma, can you just keep your opinions to yourself sometimes?"

Before she was able to answer, I said, "You know what, never mind. Forget I asked that stupid question. Just do me a favor and hold things down while I'm gone."

"Just make sure they don't have you there all day. You can't be makin' that man wait for you."

"I'll just meet y'all at the church."

I grabbed my dress and my other bag of accessories and gave my momma a kiss. "Love you, Momma."

"OK, baby. I'll see you in a little bit."

Chapter 2

When I pulled up at the beauty shop, the parking lot was packed. I figured as much, especially with it being Saturday. All the chickenheads had to get their wigs laid to hit the hottest clubs in the Chi this weekend. I walked in the shop at 12:25, and the couches and salon chairs were full of clients. I got furious when I saw a woman sitting in Phelecia's chair with her hair half done. Phelecia was supposed to be doing my hair today, and she knew I had to be on time. No way in hell was I gonna let this girl make me late for my wedding.
I looked over at Sabrina, another stylist in the shop, and said, "Where the hell is Phelecia?" "I think she went in the bathroom."

I walked to the back where the bathroom was, and a woman who had barely enough hair to curl walked out. Then I turned around and saw that the back door was open. I went outside and saw this bitch out there smoking a damn cigarette.

"Phelecia, if you don't get yo butt in here so you can do my hair, I'm gonna kick your cigarette-smokin'-while-you're-pregnant ass!"

Phelecia was only a month pregnant, but I couldn't stand it when women smoked when they knew they were pregnant.

"Oh, girl, I just needed a stress reliever. You know I'm goin' through a lot right now."

"I understand that, but I'm getting married in two and a half hours, and I need your undivided attention in my head right now."

"OK, girl." She threw her cigarette down in the dirt and put it out with her worn-out Reebok. I couldn't understand how a person could be making all this money doin' hair and couldn't afford to buy a new pair of kicks. Phelecia was my coworker though, and she was cool most of the time. She just had a lot of issues with men. She wasn't bad looking, but wasn't fine neither. She was tall, thin, and caramel-complected like me with a cute, short haircut that she wore spiked. She just let men run over her and always felt she was at fault when they left her knocked up or beat her ass. I had known Phelecia in high school, and she hadn't always been that way. Everyone always knew her as being conceited and wouldn't take shit from nobody. I didn't know what happened to her within the past five years, but she was not herself.

Phelecia was finishing up the lady's hair that was sitting in her chair. I looked up at the clock. It was twelve-fifty-five. I was getting so nervous. Not about getting my hair done, but about getting married.

"So Kellie, are you ready for this, girl?" a country, shrieky voice said from behind me.

I looked back. It was Rhonda, the salon owner. She was struggling, trying to put some twisties in this little girl's hair. The little girl was frowning, trying to get her hair out of Rhonda's grip.

I hesitated a little when I said it, but I said, "Yeah. I feel like this is it. I love this man, and I don't think anyone can love me more than he does."

I knew Terrance was a good man, and I probably would never find anyone better than him, but I sometimes thought that it was all too good to be true. I wondered if I was just being paranoid, pondering so much about what I did to deserve such a wonderful man in my life, and whether or not all women went through this before their big day.

Then Cameron, one of the older hairdressers, jumped in. "That all sounds real nice, Kel, but that's how it always is at first, baby. They love you to death until they see a better model. Then they kick yo ass to the curb. Nowadays men are so good at lyin'. They can make you believe anything. They always sound and look so damn sincere, when all they're thinkin' about is getting' with their side chick later on that night."

Cameron was thirty-seven. She had already been married three times. The first time, she caught her husband fuckin' her best friend. She caught her second husband fuckin' her sister and her third husband fuckin' her friend, Aaron. Yes, Aaron was a man, but a pretty-ass man! I just thought maybe since she was older, she needed to learn some of us young girls' tricks in the bed. She did get me to thinking about my past experiences with men. I was in deep thought.

"Kel. Kel! Come on, girl. You wanna rush me! You betta bring your butt on and get in this chair!" I went and plopped down in Phelecia's chair. I pulled out my custom-made tiara to make sure it fit over whatever hairstyle I got.

"What do you want done with all this hair of yours?"

"Just give me a pretty updo. Something elegant. Not ghetto."

"Now you know I don't do ghetto." Everybody in the shop looked over at her like she was insane. Phelecia could do some hair. Not better than me, of course, but she also did some ghetto shit at times, like the time she put some purple hair in this chic's head, fingerwaved it, crimped the ends, then had the nerve to spray it with gold hairspray! That girl walked out of there like she was really doin' the damn thang and everybody burst out laughing when she walked out the door.

"How did you find one of the good ones?" Phelecia asked.

"What?" At first I thought she was talking about tiaras. She caught me off guard.

She said, "Good men, girl! How did you find one?"

"I don't know. I guess it was just luck because you can't find too many good men in the club. All they usually want is someone to take home that night and be done with it, and I thought Terrance was the same way when he first approached me, but he proved me wrong."

"I know, girl. Terrance is a very rare man. I bet he's the type that don't wanna go anywhere without you. That's the type of man I need. I get sick of wonderin' every time my man walks out the door—where he's goin' or who he's goin' to do. It drives me crazy, but I deal with it because he gets mad whenever I ask him where he's going."

"Phelecia, you know you deserve better than that. Why do you let men treat you like that? If he is supposedly your man, he should have no problem telling you where he's going! You shouldn't even have to worry when he's walking out the door. Trust is a must, girly."

Phelecia lowered her voice even lower than she had already been talking. "He loves, me and that's all that really matters. He's really a good person. You can't ask for too much out of a man. A man is going to be a man. I've learned that, and you should've learned that by now from all the heartbreaks you've had."

I had been scorned in the past, and it caused me a lot of pain, but I was not about to let Phelecia and all these other women get in my head. I knew that I had a good man, and that's all I needed to know.

Chapter 3

After I got my hair done, I was trying to hurry to get to the church. Traffic in Chicago on a Saturday is horrible. "Please, Lord, let these girls have their shit together." I had to get to this church, get dressed, and do my makeup. I pulled up to the church and ran in. It was decorated so beautifully. I found the dressing room where my momma and the girls were. My momma's loud voice led me right to it. "Tasha, now you know I ain't gon' let you walk down my baby's aisle with earrings in all ten of those holes in your ears lookin' crazy!"

They all listened to my momma, 'cause they knew she wasn't gonna shut up. When I walked in, my momma ran and gave me a hug.

"Hey, baby! Your hair looks so pretty!"

Phelecia had upset me a little with her comments, but she still hooked my hair up. I had long, silky jet-black hair that I got from my daddy, so it wasn't hard doing something pretty with it.

"Let's get you in this dress. You are gonna look gorgeous," my momma said, smiling from ear to ear with her freshly whitened teeth.

"Tasha, how did you do with the blow-dryer and your dress?" I asked.

"Girl, that shit . . ."

"Tasha, now you know better than cursing in the house of the Lord, or anytime I'm in your presence as far as I'm concerned! You just don't have any manners."

"I'm sorry Ms. Armstrong. Yeah, but it worked. You can't even tell."

I looked over at Tiffany. "Tif, you need something for your eyes 'cause they are redder than that lipstick you got on. Let me find you something, and wipe that lipstick off. I got something better." I walked past Bri as I went looking for my makeup bag.

"Briana, you look so pretty. I might have to black your eye. You can't be walking out there lookin' better than me!"

Briana laughed, but I wasn't playin'. Girl was lookin' good. Briana was dark-skinned with shoulder length hair that she wore in a silky bob. She had gorgeous dark chocolate skin that I was envious of. She was a gorgeous girl, but she let men run over her like the rest of my friends.

My mother left out the room for a few minutes, so I took the time to address Tiffany. "Tif, we gon' have to talk after all this is over. I think you need to slow down. I don't know what's happened to you, but I've never had to worry about you. You got me worried, girly."

"Girl, please. I'm not married and not getting married for a while, so I'm having fun while I can. I don't know how you gon' do this, but I wouldn't if I was you. We're too young to be tied down. This is our time to have fun and enjoy life. You have the rest of your life to get married."

"Look, I found me a good man. There aren't that many left out there. I hope you find one because I'm holdin' on to mine."

My mother walked back in. "Holdin' on to what?"

My momma was so nosey!

"My flowers. I was tellin' Tif to hold on to my flowers while I put my garter on."

"OK, well, they ready out there, so make sure you look good 'cause I know I do. How yo momma look, baby?"

"You look good, Ma."

My momma came and gave me a hug. She whispered in my ear, "You found you a good man. Hold on to him. He loves you so much."

A tear fell from my eye.

"Girl, don't mess up your makeup! It's not time to cry yet!" my momma said with a shaky voice, trying to hold back her tears.

"It's your fault. You makin' me all emotional."

My momma went to the door and opened it. "Come on, y'all. Let's take our fine butts out there. Kellie, you stay here until they tell you to come out."

"OK, Ma."

"Bye, baby."

As soon as my momma walked out the room, I got so nervous. I didn't know what to do. I almost started biting my nails until I realized they were acrylic. I knew I was doing the right thing. At least, that's what I kept tellin' myself.

I stood in the room for about five minutes by myself, then there was a knock on the door. It was my daddy with his fine self. It runs in the family. He had on a black tux with a white shirt and black tie. It matched his salt-and-pepper hair and goatee. My momma and daddy had gotten divorced when I was about thirteen. He was too much of a playa. He had never been faithful to my momma, so she finally got tired of it and gave up. They got along better now than they ever did when they were married.

"You ready, sweetheart?" he asked in his comforting voice.

"As ready as I'm gonna be."

He gave me a hug, and we slowly walked out to the closed double doors. I could hear my grand entrance song that I had chosen, and the doors began to open. The sound of Eric Benet and Tamia's voices singing "Spend My Life With You" put a lump in my throat so huge, I could hardly swallow. Everyone stood up and looked back at me. First I looked at the girls standing up there, and I thought, *What the hell was I thinking when I picked those ugly peach dresses?* Then I looked at Terrance's fine ass standing up there, staring and smiling at me, and it made me feel a whole lot better about those dresses and any doubts that I had. I couldn't hold back my tears any longer. I started crying, and not just a few tears here and there—I was crying hard! My momma stood up while I still walking down the aisle and wiped my face with a tissue she was obviously holding on to for herself.

She whispered, "Cry pretty, girl. Cry pretty!"

Tell me, how does a person cry pretty? I finally got to the altar, and Terrance grabbed my hand. He had tears in his eyes. In the two years we had been together, I had never seen him cry. He mouthed the words "I love you," and I did the same. It was such a good feeling standing up there with the man of my dreams, because I knew everything was being made official. He would now be the last person I would see before I went to sleep every night, and the first person I would wake up to every morning. We would share so many special moments together, learning something new about each other every day. We would grow old together, just as we were meant to.

When it was time to say our vows, Terrance shocked me. I didn't realize he had written his own.

He looked at me and took both my hands in his large hands and said, "Kellie, you're what I've been waiting for all my life. You're beautiful, smart, loyal, passionate, and everything else a man could possibly want in his wife. I know what other men have put you through, but I promise that I'll always be there for you no matter what, until death do us part. I always want you to be part of my life."

While he was saying his vows, I was reminiscing about the first time we met.

One Friday night, two years ago, my girls decided to take me out because I had been so depressed about my last breakup. My boyfriend of two years who had proposed to me six months prior to our breakup finally had gotten caught up. He felt like my soul mate, and it still ended disastrously. Jaleel seemed so sweet at first. He was always buying me something and always wanted to be around me. Then, it seemed like he got too comfortable. I had to ask him to come see me, and he wasn't romantic like he previously had been. My momma never liked him because she saw straight through him, and he knew it. I figured out that that was the reason he never came by when my momma was around. He didn't feel comfortable around her because he had to walk on eggshells. She deeply analyzed every word that came out of his mouth so he had to be very careful of what he said, and how he said it. Anyway, about a year and a half after we had been together, he came by my momma's house, where I was living at the time, and said it was important that he talked to me. My heart dropped because I knew what this meant . . . Another heartbreak for Kellie.

"What's wrong, Jaleel?"

"I just want you to know that I love you so much, and I think you already know that, but things ain't where I want them to be right now."

"Where do you want them to be? I try to spend as much time as I can with you. Baby, you know I'm in beauty school and working full-time, but I still manage to make time for you. I don't know what you want . . ." I saw Jaleel getting down on one knee, and I just started crying.

He looked up at me and said, "Baby, things ain't the way I want them to be because I want you to be completely mine. I wanna wake up next to you every morning. I've never felt like this about anyone in my life, but I love you so much, Kel. Will you please marry me?" I couldn't believe what had just happened. I was still in shock but managed to kneel down beside him.

I gave him a peck on the lips and said, "Yes. Yes, baby. I'll marry you."

It was the happiest time of my life, and I thought it was the happiest time of Jaleel's, but I found out how far from the truth that was about five and a half months later.

I had just begun working in the shop, so I didn't have a lot of clientele. One day I got tired of sittin' in my own chair, watching everybody else do hair, so I left early for the day and decided to go by Jaleel's apartment. I had practically moved in since our engagement. I pulled in the parking lot and went in the building. I didn't have to buzz in because Jaleel had given me my own key after he proposed. He told me he didn't have anything to hide from me, so I could come whenever I felt like it, even if he wasn't home. I went in the apartment and it was so dark. The blinds were closed, and the shades were drawn. I knew he was there because his car was in the parking lot, unless he had ridden with one of his boys somewhere.

"Jaleel." Maybe he wasn't home.

No one answered. I looked in the fridge to see what I could eat real quick, and then I heard music. I walked towards the bedroom and the door was cracked. I peeked in and saw this black, ugly-ass bitch ridin' the hell out of my man's dick. I didn't even say nothing. All I remember is jumping on that naked bitch's back and pulling about five tracks out of her head. I scared the shit out of both of them.

Jaleel grabbed me off of his tramp and said, "Kellie, what the fuck!"

"What you mean what the fuck?' I come home to find my fiancé fuckin' some other bitch in the bed that I sleep in almost every night, and all you can say is 'what the fuck?' What kind of shit is that?"

That bitch had the nerve to speak, with her skinny black ass.

She said, "Fiancé? What you mean fiancé? We've been engaged for almost a year!"

"A year! Jaleel, you betta change your locks because I'm gon' come in here and tear up the little bit of shit that you do got! Have a nice motherfuckin' life. You and this black-ass tramp!"

I walked out and left all my dignity behind. I was so embarrassed and so tired of men doggin' me that I had vowed I would never love again. Jaleel kept calling tryin' to apologize, but I couldn't give in like that, no matter how much I loved me some Jaleel. He had hurt me too badly.

A couple of weeks later was when my friends took me out. Tasha, Tiffany, and I were sittin' at the table havin' a few drinks. I needed it. I still felt so bad, I thought the pain would never go away. I even thought about going back to Jaleel's ass a couple of times. I would pick up the phone, dial six digits of his phone number, and hang up.

Tasha got up and said, "Come on, y'all. Let's dance."

She was drunk by now and ready to party.

Stirring up my Tequila Sunrise, I said, "Y'all go ahead. I'm about to sit here for a minute and maybe get another drink."

Tasha had already started dancing as she walked away from the table.

"OK, girl," she said.

"We'll be back in a minute, Kel," Tif said.

She gave me a concerned look, like she really felt bad about leaving me at the table. Tasha found somebody to dance with real fast. He was a thuggish-lookin' nigga. Definitely Tasha's type. The DJ was a little whack until he went way back and played "Seems Like You Ready" by R. Kelly. That was my shit. Anything written by R. Kelly was my shit. Most of his songs made me horny as hell, and honestly, this was the wrong time for that. I sat there and watched everybody grind on each other. This one couple caught my eye. The man was tall and dark but not too dark. He was very clean cut and had a goatee, which I found very attractive on a man. He had on some straight-leg Levis that fit his nice body perfectly and a fitted short-sleeved shirt that showed off his big, sexy arms. I thought, *How I would love for those big strong arms to be wrapped around me.* Jaleel had arms just like that. The woman had on a slinky red dress and some red pumps that I couldn't believe she was dancing in. They had to be at least five inches. The man caressed her curves as they danced closely. He ran his fingers through her hair and grinded on her like they were in the bedroom. I sat there and began to imagine that it was me he was dancing with instead of her. I crossed my legs as I listened to R. Kelly and watched the couple make love on the dance floor.

"Kellie. Earth to Kellie!" Tasha was standing over me.

The song was over, and the couple had disappeared.

"You gotta get up and dance or something. We're supposed to be cheering you up, and we're having all the fun while you're sitting here looking all depressed."

"Girl, I think I'm gonna just let y'all have a good time. I'm gonna go home . I'm really not in the mood to party."

"Well, just wait. Let me find Tif so we can all leave."

Before I could say anything, Tasha was gone.

I heard a deep, sensual voice behind me say, "Hi, beautiful. How you doing?"

Here goes another lame, ass nigga trying to pick me up with the "Hi, beautiful" line. I turned around with an attitude, ready to go off on the person whom the voice belonged to. I looked up and it was him. The man I was watching on the dance floor. My whole attitude changed. He was even finer up close.

"Hi. I'm doing ok," I said in my most innocent voice.

As he sat down he said, "You don't look ok. You look a little lonely, if you ask me."

Lonely. Did he just call me lonely? I didn't ask his fine black ass to sit down. Instead of losing my composure, I simply said, "No, I'm not lonely, and I see that you're not lonely either."

He gave me a confused look and said, "What do you mean by that?"

"Well, what I'm trying to say is that you're just like all the rest. What, did your woman go to the bathroom or somethin', and the first second you got, you came, trying to holla at another female? Have some type of decency for yourself and your woman!" I had my finger pointing and head moving just like my momma!

"Wait, wait a minute. My woman? I don't even know you, so how could you possibly assume that I have a woman? I just came over here to try to have a nice little conversation with someone who looked like a person I would like to get to know."

I saw Tiffany and Tasha walking towards me, so I grabbed my purse so I could get out of the presence of this loser.

"I saw you on the floor, grindin' all up on your woman, so if you'll excuse me, I have better things to do than talk to you.

I started standing up, and his bold ass grabbed my arm and started laughing. Normally, I would've started swinging on a nigga and cussin', but I couldn't bring myself to do that for some reason.

"Are you all right, girl?" Tasha asked.

"I was just telling this loser to go ahead on about his business cuz I don't have time for him and his lies."

He didn't let my arm go, and I wasn't trying that hard to get away. I noticed how beautiful his smile was as he laughed, but it didn't stop me from saying, "What the fuck are you laughing at?"

"I'm laughing because you have it all wrong. That wasn't my woman on the floor. That was just somebody I was dancing with. This is a club, right? Turn around and look at the dance floor."

I slowly turned around and saw the same woman he was dancing with earlier, grinding on another man. I felt like such an ass. Tiffany and Tasha were just standing there looking at me like, "What the fuck just happened?" I turned around and looked at the man who I had just insulted for no reason. I was at a loss for words, but obviously he wasn't.

He said in a low, sexy voice, "Now, can we start this conversation over?"

That man is the same man that proposed to me a year later and who I am marrying today.

"I now present to you Mr. and Mrs. Terrance Moore," the pastor announced right before my new husband and I shared a long and passionate kiss.

Chapter 4: One Month Later

My baby and I had been married for only a month, and it seemed like we saw each other less now than we did when we weren't married. Before we were married, I lived in my apartment, and he lived in his. I didn't try to move in, especially after what I had experienced with Jaleel. We found a house in the suburbs about a month before we got married, so that we would have somewhere to move after the wedding. We went to Jamaica for our honeymoon, and it was awesome. It looked exactly how it looked from what I saw on *How Stella Got Her Groove Back*. We stayed in a cabana, which was really nice!

When we got there, I found my red suitcase that I knew had my red bikini inside. I was ready to go enjoy the clear, pretty waters. As I was looking through my clothes searching for that one tiny item, I felt my man's strong arms around me, and it felt so good, especially since we now shared the same last name, and everything intimate that we chose to do was now legal in the eyes of God. He pushed my hair back behind my ears and started kissing me on my neck while he grabbed my ass and squeezed it gently. He turned me around and slid his hand under my short yellow summer dress and caressed my nipples. My nipples were always so sensitive, and he knew that. As soon as he touched them, they would get erect. My clit started throbbing. I moved my hand down under my dress and started relieving it. Terrance pulled my straps down off of my shoulders and began aggressively sucking on one of my twins while he squeezed my nipple on the other. He lifted me up off the floor, and I wrapped my legs around him tight enough so my clit could rub up against his six-pack. He sat me on the cream-colored marble dresser and took the rest of his clothes off while still gazing at me.

Terrance always knew how to get me to this place where I just felt like screaming. It felt like an out-of-body experience. I looked at his long, thick black dick that was standing out like it was lookin' for me. He kneeled down and spread my legs as far as they would go. I held on to the edge of the dresser biting my bottom lip like I always did when we made love. Terrance licked my clit and then looked at me like he was teasing me. Then he stuck his tongue inside my already wet pussy. He went in and out, then around my lips until he made me cum in his mouth. I screamed out his name, and he picked me up and laid me on the bed. He got on top of me, and I already knew what to expect. He put that big dick inside me, and I let out a sensual moan. He started stroking back and forth, pounding every wall in my pussy, then that moment came when he let out the moan of a grizzly bear and laid on top of me. Yes, Terrance was a minuteman, but I didn't care because he was a good man. I never addressed it because he always made sure he pleased me by giving me an orgasm orally before he satisfied himself. I always wondered though how a man could be so blessed in the pants and not know how to use it to my satisfaction. Then I thought, maybe I'm just that good, he can't help it. Before Terrance, I was used to fuckin' for at least forty-five minutes at a time, and then go at it again ten minutes later. I looked at it as a sacrifice. I had to sacrifice the good dick for a good man.

Terrance's and my schedule always seemed to conflict these days. We still had lunch sometimes, but Terrance had a lot of studyin' to do, and I understood that.

Ring! Ring!

There goes that damn phone. I rolled over and looked at the clock.

"Eight-thirty? Who is callin' so early?" I asked.

I felt Terrance on the side of me. He said, "Probably Tasha. You know she calls early Monday mornings since you don't have to work."

Terrance was right, but I let the voice mail pick up. Terrance got up and went in the bathroom. He had to be at work at ten. I hated the fact that I had to be home alone on my off days. I wished that we could just spend the whole day together. I got up and went in the bathroom. Terrance was pissin', and he hated when I came in the bathroom with him, but I stood behind him and wrapped my arms around his strong body.

"Come on, Kellie. You know I don't like when you come in the bathroom while I'm tryin' to piss."

"Baby, why don't you call off today so we can spend some time together. We need it."

"You know I can't afford to do that. I wish I could, but I gotta pay for law school and help pay the bills around here. I don't want you trying to do everything by yourself." He shook his dick and stuck it back in his boxers. I pulled my pink lace boyshorts down and sat on the toilet. Watching him piss made me have to.

"Well, what time are you gonna be home today?"

"I have class right after work, so I'll probably be home around eight or eight-thirty."

Terrance turned on the shower, pulled his boxers off, and stepped in. He started talking to me from behind the curtain.

"Don't you have to go to the license bureau today and get your plates renewed?"

"Oh shit. I almost forgot. I refuse to pay a damn late fee again this year like I did last year."

"You betta get there early cause you know how packed it is on the last day."

I stood at the sink and started washing my face, then I decided to take off my clothes and step in the shower. I stood in front of Terrance. He lathered my titties with soap. I played with his dick until it got hard, then got on my knees and licked the head. I could already taste the pre-cum on the tip. I licked around the shaft and

waited until it got rock hard before I took his dick all the way in.
He had to balance himself up against the wall and he looked up to
the ceiling. I stuck his dick down my throat as far as I could get it I
had successfully conquered the gag reflex. I grabbed his balls and
licked and sucked on them while I jacked off his dick. When his
dick got hard as a brick, I sucked it hard and fast, the way he liked
it until he busted in my mouth. I knew I wasn't gettin' any dick
after that. After Terrance came, that was a wrap. We washed each
other's bodies and held each other for what seemed to be eternity.

Terrance got out before me. I heard him close the bathroom
door, and that's when I had to finish the job. I lifted my leg up
against one of the shower walls and started massaging my titties.
Then I put my index and middle finger in my mouth and moved
them down to my pussy, fingering it and massaging my clit. I felt
my clit begin to throb and I moved my fingers faster over it. I was
trying to hold in my scream so Terrance wouldn't hear me. I didn't
want him to feel less of a man by knowing that I had to satisfy
myself. I came so hard that I found myself sittin' on the shower
floor. I could barely catch my breath. I heard the bathroom door
open.

"Kel, you ok?"

"Yeah. I'm about to get out. I was just relaxing."

I didn't know what the hell to say.

He peeked in the shower and said, "I'm about to go. I'll see
you later."

"OK. Call me if you get a chance."

"I'll try," Terrance said, like it was nothing.

It didn't used to be "I'll try." He used to always say "most
definitely" if I told him to call me if he got a chance. I started
thinking about the conversation I had in the beauty shop on the day
of the wedding. I remembered how the other women in the shop
were talking about how everything started off wonderful and then
it goes downhill. I still believed that Terrance and I were different
though. We were made for each other.

I jumped on the bed after I finally got out of the shower and
picked up the phone. I saw that I had a message waiting.

"Hey, Kel. I know it's early, but I wanted to catch you before you made plans. I'm goin' to the mall. Call me and let me know if you wanna go."

It was Tasha. I loved Tasha like a sister, but it just seemed so different now that I was married. I couldn't do the things that she, Tiffany, and Briana did. Terrance definitely didn't want me going out to the clubs with them anymore, but it kinda hurt my feelings when the bitches were going out and they didn't even ask if I wanted to go. They knew that I would say I couldn't, but they could've still been considerate and asked. All they ever asked me these days was to go shopping or out to lunch.

I picked up the phone to call Tasha back. When she answered, she sounded like she was out of breath.

"Hello?"

"Hey, girl. I was just callin' you back."

"So you wanna go?" she said, still sounding like she was trying to catch her breath.

"What the hell you doin' over there, girl? You want me to call you back later?"

"Naw. I just ran downstairs to get my shoes and the rest of my clothes out the car. I had a long night."

Tasha worked at The Havannah. That was a casino about twenty minutes away from where I lived. A lot of times, straight after work, the girls would go out to the clubs and end up in somebody's bed, so I already knew what she meant by a long night.

"Right. Well, I got a few errands to run. What time you gotta go to work?"

"I'm off today. Just call me on my cell when you get done doin' whatever you gotta do."

"OK."

After I hung up the phone from with Tasha, I got up and opened my closet to see what I could put on. It was already seventy degrees outside, so that meant I could wear something really cute. I pulled out my cream-colored capris and my orange-and-cream halter that tied around the neck. I set it off with my orange open-toe wedges that I could show off my freshly manicured toes in. I went in the bathroom after I put my clothes on and combed my hair. It was still a little wet from the shower, but it was always manageable. I just threw it up in a high messy bun (the style everyone is wearing after Evelyn from *Basketball Wives* started the trend), and put on my MAC lipgloss. When I left out the house, I saw my fine-ass neighbor outside watering his grass. He was tall, but not as tall as Terrance, light-skinned, and had jet-black wavy hair that he kept cut low. He had very dark features which was a turn on, especially on a light-skinned brotha. He was almost the complete opposite of Terrance, but I still thought he was sexy.

"What's up, Kellie?" he said as soon as he saw me walk out the door.

"Nothin' much. About to enjoy this nice-ass weather a little bit."

"I don't even blame you."

"You're not gonna get out today and let your top down?" I asked him.

Mike had a black Porsche that he always kept clean. I never saw him with a woman. Sometimes I thought maybe he was gay. It's always the fine-ass men who are the straight-up gay or down-low brothas. I couldn't understand how a man could have a car like that without having a woman to flaunt in it. He was a handsome man. I never asked him how old he was, but I was pretty sure he was probably between thirty and thirty-five. I didn't know what he did for a living, but I could tell that he had money. I always had an eye for that kind of thing.

"I'll probably let it down later on today. I would let it down more often if I had a woman like you to show off."

Wow. I knew I was blushing, and he gave me the sexiest smile ever. I didn't know what to say after that comment.

"Thank you, but I know you have plenty of women trying to get at you."

"Yeah, maybe so, but none of them with pretty, almond-shaped eyes with a sexy little dimple in their chin that turns me on."

On that note, it was time to go because if I didn't I was gonna have to go right back in that house and change my panties.

"Well, I gotta go, Mike. I got a lot of business to take care of. I'll see you later."

"OK, sexy. Have a good day."

"You too."

I jumped in my red BMW and made my getaway before I could even let the top down.

Once I got a mile down the road, I finally let my top down and continued on to the license branch. I started thinking about Mike. He had really turned me on to a point where I started wondering what he looked like under all of his clothes. I had seen him walk out to the mailbox without a shirt on many occasions, and it was a beautiful sight. Terrance had a wonderful body, but I wondered what Mike had that Terrance didn't. My mind began roaming so much, to the point that I found myself thinking about if Mike's dick was bigger than Terrance's. I didn't understand how I could love my husband and be thinking about another man in this way. Mike's smile kept entering my mind and the way he had called me "sexy." Out of all the times I had seen Mike, he never flirted in that manner, but to think about it, Terrance was always around.

When I pulled up to the license branch, I looked at all the cars in the parking lot and almost turned my ass right back around.

"I don't have time for this shit!" I said.

I've always hated spending my days off doing stuff that had to be done. I just wanna do what I wanna do. Is that too much to ask? I should've gone during my lunch break one day last week, but us black folks never do stuff on time, especially me. I grabbed my registration out the glove compartment, looked in my rearview mirror to make sure I was still flawless, and prepared for my long day at the license bureau.

As I sat there waiting for my number to be called, I felt someone sit next to me, but I didn't bother to look to see who it was. Then, I got this feeling that somebody was staring at me, so I slowly looked to the right of me.

"About time you decided to look over here."

"Reggie! Hey! How you doin'?"

I jumped up and gave him a hug and a kiss on the cheek.

"I'm ok . . . especially now that I'm in your presence. I been askin' everybody about you. It was like you dropped off the face of the earth."

Reggie was . . . well, I wouldn't exactly call him an ex, but more like somebody I used to mess around with . . . A friend with benefits, I guess you could say. We began our "friendship" our sophomore year in high school. No one ever knew about us. Not even my girls. Not even my best friend Tasha because I knew she could run her mouth at times. I always knew Reggie had a girlfriend, but that didn't stop us from fuckin' whenever and wherever we had a chance. Whenever I broke up with a boyfriend, I would always run back to Reggie and he was always there for me. I vowed that I would never sleep with Reggie while I was in a relationship and I never did. I wasn't the cheating type. Our so-called relationship ended a few months after we graduated. One night when we had just finished doin' what we did at his house, we were just lying there, and out of the blue, he said, "So when you gon' be my woman, Kel?"

That shit scared me. I wasn't expecting it at all. I was completely silent for a while which made the situation very uncomfortable so I got up, put my clothes on, and left. I guess Reggie had gotten a little embarrassed, so we hadn't spoken since then.

"Naw, I didn't drop off the face of the earth. I been around."

"Well, what you been doin' with yourself?" he asked curiously.

"I'm a hairstylist now. I've been doin' that for a couple of years."

"Anything else?" Then I saw him look down at my ring finger.

"Oh yeah. I got married about a month ago."

"Oh, really."

He had this disappointed look on his face. Almost like the look he had when I left his house that night. Reggie was still a fine-ass nigga. I didn't mess around with anyone who wasn't fine. That was one of my major criteria in a man. The only difference about him was that he had cut his hair. Back in the day, he had braids that were always neatly done.

"So since you're married, I guess that would mean I couldn't take you out for a friendly lunch."

"I would, but I still got a lot to do today. I told my friend Tasha . . ."

"Tasha? You still hang with her, huh. Obviously, you didn't give up all your ways."

"What are you tryin' to say?"

"I remember how y'all used to be. You, Briana, Tiffany, and Tasha."

"Boy, whateva," I said with an attitude.

"I'll show you how much of a boy I'm not, but I'm sure you already know."

He gave me this sneaky little grin, and I looked up to see what number they were on. I needed to get out of there. They were on thirty-eight and I was forty. I peeked over to look at Reggie's number and he was forty-one. I was trying to estimate how much time I needed to get out of here before he did.

"So you still didn't answer about lunch. Can you make time for me?"

"Um . . . I gotta go home first because I forgot a few things while I was rushin' out the house, so maybe I'll see you out another day."

Actually, I had forgotten my cell phone and I felt lost without it.

Finally, they called my number and about ten seconds later, they called Reggie's. I was sittin' at the counter callin' the lady that was waiting on me all kinds of bitches in my mind because I needed her to hurry her black ass up. When I was finally finished, I looked around and Reggie was gone, thank God. I spoke too soon because, low and behold, as soon as I walked out the door, there he was, standin' there waiting.

"I told you we'll do this another day, Reggie."

"That doesn't make much sense to me since we have nothing but time and opportunity now. What if I don't run into yo ass for another few years? It's not like I can call you, can I?"

Then I started thinkin' about my cell phone again. How it was probably ringing off the hook right now.

"Reggie, I really gotta go home. I left some important things I need."

"Let me follow you home so you can get what you need and then we can go to lunch."

I actually stood there and thought about it and did the dumbest thing ever.

I said, "OK."

The whole way home, I was thinkin' to myself, "What the hell are you doing, Kel?" I kept lookin' in my rearview mirror hoping some miraculous way Reggie would've disappeared. When I pulled up in my driveway, I looked around to make sure none of my neighbors were around, especially Mike. Reggie pulled up behind me. I got out the car before he had a chance to and went over to tell him I'll be right back. Reggie must've had a nice job cuz he was sportin' a 2012 Lexus. I didn't know which Lexus model. I wasn't good with all those letters at the end, but I knew it wasn't cheap. I ran in the house, went upstairs, and grabbed my phone off the bed where I had left it. To my surprise, no one had called me. I needed to hurry up and get this dude out of my driveway. I ran back down the stairs and ran right into Reggie's ass, standing in my living room.

"What the fuck, Reggie! You know you can't be comin' up in here like this. It's not like it was back then. I'm married."

He grabbed my hips and said, "You know how much I wanted you then, and I want you even more now. I fell in love with you back then, and I never found anyone that even compared to you."

I felt my panties getting wet for the second time in one morning. *What the hell is goin' on?* I thought to myself. I started counting days to see if it was that time of the month. I know I'm extra horny during that time. Nope, still got a couple of weeks! Is God tryin' to tell me something? Shit, He should've given me this sign a little over a month ago.

"I understand all that, Reggie, but this can't happen. I'm married."

"Yeah, you already said that. Are you happily married is the question."

He started kissing my neck, as his hands wandered down to my ass. I was pulling away from him, but not with all my strength. I felt like part of me might've wanted this.

"Yes."

"Yes, what, Kel?"

"I am happily married," I said as I struggled to push him away.

"We're about to find out if that's the truth cuz honestly I don't believe that."

He started unbuckling my capris, and I let him. My emotions were all over the place and I couldn't control them. My cell phone was still in my hand and it started ringing.

"I need to get this Reggie. It could be Terrance."

"Oh. Is that his name?"

Reggie grabbed the phone out of my hand and turned it off. Then he put it on the floor and slid it into the dining room. He pulled my capris down and kneeled down and starting kissing and licking my thighs.

"Your body is still so beautiful." he whispered from below.

I let out a soft moan. I knew this was wrong, but it felt so right. I lifted my feet up one by one so Reggie could take my pants all the way off and he picked me up and laid me on the couch with nothing on but my halter and black thong. He took off his shirt, which was nothing but a wife beater. I wanted to tell him that his body was still beautiful too, but I was in a trance. Reggie got on top of me and tongued me down. He pulled off my halter and exposed my bare breasts. He looked at them like he had never seen titties before and started tonguing my nipples. He licked me all the way down to my navel and pulled down my thong with his teeth. When he got all the way down my legs with my thong, he did something that Terrance had never done before. He put my big toe in his mouth and sucked it so good that I almost had an orgasm just from that. I started rubbing my clit and Reggie moved my hand.

He said, "Naw, baby. That's what I'm here for."

He stood up and took off the rest of his clothes. His dick was juicier than ever. He had definitely grown since the last time we had been together. He climbed on top of me while his dick searched for my pussy. When he found it, he worked the hell out of it. He worked it, then ate it, worked it, then ate it again. He hit my G-spot so hard and so many times, that I screamed like somebody was killin' me. I hadn't had dick like this in so long, I forgot how good it could be, but how would I feel when I was all over? Honestly, I never wanted it to end.

Chapter 5

An hour and a half later, I lay there with a nigga' on top of me who wasn't my husband. I wondered how I would act differently around my Terrance, or if I would act differently at all.

"Get up, Reggie. I need to go take a shower."

He rolled off of me, and I grabbed my clothes and cell phone and ran upstairs. I closed and locked the bathroom door behind me and stood in front of the mirror and stared at myself. I turned my phone back on. Tasha had called me three times, my momma called, and my baby, Terrance, called. Tasha had just called to see where I was all three times. I never understood her. She didn't care how many times she called somebody, she left a message every single time. I heard my momma's voice in the next message.

"Hey, baby. It's me. Just callin' to see if you can fit me in tomorrow 'cause I need a perm bad as hell. I couldn't comb through this mess this mornin'. Call me back at the office when you get this. Love ya."

She was calling from work. She had been working as a
secretary in the same doctor's office for about twenty years. The
next message was from Terrance.

"Hey, Kel. I'm at lunch right now. I was gonna come home but
decided just to go eat somewhere around here. I'll probably just
pick up a burger or somethin'. I miss you, baby, and I love you.
See you tonight." I felt kinda bad, but I didn't really regret what I
had done. Maybe it just hadn't hit me yet. Shit, I hadn't been
fucked longer than five minutes in about two years and I didn't
realize what I had been missing until now. I started the shower and
waited 'til the temperature was just right. While I was waiting, I
unlocked the door and peeked outside. I guessed Reggie was still
downstairs. Thank God Terrance hadn't come home. I closed the
door back and got in the shower. I felt like I was starting my
morning all over. *Knock! Knock!*

"Yeah," I said nervously.

I heard Reggie's voice outside the door. "You almost done?
I'm getting' hungry."

"Yeah. I'll be done in a minute."

I heard the door open so I opened the shower curtain a little so
I could see. Reggie was still naked. He grabbed a face towel out of
the linen closet.

"Kellie. You got another bar of soap?"

"Yeah. Look on the shelf above the towels. There should be
some up there." I finished washing myself up but started
wondering if lunch with Reggie was a good idea. I didn't know
what my trip was. I had just fucked the boy, but couldn't go out to
lunch with him. I stepped out of the shower and didn't see my
towel so that I could dry off. I looked over and Reggie was drying
off with it.

"I guess we found out if you're happily married, didn't we?"
Reggie said, playfully.

"Reggie, I know what just happened, but I guarantee you that
I'm happily married."

"Kel, you can't fuck somebody else with that much passion,
then honestly say that you're happy, can you?"

I didn't know what to say because to tell you the truth, I was
confused. I knew I was young to be getting married, and I'm still

young, but I felt like it was the right thing to do. Maybe I married Terrance because I didn't want him to get away.

"I don't know, Reggie, but I do know that this can't happen again. You threw off my whole day."

"It was worth it wasn't it?" he said while he licked his lips and looked my naked body up and down.

Even though I felt like I didn't regret the whole thing, I knew that it would hurt Terrance so much if he ever found out. I went in my room and got dressed again. Reggie followed me around the whole house until we got ready to leave. Before I opened the front door, I turned to Reggie and held his hands and said, "Reggie, if this had been about a year and a half ago, I would give us another chance, but this is bad timing, and you know it. I can't go to lunch with you. This is as far as this goes."

"Kel, how you gon' do this to me. You know you not happy."

"That's the thing. I am happy, and I can't mess that up with a good man." I gave Reggie a hug and we walked out.

"Hi again, Kellie." I felt as though my heart skipped a beat. Oh my god. It was Mike.

"Hey, Terrance," he said and smiled.

I could've killed Mike. He knew damn well that wasn't Terrance. Mike started walking towards us.

"Oh, that's not Terrance. I'm sorry, man."

"Mike, this is my cousin Philip from out of town."

I used the name Philip because I did have a cousin named Philip who lived in California.

"Oh. How you doin', Philip? I'm Mike." He shook Reggie's hand.

Reggie said, "What's up, man?"

"Nothin' much. Just about to enjoy the day. I'll catch y'all later."

"OK. See you later, Mike," I said, trying to sound calm as hell.

He winked at me and said, "OK, sexy." Mike went and got in his car, let the top down and sped out smiling.

"Reggie, that was too close. That's exactly why it has to end now."

"Kellie, I told you how I feel about you. Can't we at least talk? Give me your cell phone number."

"No, Reginald." That's what I used to always call him when he would frustrate the hell out of me.

"Wait a minute," he said before he started walking to his car. He went and sat in his car. He was sitting in there doin' somethin', but I didn't know what. I sat in my car and waited. I looked in the rearview mirror and saw him coming with something in his hand.

"Here, Kel. Here's my home and cell number. Please feel free to use it."

I took it and said, "Talk to you later," even though I didn't intend on ever calling him because I knew how it would end up.

"I'll talk to you later, Kellie." He walked back to his car and drove off.

I sat there in my car for a minute so I could regain my composure. I felt like I had dreamed the whole thing.

I cranked up my car and Destiny's Child was singing "Cater to U" on the radio.

"Ain't that about a bitch?!" I said to myself. About a week ago, I wanted to do something different and special for Terrance to spice things up a little bit, so I got off work early so I could drop by Seductress, one of the hottest lingerie stores around, to find something sexy to wear in the show that I was gonna be performing for my man when he came home later that night. I set up strawberry-scented candles everywhere and put pink and red rose petals on the bed. When Terrance walked in, all the lights were out, and I played "Cater to U" on the CD player, and I catered to him all night long.

After the Reggie ordeal, the rest of my day was full of confusion. I forgot I was supposed to be trying to get up with Tasha. I grabbed my cell phone from off my lap as I pulled out of my driveway and dialed Tasha's number. She obviously looked at the caller ID before answering because she didn't even say hello when she answered. She just got to snappin'.

"Where the hell have you been? I been sittin' here waitin' on you for two hours to call me back."

I heard another voice in the background say, "Everybody don't got the luxury of being off today!"

"Who is that?" I said in an irritated voice.

"That's Bri. She over here with me waiting on your slow ass. She gotta be at work in a couple of hours."

"You didn't ask Tiffany to go?" I asked, surprised.

"She not answerin' her phone. I don't know where that girl is. I haven't talked to her since we split up last night at the club. But anyway, we wastin' time. You gonna pick us up or you want us to meet you at your house?"

"I already left home, so I'll just pick y'all up from your house. I'll be there in about five minutes."

"OK."

Those seemed like the longest five minutes ever. I just kept having visions of Reggie and how he had just rocked the hell out of my world. I knew one thing for sure. My girls are my girls, but they could never know anything about this. I wouldn't hear the last of it. As far as they were concerned, I was the one in the group that had all the sense, and they didn't need to know otherwise. Their belief was that Kel just didn't do shit like that.

When I pulled up in front of Tasha's apartment building, she and Bri were sitting on the steps. Bri was looking so damn hoochified it didn't make no sense. She had on a neon pink belly shirt with her navel ring showing, some denim daisy dukes, and some neon pink, three-inch pointy-heeled sandals that looked like they came from Payless. Like I said before, Bri was a pretty, dark girl, but there were still exceptions to what colors dark-skinned people could wear, and neon pink was one of those exceptions. I was surprised to see that Tasha wasn't just as tacky as Bri, because Tasha was the definition of ghettofabulous. She had on some cute, tight Bermuda shorts and a sassy, pink embroidered top. Tasha had a beautiful complexion, so she looked good in most colors, except that platinum blonde weave she had hanging all down her back. They came walking towards the car like you couldn't tell them shit. Tasha was about to sit down then she reached down and grabbed something. I didn't realize what it was at first, then Tasha said, "The weather den got nice and yo ass already picking up numbers!"

It was Reggie's number. I had just thrown it over in the passenger's seat. I didn't know why I just didn't tear it up and throw it out. Maybe I subconsciously had intended on calling him.

"Girl, please. Give me that. That's one of my client's numbers. She told me to call her if I got an opening for her tomorrow." I thought of that shit fast as hell.

Tasha sat down after I snatched the small piece of paper from her and immediately started complaining. "Girl, you need to let the top up on this, bitch. My weave ain't made for this!"

"Girl, please. I'm not even thinkin' about you. You betta hold on to that shit!" Briana screamed from the back seat, "Turn that up, Kel. That's my shit right there!"

Keri Hilson's "Pretty Girl Rock" was on. Briana started dancing in her seat and singing. The piece of paper with Reggie's contact information was still in my hand. I stuck it in my purse for the time being until I decided what I wanted to do with it. I headed to the mall with my girls to take my mind off of some of the things that I had already endured for the day.

Chapter 6

The mall was packed, especially for a Monday afternoon. "So what y'all do last night since y'all didn't have the decency to ask nobody if they wanted to go."

Bri said, "I told them to ask you, but they didn't wanna spoil your time with yo man."

Tasha looked at Bri, and I knew she was about to snap. She just always got this look when she was ready to go off on somebody.

She stopped Bri before she said anything else and said, "You know damn well you didn't even mention Kellie. Quit tryin' to act like you was so damn concerned if Kel came with us. All you was worried about was finding you a man!"

"I was not looking for a man. I don't go out lookin' for a man like you and Tif. I go to have a good time," Bri said defensively.

"Y'all, it's ok. I had better things to do anyway. I got all I need right at home. So again, what did y'all skanky asses do?"

Tasha looked at me and rolled her eyes and said, "Whateva. Briana, why don't you tell her since you wanna talk so damn much."

"Anyway, girl, we went to Pueblos," Bri said.

"Y'all went to Pueblos? Why y'all go there out of all places?"

Pueblos was this lame ass restaurant-lounge where people went just to get a little buzz.

Tasha butted in. "Cuz it was Sunday and that was the only place people had to go on a damn Sunday."

"Oh yeah. I forgot it was Sunday, but you can keep your attitude to yourself!" I said, looking at Tasha and pointing my finger in her face.

Bri continued, "Girl, we had so much fun. We got up there and did karaoke sounding like some damn fools! We had the crowd goin' though. Everybody in there was drunk as hell."

"What yo crazy butt sing?"

"Me, Tasha, and Tif sang "Cater to U.""

I couldn't believe it. There it was again. That damn song.

"We sounded pretty good though. We went through the crowd and grabbed a few men. We were like the real-life Beyoncé, Kelly, and Michelle. I was Beyoncé of course!" Tasha said while laughing. I miss those fun times with my girls.

While we were in Macy's Tasha wanted to go over and look at the Coach purses. I followed her while Briana went to the shoe department.

"What happened with Tiffany, Tasha?" I asked, inquiringly.

"Girl, let me tell you about yo girl. While we were singing our song, she was so drunk she started walking through the crowd. She stopped at this fine nigga's table. He was sittin' there with two other guys and she started giving him a lap dance!"

"Shut up! No she didn't!"

"Yes she did, and he was likin' that shit too. She looked like a damn pro. I wanted to ask her if there was something she'd like to share about her real occupation, but I left it alone! When we finished the song and sat back down, he came over to our table. He told us how much he and his boys enjoyed our show and asked us what we were doin' after we left there 'cause they was lookin' for somebody to chill with."

"So that's where y'all ended up?" I interrupted.

"Hell naw! His boys were ugly as hell!" I told him I was calling it a night and Briana told him the same thing. Tif kept talking to him and we waited around for her, but she told us to go ahead and leave. She said she was gon' hang out."

"Why did y'all leave that girl? You know she don't have no kind of sense right now! I know we all make some bad decisions sometimes, but she been crazy with it!"

"You haven't been out with us in a long time, Kel, so you don't even know the half of it. She don't listen to nobody. She does that mess about ninety-five percent of the time we go out. She gon' leave with somebody."

"I don't know what's wrong with Tif lately. She was wild, but not this wild. She used to know how to handle herself with some class," I said.

"I don't know, but let me pay for this purse so we can go and find Bri. It's almost time for her to go to work."

Tasha had picked up this cute blue Coach purse. She probably couldn't afford it without skipping one of her major bills, but she didn't care. The bill would just have to wait. One thing I could say about Tasha was that she always had the cutest purses . . . one to go with every outfit. She paid for her purse, and we went and found Bri. She had gone over to the jewelry department looking at earrings.

"Come on, girl. I gotta get you home so you can make some money," I said jokingly.

She came walking towards us with a bag in her hand. She had bought some sandals, thank god. I was sick of those Payless shoes she was wearing. I hadn't bought anything. That wasn't like me, but I have to go to the mall and take my time. I decided that I would just probably go back by myself another day.

When we got in the car, I thought about something. I said, "Tasha, where did you go last night? When I called you this mornin' you said you was getting your clothes and shoes out the car."

"You are so damn nosey! Naw, but when I got home last night, Malik had called me." Malik was this dude who I couldn't stand. Tasha had been messing around with him off and on for the past few years.

"I called his ass back cuz I hadn't had none in a while, and you know what Hennessy does to me."

"You wrong for that. Yo fast butt was drinkin' Hennessy?"

"Don't trip. Briana was too."

"I had one shot, Tasha!" Bri explained from the back.

I knew my friends were wild, but they were young and just havin' fun. I wished I did still have that option sometimes.

After I dropped my girls off, I called Tiffany to make sure she was ok. I didn't get an answer, so I drove over to her apartment. Her car wasn't outside, but I still got out and went to the door. I knew that she sometimes let her sister drive her car when hers was in the shop. That was almost all of the time since her sister had a 1995 Grand Am that broke down every time you looked at it wrong. I rang her buzzer and she didn't answer. Knowing her, she probably still had a hangover from the night before. One of Tiffany's neighbors, Angela, recognized me and let me in the building.

"Have you seen Tiffany today?" I asked.

"No, but when I got off work this morning around seven-thirty, her car was here."

"Oh. Ok. Thanks so much."

At least now I knew that she had been home. That made me feel a little better about the situation. I went upstairs and knocked on her apartment door. She didn't answer, so I put my ear up to the door and I heard complete silence. I tried turning the knob, but it was locked, so I went and got back in my car and headed home. This had been a long day, and it was still early. I had decided I was gonna go home, soak in my Jacuzzi tub, and cook my husband a nice dinner.

Before Terrance got home, I pulled Reggie's number out of my purse and stared at it. I wanted to get rid of it because I knew it was nothing but trouble, but then on the other hand, what if I wanted to talk to him one day or I needed him for something. I stuck his number under the mattress on the side of the bed where I always slept. I told myself I would decide at another time what to do with it. I still wasn't thinking rationally. I looked at the clock and it was around eight-forty-five, so I ran downstairs to take our steaks out the oven. Terrance would be home any minute. While I was waiting, I made sure there was no evidence anywhere of what

I had done. I heard the front door open, so I went towards the door to greet Terrance with a big hug.

He said, "Hey, baby. I missed you so much." He put his stuff down and gave me another hug and a kiss.

I told him, "Go get comfortable so we can eat dinner."

"It smells good, baby. Smells like steak. I'm hungry too."

"What did you end up having for lunch?" I asked him, referring to the message he had left me earlier saying that he would probably pick up a burger.

"That's why I'm so hungry. I didn't end up eating. I sat in the car during lunch and studied some things. I learned a lot of things I didn't know. I wish I would've learned this stuff earlier, now I gotta study extra hard so this shit will stick."

"Baby, you know it don't take much for you to learn something."

"Yeah, but some of this stuff can be real tricky."

Terrance went upstairs, so while I waited for him to come back down I fixed our plates and poured us a glass of wine. I sat at the table feeling worse and worse every second. The guilt was beginning to get to me. I sat there with my hands clasped under my chin just thinking . . . thinking real hard. I was thinking so hard I didn't hear Terrance come back downstairs.

"Baby, what's wrong?"

"Nothin'! I was just sitting here waiting for you."

He sat down at the table across from me and started eating.

"This steak is good, Kel."

"Thank you. I felt like you deserved a good dinner. You've been working so hard."

"I do it all for you. You look nice today. What did you end up doing?"

"I went and renewed my plates. The license branch was packed. That's where I was when you called and I had left my cell phone at home. After I finally left there, I hung out with Bri and Tasha."

"What's up with them?"

"Nothing. We went to the mall, and they were just telling me about their night out. You know them."

"Yeah, I know them," Terrance said, as he chewed his steak.

After that conversation, there was dead silence at the table until we finished eating. I started putting the dishes in the dishwasher. Terrance came up behind me and started kissing my neck. He turned me around and said, "Let's go upstairs. I'll finish this later."

I knew what that meant. He wanted some, and I couldn't refuse because I had never refused. I knew that I couldn't act any differently. We went upstairs, and he undressed me and kissed me all over. He stood up and took his clothes off and got on top of me. I just couldn't get into it. I gently pushed him off of me and said in a low voice, "I'm really tired, baby. I'm sorry." Terrance looked at me in a way that almost made me cry.

He said, "OK. No problem. Just get some rest." He gave me a kiss, and I turned over but couldn't even close my eyes. I felt Terrance move closer to me and wrap his arms around me. He gave me a sense of security. After that, I fell asleep.

I jumped up when I heard my phone ringing. I looked at the clock, and it was two-thirty in the morning.

"Hello," I whispered.

I heard Tasha's voice. She sounded frantic and like she was crying. I could barely understand what she was saying.

"Kel, it's me. They found Tiffany."

"Who found Tiffany? What happened?"

By this time, Terrance had jumped up trying to find out what happened.

"This is Tasha, Terrance. Something happened to Tif!" I started crying before Tasha could even finish telling me because I knew I had gone to her house, and I sensed something wasn't right. Now she's dead.

Tasha continued talking. "Her sister found her unconscious in her apartment. She had been beaten and raped. Then the motherfucker had the nerve to steal her car! She's at St. Mary's hospital."

I felt so relieved. Not relieved because she had been beaten and raped, but because at least she was still alive.

"Well, can we see her?" I asked

"Her sister said not right now because the police are still there and they are still doing a lot of tests. They out looking for her car now."

"Was it the dude she left the club with last night?"

"They don't know yet, but probably so, so I know they gon' be comin' to question me and Bri. I haven't told Bri yet. I'll wait 'til the morning when we can all go see Tif. I don't wanna freak Bri out right now."

"OK. Well, call me first thing in the morning. I'm gonna cancel all my morning appointments."

"Alright, Kel, and our girl is gonna be ok, right?" she asked as though she needed confirmation from me.

"Yes, she is Tasha. I love you, girl."

"I love you too, Kel. Bye."

"Bye."

When I hung up the phone, Terrance was still sitting up, waiting for me to get off the phone. I told him what happened to poor Tif and how I had gone over her house to check on her. He couldn't believe what had happened either. My girls treated Terrance like a brother, and he treated them like sisters. He would do anything for them. That night, he told me he was gonna buy me a small gun to protect myself because people were crazy. I didn't like the thought of having a gun, but after what had just happened to Tif, I agreed. I was kinda upset with Bri and Tasha too because they shouldn't have left her with those niggas that night. I couldn't really think about that, though. All I was really concerned with was that they caught him and that Tif was safe. I felt bad because I promised that I would talk to Tif after my wedding because I could tell she wasn't herself lately. That was a month ago, and I still hadn't talked to her the way I intended to. This probably could've all been avoided. My girls looked up to me, and I'm sure she would've listened.

Chapter 7

I really couldn't sleep the rest of the night after I had received the call from Tasha. I really felt that it was partially my fault because I didn't do all I could've done as a friend to help prevent something like this from happening. Terrance sat up with me most of the night, even though he had to work the next morning. He told me he would call in sick, but I told him it wasn't necessary and that I would be all right. Terrance was my best friend. I could talk to him about anything, but it was impossible for me to talk to him about what I was going through with the Reggie situation.

By the time Terrance and I had finished talking, it was already five-thirty in the morning. I remembered that I had a seven o'clock and a seven-thirty appointment this morning, so I got up and went downstairs to get my phonebook of all my clients and called the ones that I had appointments with this morning to let them know that they would have to reschedule because I had a tragedy in the family. I didn't lie. Tif was my family as far as I was concerned. I planned on spending the whole morning with Tif. I knew my momma was gon' kick my ass. I forgot she had called yesterday and left me a message asking me to fit her in to get her hair done today. I called her after I called my other clients, but I got her voice mail and told her tomorrow would be better. I didn't go into detail because I knew how dramatic she could be sometimes. I didn't really feel like talkin' about it anymore. I was just ready to see my girl.

I got up, showered, and put my clothes on. By the time I finished getting dressed, Terrance had just rolled out of the bed. I felt bad for keepin' him up all night, but he'd get over it. I went in the kitchen to get a banana and sat on one of the stools at my granite-covered island. I heard Terrance come downstairs and go outside to get the newspaper. All of a sudden, I heard a lot of laughin' and talkin' so my nosey ass (just like my momma), went in the living room and looked out the window. It was Terrance talking to Mike. That caused me to get a little nervous. Mike had on a black suit with a tie and some nice black shoes. They had to have been Stacy Adams. I thought he was lookin' good yesterday, but he was fine as hell today. I needed the attention, so my crazy ass opened the door and went outside. I also wanted to make sure that Mike didn't mention "Philip" being at the house with me yesterday. Then I would really have some explaining to do. I walked over towards the both of them. *Damn, all eyes on me!* I thought to myself. I tried to not make it seem so obvious that I was just tryin' to get Mike's attention, even though I didn't even know why I wanted his attention.

"I'm sorry to interrupt, y'all. Baby, let me see the paper before I go," I said.

"Oh. My fault. I got to talkin' to Mike and forgot I had it."

"That's ok, babe. Hey, Mike. How you doin' today?"

"I'm all right. 'Bout to get ready to go make some money. I like the finer things in life, so I gotta work to keep 'em, right?"

"Yep. I heard that, man!" Terrance said.

Mike smiled at me, and I rolled my eyes, trying to pretend I didn't like it. I knew exactly what he meant by saying he liked the finer things in life.

"Well, I'll see you later, Mike," I said.

I think Terrance might've sensed Mike's flirting because as I was walkin' away, he squeezed my booty and said, "I'll be in in a second, baby."

Men are funny. His ass was just trying to show Mike who I belonged to.

When I went in the house, I sat in the living room and opened the newspaper. The headline read: "Woman Raped and Beaten After Leaving Local Bar." *Wow, news travels fast as hell,* I thought. I was just glad that they didn't mention Tif's name in the article. It said that the victim would remain anonymous. Tif was the type that wouldn't want it to get around that she was raped. While I was sitting there reading the article, the phone rang. It was Tasha. "Hey, Kellie. What time are you goin' to the hospital?"

"I'm about to leave in about five minutes. Did you see the article on the front page?"

"Naw, girl. They got it in the paper already?"

"Yep."

"I'll pick up a paper on the way. I'm gonna leave in a few minutes too, but I gotta pick up Bri. Her car is in the shop, so I'll just meet you there."

"Alright then. Bye."

Tasha sounded much better than she did when she called me last night. I was glad because someone needs to be strong for the group.

Terrance finally came in the house. "You betta hurry up and get ready for work. You out there runnin' your mouth and forgot you had to go make me some money."

"No I didn't. I was just tryin' to see how I could be like Mike." He started laughing, and then I remembered why I loved Terrance and how much I loved him. He tried to crack jokes, but didn't nobody ever laugh because half the time he was foul as hell, but I always laughed with my baby.

"That man is ballin' out of control," he continued.

"Well, we'll be ballin' too when you finish law school and get yourself established. We're not doin' too bad right now if you ask me."

"No, we're not, but we could always do better."

I gave Terrance a kiss and said, "Make sure you brush your teeth! That don't make no sense at all how your breath smell!" He started laughing like I was playin'. "You laughin', but I'm so serious!"

"Gone and get out of here girl. Tell Tiffany I said hi and I hope she feels better."

"OK. Call me later."

"Most definitely, Kel." That's what I was talkin' about. I liked to hear "most definitely." Forget all that "I'll try" shit.

When I got to the hospital, I parked and waited a few minutes to see if I saw Tasha's car pull up. I finally pulled out my cell phone to see where she was.

"Hello?"

"Hey, Tasha. Are you close to the hospital yet?" There was a parking space right next to me, and I heard a car pull in. It was Tasha's baby blue Malibu.

"Yep, I'm there right now."

"I see you now, smart ass!" I hung up the phone and started getting out the car. I'm usually not scared of anything, but I was scared to go in that hospital alone. I was scared of what I might see. I didn't know the first thing to say to Tif if she was awake. Bri got out the passenger side of the car. "Hey, Bri."

"Hey, girl," she said without any energy whatsoever. I could tell she had been crying because her eyes were puffy as hell with dark circles around them. We got up to the front desk, and I think all of us were scared. The lady at the desk said, "Hello. Can I help you?"

We all just stood there lookin' dumbfounded for a second and then finally, I said, "Yes, we're here to see Tiffany Lucas."

"Does she work here or . . ."

Tasha interrupted, "Oh no. We sorry, she's a patient."

"OK. Well, for security purposes, she has a list of people who can see her, so I'll need each of your IDs before I can let you go up."

The fact that we had to show our IDs to see our friend really scared me. The hospital or police must've felt that she was still in danger. We all showed our driver's licenses and she gave us visitor passes to go up to the fifth floor.

We walked down the long hallway until we got to room 5125, which was Tiffany's. There was a police officer sitting outside the room with something that looked like a notebook. He asked for our IDs and opened his notebook. He had a list of people who were allowed to visit, too. At least her room was secured. I took a deep breath before I walked in. We all walked in together and stood over Tiffany. I couldn't believe what I was looking at. My girl was layin' up here in a hospital bed lookin' like she got hit by a car. Her whole face looked bruised. Both of her eyes were black, her nose was swollen, and the whole left side of her face was swollen. Tif was always so pretty. That's why I couldn't understand why she acted the way she did—like she was desperate and worthless. She could've easily had any man that she desired, but for some reason, she didn't deal with any man who she would seriously consider settling down with. I walked over to the window and looked out, trying to stop myself from crying, but the tears eventually rolled down my face. Bri came over, hugged me and started crying too. I looked back and Tasha was still standing over the bed, holding Tif's hand. I went in the bathroom to get some tissue and I heard some coughing outside the bathroom door. I came out the bathroom and Tasha was pressing the button for a nurse's assistance. One of the nurses and a doctor came rushing in and told us to wait outside in the hallway.

"Why did this have to happen to her?" Briana said in a low, shaky voice.

I think she was feeling a lot of guilt for leaving Tif that night. Tasha was too, but she would probably never admit it. That's just how she was—stubborn as hell.

While we were waiting in the hallway, we saw Tif's sister, Theresa, walking briskly down the hall. When she got close enough to us for us to hear, she said, "What's goin' on, y'all?" looking a little worried and came over to hug each of us.

Theresa was two years older than all of us. All Tif and Theresa had were each other and us, of course. Their parents had died before we met them, so their grandmother, who had died last year, raised them from the time they were eleven and thirteen. Bri, Tasha, and I met Tiffany when she transferred to our school in the seventh grade. She was always sittin' all by herself at lunch, lookin' depressed, so we decided one day to go over and talk to her. She ended up bein' cool as hell, and we pulled her into our little circle. Now I couldn't imagine us without Tif. I always thought of her as being so strong. It had to be devastating to lose both of her parents at such a young age. She never talked about it, and we never forced her to. 'Til this day, we didn't know how Tif's momma and daddy died.

"Hey, Theresa," Tasha said. "Tif got to coughing, so we had to leave the room. Hopefully we can go back in soon . . . So what's the latest news?"

"He left my baby sister for dead!" Theresa said and started crying.

I held her until she calmed down.

"I'm sorry y'all. I'm just so mad I could kill somebody.

"Don't apologize," I told Theresa. "This is hard on everybody."

"She told me what he did to her, and I just wanted to go out there and find and kill his ass myself! I don't understand how somebody could do somethin' like this. Last night, the doctor checked Tif for any evidence that would help the police find the muthafucka. He used a condom, so they don't have much to go by with that, but they did find skin under her fingernails where she had scratched him. That won't do any good if they don't have him in custody to match the DNA, right?

Everyone looked at me like I had all of the answers. I didn't know much about the law, so I just shrugged my shoulders. *Too bad Terrance isn't here,* I thought.

I said, "Anybody who could do somethin' like this to a woman has to have a record, right?"

"Not if he's never been caught," Theresa answered. She continued and said, "They did find her car early this morning, though. Maybe they'll be able to find some evidence inside."

Looking down at the floor, Bri said, "I knew we shouldn't have left her there. I had a feelin' somethin' wasn't right."

Theresa had a confused look on her face. "What? What you talkin' about?" Tasha gave Bri one of her "shut yo ass up" looks and turned around with her back facing us and her arms crossed. Theresa was lookin' around at all of us and I didn't say a word.

Bri looked up and began to talk again. "Tif was with us that night. We went to Pueblos to have a few drinks and she told us to leave her."

"Y'all bitches left my sister by herself? What is wrong with y'all? She would never do that to any one of y'all." Theresa took a brief pause, shaking her head and taking deep breaths. "That's just wrong, and she's supposed to be your friend? Bullshit!"

The officer who was sitting at Tif's door stood up and looked like he was ready to take somebody out. He didn't look that big and tall while he was sitting, but as soon as his six feet five–inch, three-hundred-pound ass stood up, everybody shut the hell up. One of the nurses at the desk came over and said, "You all are gonna have to keep the noise down or leave. The next time it happens, I'm gonna have to have you all escorted out."

Tif obviously hadn't told Theresa that she was with Bri and Tasha that night. She knew how upset Theresa would've been. That answered why the police hadn't contacted them yet. I'm sure they would've wanted a description of the dude Tif was with and his friends. I tried to put my arm around Theresa, and she pushed me away and said, "Don't put your goddamn hands on me!"

"Come on. Just walk with me for a minute." She hesitated for a second, and then she came around. I told Bri and Tasha we would be back in a little while. I just wanted to shed some light on what was goin' on because I knew Theresa was a little confused. While we walked around the hospital, I told her exactly what Tasha and Bri had told me.

"Theresa, I don't know what's been goin' on with Tif, but right before the wedding, she started acting different. She doesn't seem herself at all. I never had to worry about Tif before because she was so independent and knew what she wanted. Now she seems like she's tryin' to find herself in all the wrong places."

"I know that she acts crazy sometimes. Me and my sister went through a lot when our parents died, and it is coming up on the ten year anniversary of when we lost our parents. It really took a toll on us. We could have some real serious issues, but we made it through. Howeva, the way she acted that night still didn't give them bitches a right to leave my little sister with a group a niggas that none of them knew."

"I'm not saying that that was right either, but we all make mistakes and misjudge situations sometimes. All I'm sayin' is that Tif needs some guidance. She lost sight of her morals. We need to just be happy that she's alive because she could be dead right now. Things could always be worse." I think I got through to Theresa a little bit. I saved Bri's and Tasha's asses.

When we got back outside Tif's room, Bri and Tasha were gone. The officer was still outside the room, and he let us go inside. Bri and Tasha were already inside talking to Tif since she had woken up after her coughing spell.

I walked over to the bed and gave her a hug. "I am so glad you're ok, girl."

She spoke in a soft whisper and said, "Y'all ain't getting' rid of me that easily. I'm a survivor."

We all laughed. At least she could have a sense of humor right now, but like I said, she was always strong. Theresa called the detective that was on the case and he came by the hospital to question Bri and Tasha about the incident. He said they still didn't have any leads. If that was the case, there was no way in hell Tif could go back to her apartment. That same rapist could easily come back and try the same thing. We all left the hospital at the same time, except of course for Tif. I told her I would call and check on her later. I went straight to work and one of my regular clients was already sitting in my chair. Before I started on her hair, I called my momma to tell her I would fit her in later that evening. I was feelin' a little better after seeing that my girl was gonna be all right.

Chapter 8: One Week Later

Tiffany was finally getting out the hospital, and it was long overdue. I was tired of spending my lunch hours at the hospital even though I did enjoy spending time with Tif outside of the club scene, but my lunch hour was me and Terrance's time. The police still hadn't found any leads, so Terrance and I had agreed to let Tif stay with us until either they caught the rapist or she found another apartment. Whichever came first. Theresa wanted Tif to stay with her, but she only had a one-bedroom apartment. We had two spare bedrooms, so it wasn't a problem. I took a week's vacation just so I could stay with Tif until she felt more comfortable being alone. She was still scared, especially since ol' boy was still out on the streets.

When I picked Tif up from the hospital, she looked a whole lot better than she did the first day I went to visit her. Most of her bruising was gone, and her swelling had gone all the way down.

On the way home, she said, "Are you cookin' tonight?"

"I don't know. Why?"

"Girl, I'm so tired of hospital food I don't know what to do."

"Well then, I guess I'll cook. Maybe fry some chicken or somethin'."

"Now why you figure I want some fried chicken? That's not what black folks want all the time!"

I looked at her and smiled and said, "What you want then?"

"Now you know I want some of your fried chicken!" She laughed, and it felt so good to see that side of Tif again.

When we pulled up at the house, Terrance's car was outside.

"Wow, he's here early today. It's only four o'clock."

"Well, you should be happy that your husband is home early, right? The honeymoon isn't over already is it?"

"Naw, girl. I'm just surprised. That's all."

"Well, maybe I'm just so important that he wanted to be home when I got out the hospital!

"Girl, please! Not even that can keep him from making his money!"

We got out the car and went in. I didn't see Terrance, so I went upstairs. The bedroom door was cracked, and I heard music playing. Please Lord don't let this be déjà vu, I thought. I slowly went in, and there was my man lying there in the bed by himself. I was glad because I don't know if I could've handled another Jaleel scene. I might've killed a bitch, and I wasn't tryin' to catch no case.

"Hey, baby. What you doing home so early?"

"Yo baby don't feel good," Terrance said, looking like a big-ass baby.

"Awww. Poor baby. How you want your wifey to make you feel better?"

Terrance grinned, so I knew what they meant. I forgot that Tif was even downstairs. I crawled on top of Terrance and started licking him across his juicy lips, easing my tongue inside his mouth. I put my hand under the sheet, and his ass was butt-ass naked. I grabbed his dick, and it was hard as a rock. He hadn't had no pussy since I had the little incident with Reggie. I guess it was about time I gave him some before he got suspicious. He rolled over on top of me and pulled my shorts and my thong down. He fingered my pussy while he sucked on my titties, then he lifted his body up and stuck his dick in my pussy. It felt so good for the moment. That first insertion was always the best. Then he moaned and laid on top of me. Next thing I knew, he was lying there snoring his ass off. I slid my body from underneath his and got up so I could entertain my guest.

When I made it back downstairs, I didn't see Tif anywhere.

"Tiffany." I went in the kitchen and I saw her through the glass doors, sitting on the patio. It was a very nice day, so I went and sat out there with her. She looked like she was in a trance.

"You ok, Tif?"

"Yeah. I was just thinkin' about some things."

"Anything in particular?"

"Yeah. My life. I don't feel like Tiffany anymore. I don't know who I am."

"You're not the only one. Believe me. I don't know who I am these days either."

I didn't plan on telling any of my girls what I was going through, but I felt like I had to talk to someone.

"What's wrong, Kellie? You have everything you need, so what's the problem?"

"Nothing, girl. This isn't about me. This is about you. Now, how you feeling?"

"I've just been through a lot in my life. More than you know about, and I've suppressed a lot of my feelings. Now I think it's all eating me up. I never really trusted people enough to tell them all about me."

I didn't know what Tif was trying to tell me, but I could tell she really wanted to talk, and she was just waiting for an invitation to tell me what was on her mind.

"You know it's not good to hold stuff in. That shit can mess you up physically, mentally, and emotionally. That's not healthy."

"I know that now. I realized it after all this happened." Tears started running down Tif's face. She put her hands to her face and started wiping her tears. She seemed as if she was embarrassed for crying.

"Kel. You're not supposed to see me like this. I'm supposed to be strong."

"We all know you're strong, but you can't be strong all the time. That's just impossible. You're only human just like the rest of us. We all cry."

At that moment, I had just realized I had never seen Tif cry. It was an awkward moment. Tif's voice was still shaking, and she was trying to control her breathing.

"Kel, I never told anyone about my parents. Me and Theresa don't even talk about it, but I think I need to talk about it with someone. It is really starting to affect me mentally. It's going on ten years since they've been gone, and that's how long all this has been building up inside of me."

"You know you can talk to me about anything. I wouldn't say anything to anybody if you didn't want me to, and you know it."

Tif started twiddling her thumbs and said, "My daddy . . ." Tif paused and took a deep breath. "My daddy was murdered."

I sat there in shock. I had no idea she was about to say something as deep as that. I always thought that maybe her parents were killed in a car accident or something.

"Theresa and I always thought we had a perfect family. My momma was always at home doing things with us. She would even come outside and jump double-dutch with us and our friends. My daddy supported the family, and anyone who was around my momma and daddy knew that they loved each other dearly."

After every other sentence, Tif would take a deep breath, but I never interrupted her.

"One night, my daddy said he was going out with his guys. He did that quite often. It had gotten to the point where sometimes we wouldn't see him come home until the morning when we were getting ready for school. He would just say that he got too drunk to drive home, so he spent the night at one of his friend's houses."

It looked like it was hurting Tif so much to tell this story, but I didn't stop her even though I wanted to. I felt like she really needed to let this out.

"My momma was a little naïve or tried to act naïve. That night when he left, that was the last night we saw my daddy alive. Our phone rang around three o'clock that morning, and all I could hear was my momma screaming and crying. She was saying, 'Nooooo. Not Sam. Please don't tell me this. Please tell me this is a joke.' It

wasn't a joke though. My father had been murdered in his
mistress's bed."

I raised my eyebrows and said, "She killed him?"

"No. Her husband did."

"Nooooo," I said, as if I could feel their pain.

"Her husband was supposed to be out of town and ended up
coming home early and caught them fuckin'."

"That's horrible, Tif. I'm so sorry."

"That wasn't the end of my trauma. My momma seemed to be
handling the situation pretty well after the initial shock. We had a
lot of company for the next couple of days and that seemed to
make her feel a lot better. She even talked to me and Theresa about
what happened. She did cry, but we figured that was normal. We
all cried. Anyway, three days after my daddy was killed, after all
the company left and we cleaned up, my momma went upstairs and
took a bath. She was in there for a long time, so Theresa went in to
check on her. She was in the tub staring at the wall. Theresa said,
'Momma. You ok?' My momma said she was fine, and she'd be
out in a minute. My momma got out the tub and went in her room
to put her gown on. I went in there to give her a hug and kiss and
tell her good night."

That was when Tif broke down. She put her head down on the
table, calling for her momma. I went in the house and brought
some tissue back out with me. I watched Tif as she wiped her eyes,
asking her if she wanted to finish or go lay down. She said that she
wanted to get it all off her chest, so I sat there and waited until she
was ready to begin again.

Tif continued where she left off. "When I hugged her, I felt
something powerful. So powerful it made me cry. I went in my
room, and after lying in my bed for about ten minutes, I heard a
loud noise. I got up and ran out of my room to my momma's room.
Theresa had made it there before I did, and she was crying and
trying to push me back. She kept telling me to go call for help. I
didn't go call. I just stood there, helpless, looking over my
momma's lifeless body while blood was still pouring out of her
head. She had shot herself in the head with my daddy's gun. I can
never get that picture out of my head."

Tif started crying again, harder and harder. I went over to her and hugged her and didn't let her go. Tif had a lot on her mind, and it had been there for so long. I'm surprised that she was just now breaking down. That's too much for a person to carry. After Tif shared her story with me, I felt like we had a special bond because she trusted me with something that she didn't trust anyone else with.

Chapter 9

The next morning, Terrance was feeling better, but he decided to call in sick because he wanted to spend some time with me. Tif was going with Theresa to look for a new apartment even though I told her she could stay with me and Terrance however long she needed to. I only had until about four o'clock to be with Terrance because he had class at four-forty-five, so we started the day early. I needed to relax for a minute, so I soaked in my Jacuzzi tub. While I was soaking, I was just thinking about Tif's parents. How could everyone think that a couple is so in love, when the husband is stepping out on his wife almost every night? Maybe he was still in love with Tif's momma, or is that possible? I knew that I had cheated on Terrance, but it wasn't something I did on the regular. It only happened once, and I knew I loved Terrance. I had thought about calling Reggie several times, but I knew that wouldn't be a good idea.

While I was in the tub, I just couldn't get Reggie off my mind, so I grabbed my cell phone off the floor beside me. I always brought my cell in the bathroom with me while I was taking a bath because I tended to get bored just sittin' there, so usually I would call one of my girls or my momma. After I grabbed my phone, I didn't know what the hell I was doing because the paper he had written his number on was still under the mattress. I guess that was a sign that I didn't need to call his ass.

When I got out the tub, I threw my robe on and headed downstairs. Before I made it down the stairs, I heard Terrance down there talking to someone. I went in the kitchen, and there was Terrance standing there in only his boxers, cooking pancakes. It would've been ok if Tif wasn't sitting there talking to him like nothing was wrong. They didn't see me walk in the kitchen, so I walked out before they saw me and I went in the living room.

"Terrance, baby!" I hollered from the living room. I guess he was so into his conversation that he didn't hear me. "Terrance!" I was getting irritated.

Finally he came walking from the kitchen. "What's up?"

"No. What's up with you walking around here in your boxers while we got company?"

"I didn't think it was a big deal. I was coming down here so I could surprise you with breakfast when you got out the tub. I thought Tiffany was already gone, so I didn't even think to put nothin' else on."

"Think about it, Terrance. What if you had one of your boys over here and I came down here in my panties and a tank top? Let's add with no bra under the tank top! Would you think that it was a big deal then?"

"That's different. Panties are nothing like boxers, but since you got a problem with it, I'll go put on something else." He had the nerve to walk upstairs like he had an attitude. I should be the one with the attitude. I walked in the kitchen and Tif was sitting there eating a piece of bacon.

"Hey, Tif. Did you sleep ok?"

"Oh yeah. Thank you so much for doing this for me. I really appreciate it."

"No problem."

"Theresa should be here in a minute to pick me up. We'll probably be gone most of the day."

"You got a lot of apartments to look at?"

"Yeah. Pretty much."

Just then a horn blew outside. I went and looked out the window. It was Theresa. "Tif, she's here."

"OK, girl. I'll see you later." After Tif left, I sat at the dining room table and ate my surprise breakfast by myself.

I didn't think that I had done anything wrong by being offended when I saw Terrance downstairs in his boxers, but he was pissed. I didn't want this time that we had to spend together to be ruined, so I was the bigger person and apologized for making a big deal out of nothing. After we got dressed, we left and went to the mall. I think Terrance felt bad too because he kept asking me if I wanted anything. He ended up buying me this bad ass dress I had been wanting for a while but was too cheap to buy it myself. After I kept Terrance in the mall for a few hours, we were both hungry, so we went to Applebee's for lunch. We were seated, and while I looked through the menu, I kept feeling like I was being watched. I looked up from the menu, and Terrance was staring at me.

"What?"

"Nothing. I can't look at the woman I love?"

"You're just making me feel uncomfortable," I said with a frown, "like I got somethin' on my face or somethin'."

"The only thing on your face is beauty. You are so beautiful."

I grinned a little bit, and I knew I was blushing. It felt good for him to compliment me like that because he didn't do it as often as he used to. Well, that was the excuse I was using for seeking attention elsewhere.

He said, "I'm sorry for earlier. I don't want anything stupid to come between us. You know I don't want nobody else. And Tif's your girl. Do you really think she would do somethin' like that to you?"

I thought about it. First, I thought about what my momma always said about not trusting females, then I thought about the talk Tif and I had had. Terrance was right. I didn't have anything to worry about with Tif.

Our food finally came about a half hour later.

"Finally. I should complain because we shouldn't have to pay for this after how long we waited!" I was good at complaining at restaurants—especially when I felt I wasn't treated right.

"Don't worry about it, Kel. That just gave us some time to talk," Terrance said, which was obviously true.

Terrance and I didn't sit and talk very often anymore. We didn't have time. I couldn't wait until he finished law school in a few months. Maybe it would be a lot less hectic with him not having to work, go to school, and study. I took a bite of one of my buffalo wings and happened to look behind Terrance at one of the other couples sitting at one of the other tables nearby. I couldn't believe it. I looked back down at my plate trying not to be too obvious. Terrance wasn't paying attention to me anyway. He was too infatuated with his food. He didn't play when it came to eating. Suddenly, I felt somebody standing over us.

"Hey, Kel. What's up wit you?"

I slowly looked up, already knowing who it was because I had already seen him at the other table. I was so nervous that I considered acting like I didn't even know him. I said the first thing that came to mind.

"Hey. Long time no see."

"Yeah I know. You still look the same from the last time I saw you." Reggie was trying to be funny with that comment. He knew he had just seen me last week. I just played his game right along with him.

"Terrance, this is my friend from school, Reggie. Reggie, this is my husband, Terrance."

Terrance nodded and said, "Hey, man. What's up?"

"Nice to meet you, Terrance. I never thought this girl would get married. She was somethin' in school."

I quickly tried to change the subject. "So, Reggie, is that your wife sittin' over there?"

"Nooo. I never got married. You know, that girl I used to mess around with in school, she broke my heart for the second time not too long ago, so I'm still tryin' to get over that."

"Poor baby," I said, trying to sound sincere.

"Yeah, well, again, nice meeting you, Terrance, and nice to see you again, Kel. I'll be talkin' to you."

I looked at Reggie as he walked away, wanting to kick him in his ass. When he sat back down with the woman he was with, they both started smiling and laughing. I wasn't gay or anything, but she was beautiful. She looked like a model. I wondered who she was. Was she a coworker of his? A friend? Or did he fuck her like he fucked me? I was so deep in thought watching them that I forgot Terrance was sitting across from me until he said something.

"He must really be in love with the girl he was talking about."

"Yeah. He had it bad for her in high school, but it looks like he's getting over it just fine." I took a sip of my coke and finished my food. It was hard for me to finish because I felt so sick to my stomach watching Reggie with another woman. Unless Reggie was a damned good actor and overexaggerated the situation, they seemed to me to be in love. Terrance didn't ask anything else about Reggie. He felt sorry for him and didn't even know him. I knew that Reggie was playin' games and two could play that game.

When we got ready to leave Applebee's, I had the chance to get back at Reggie. Terrance and I stood up and I walked over to Terrance, gently rubbed his defined jawline, and gave him a kiss.

"I love you, baby." I said in a sensual voice.

"I love you too, boo." Terrance walked in front of me as we slid between the tables. I switched my ass so hard right past Reggie's table that I felt like I was about to break a hip. As I walked past and noticed I had his attention, I winked and gave him a sneaky grin. No one outplays me.

When I stepped into Terrance's black Impala, I said, "That was nice, baby. We need to try and do this more often."

"We'll be able to soon. Don't even worry about it. I'm just trying to get to where I can get my boo anything she wants."

"And who is your boo?" I said, turning sideways in my seat, looking at his sexy profile.

"You know you my boo, so stop playin'. You been my boo since the night I came and talked to you after dancing with my "woman" on the dance floor!" We both started laughing. Now when I think about it, I should've been embarrassed as hell.

"I'm surprised you still attempted to talk to me after I made such an ass of myself."

"I couldn't resist your sexy ass. You was lookin' too good to let somebody else snatch you up. I would've never forgiven myself for that."

"Awww. That's so sweet."

I thought we were going home after we left Applebee's, but Terrance was going in the opposite direction. I didn't even ask where we were going. I just enjoyed the ride. Terrance used to always just ride me around to flaunt me. I could always tell that he was so proud to have me on his arm, and I was proud to have him on mine. We ended up in a neighborhood that didn't seem to be one of the nicest, and Terrance started slowing down and parking in front of a small brick building. I raised my sunglasses up to see exactly where we were. It was a gun shop. Terrance was serious about getting me a gun. He already had one, but I didn't even know if he ever even carried it. I barely ever saw it. I didn't even know where he kept it, and I really wanted to keep it that way. I didn't know much about guns, but the salesman showed us a lot of them and how they worked. Terrance ended up buying me a silver Derringer, so that I could fit it in my purse. Now I just needed to get my permit.

By the time we got home, unfortunately it was almost time for Terrance to go to class, so I would have to find something else to occupy the rest of my day. I knew that Tasha and Briana had to work today, and there was no telling when Tif would be back. I was gonna get out the house by myself, but gas was way too high to just be driving around for no apparent reason. I took my bored ass in the living room and tried to watch TV, but that was not even workin' for me. I was never big on television. I would rather go to sleep most of the time, but it was too nice of a day to just lay around. I almost took my ass to work, but

I hadn't scheduled any appointments for the week, and I hated sittin' around there waiting for walk-ins. I was in the mood to have a drink, so I went in the kitchen and took my blender out so I could make me some strawberry daiquiris. After I finished making them, I poured me some in a tall glass, cut up some fresh strawberries, and grabbed my radio from off the top of the refrigerator. I plugged my radio up outside on the patio and enjoyed myself, my music, the weather, and of course, my daiquiri.

After I had been sitting outside for almost a half hour, I heard someone walking on the side of the house. I pushed my sunglasses down towards the end of my nose, and I saw Mike coming around the corner. At first he didn't look in my direction, but I guess he heard my music. He had gloves on his hands to probably work in his yard. He did a lot of that landscaping type stuff in his backyard. It was a beautiful view. He had flowers everywhere and even a fountain. It reminded me of Sanaa Lathan's backyard when that white man finished it in that movie *Something New*. He had shorts on, which I had never seen him in. When did the sexiness end? He had big, sexy, bowed legs. When he looked over at me, he waved, which was strange. It was strange because he always spoke and usually would come over to talk. When I looked over at him again, I noticed he had his Bluetooth in his ear, so I assumed he was on the phone. I figured he was talking to a woman because he was talking so low that I could barely even hear him.

I got up, grabbed my glass, and went back in the house to get another daiquiri. When I slid my patio door open, I could see Mike in the corner of my eye turn around and watch me walk inside. While I was in the house, I checked my caller ID to make sure no one had called while I was outside. When I arrived back outside, to my surprise, Mike was sitting at the patio table.

"Well, hey there, beautiful. I hope you don't mind me barging in on your little party."

"No. That's cool. I was so bored sitting in the house, I had to find something to do."

"Yeah, I know what you mean. At least you have somebody. I'm a single man living in all that house by myself. So where's Terrance?"

I was so spellbound by his eyes, his lips, his smell, and his sexy legs that I said, "Who?"

"Terrance. You know, your husband.

"I knew who you were talking about. Don't play me like that. I was just messing with you. But anyway, he's in class. He's there a lot these days."

"Yeah, well it'll all pay off soon. I didn't realize he was in law school until he told me the other day. I might need a good lawyer one day."

"Well, sometimes I don't know if all the time we lose together is even worth it. Sometimes I think it might get even worse once he does actually become a lawyer."

Mike pushed a piece of my hair behind my ear that was flying in my face.

"I understand how you feel. There's no way in hell I'd let my beautiful wife be without me all day. I would just have to make some sacrifices so that I could spend time with her." He gazed into my eyes as he spoke and I felt like I had known him all my life. I watched his pink, juicy lips every time he spoke.

"I'm sorry. I didn't even ask you if you'd like a drink. You like strawberry daiquiris?"

"It's a woman's drink, but I'll take one to cool me off."

I laughed and said, "A woman's drink? You are so crazy!" I got up and went in to get him a daiquiri. As I walked to the door, I could feel him looking at my ass, but it was all good. I locked the door behind me. I had learned my lesson after the Reggie incident about going in the house and leaving a fine-ass man outside. They tend to barge their way right on in.

When I came back out, Mike was on the phone again. I put his glass in front of him and listened to his conversation, even though I wasn't trying to. He was laughing and smiling. I knew for a fact that this time it was a woman. Maybe he did have someone he was dating, and I had just never seen her.

"Baby, I'm a little busy right now, but I promise I'm gonna call you back. I miss you too. OK. Bye."

He hung up the phone, and I didn't wanna act like I was listening, so I said, "So Mike, what do you do for a living?"

"I own my own brokerage firm downtown. It's called Travis Inc."

"That's yours?" I asked, astonished.

"Yeah. Has been for the past six years. It was my father's, but then he passed away, so I inherited it. I could've just sold it, but I chose to live out his legacy. He lived for that place. I wanted to make him proud."

"Well, how in the world are you at home so often?" I asked curiously.

"When you own a business, you tell your employees what to do. As long as you have people working for you who you can trust, you go to work when you want to. That's the sweet thing about it."

"When and if you ever get married, your wife would never have problems spending time with you. Must be nice."

"Must be nice what?"

"Being you. Being so young and well-off. How old are you anyway?"

I don't think I had ever had such an engaging conversation with my own husband. It felt so nice to just be able to sit and talk to someone of the other gender without being physical. Terrance and I had had a nice time earlier today, but I wasn't as engaged as I was right now.

"Damn, girl. You don't care what you ask a person do you? I'm thirty-three, if you must know. And as for 'being me . . .'" He laughed and shook his head. "Being me has its advantages and disadvantages. I never really know if I woman is feelin' me or my money." He took the straw out of his glass, put the glass to his mouth, and took a sip of his daiquiri. He then licked the slush from his lips. I could just imagine what his cold lips would feel like up against mine.

"Well, I think you're a nice person, except when you call yourself hittin' on a married woman."

"I think you like it. Don't you?"

I was beginning to feel really uncomfortable, but I brought it on myself. I didn't think he was actually gonna admit to coming on to me, but he had no shame.

"Well, I'm not even gonna lie. It does make me feel good sometimes. It makes me feel like I'm still desirable to men. I used to feel like that all the time with Terrance, but I guess that has to end at some point."

"No, it doesn't. Especially not with a woman like you. I would always adore you . . . Well, I mean, a woman like you."

Mike stood up and walked behind my chair. I looked around at him trying to figure out what he was doing. He took his work gloves off and sat them on the table.

"Don't look at me like that, Kellie. Just relax and enjoy." He put his soft, warm hands on my shoulders and started massaging them. He felt like a professional masseuse. I moved my neck around in a circular motion with my eyes closed. He said, "Kel, I've been yearning to touch you for so long. Every time I see you, I just wanna touch your skin. You are so beautiful." I suddenly felt him massaging my shoulders, then, I could hear him making his way in front of me. I kept my eyes closed the whole time. The next thing I knew, Mike's lips were pressed up against mine with his tongue making its way inside my mouth. I slowly opened my mouth, trying to debate if I should, or end it right there. I was still sitting in the chair, and he was kneeling between my legs and continued to gently kiss me.

"Kellie!"

At that moment, everything seemed to stop—even the song that was playing on the radio, which I had no idea what it was because I wasn't thinking about the damn radio.

Our lips slowly parted. I looked up, and it was Tif standing about three feet away from us. I was at a total loss for words.

"You wanna try to tell me something about how I live my life and you out here hoeing around on your husband, who is more than just good to you. I really looked up to you, but you ain't no better than me, Tasha, or Bri!"

Mike stood up and said, "Look. I don't know you, but I want you to know that this isn't Kellie's fault. She was minding her own business, and I came over here and came on to her."

"Whateva!" Tif said, and stormed in the house slamming my patio door.

"Shit, Mike! I knew I should've stopped. Why didn't I just stop?"

"Because you feel something, and I do, too. Something real special."

"You are my fuckin' next-door neighbor. You speak to my husband almost every day! This is too close to home!"

"And what? That's supposed to make me not have feelings for you?"

"You don't even know me. Now ain't no telling what my girl thinks of me. I try to keep my life private, and here I go putting it out there for everyone to see. I can't do this, Mike. It's just wrong."

"It wasn't so wrong when you fucked your so-called cousin, Philip, now was it?"

"What! You are a low-down nigga. How could you come to me with that after you said you felt something special with me? Don't fuckin' talk to me ever again!"

I stood up and was about to swing my patio door open when Mike grabbed me and said, "I'm sorry, I shouldn't have gone there, but I just don't understand how you could give him a chance and then say it's wrong when it comes to me."

"You don't know what went on that day, so just get a life." I walked in, locked the door, and closed the blinds.

Tif was sitting in the den watching TV. I don't know if she was actually watching it, but she stared at it. I stood in the doorway, and she didn't even look my way.

"Tif, I'm sorry that you saw that. I know how uncomfortable you must've felt, but nothing has ever gone on with us before."

"I know I overreacted, but I was just shocked. I'm used to seeing you so happy with Terrance, and it's just so beautiful to me. You two give me hope of finding someone and having something special like you two have . . . or had. You don't have to worry about me sayin' anything. You were my friend way before I even knew Terrance. Even though I feel bad for Terrance, I can still see, and your neighbor is fine as hell."

I smiled a little bit and sat next to Tif on the couch. "Tif, I'm not perfect. You can't base your life on me and mine. I've been going through a lot, and I'm not happy all the time, even though I feel like I should be. Terrance is a wonderful man, but I just feel like I'm missing something sometimes. Something happened a little over a week ago that I haven't been able to talk to anyone about, and it hurts not to be able to let it out, but at the same time, I feel like I don't regret my actions. It's complicated."

I sat there trying to ponder on whether or not I should share my secret with her. After a few minutes I said, "Tif, if I tell you something, it has to stay between us, and never leave this room."

"After all I told you about my family, you should know you can trust me."

Tif seemed really sincere, and she had shared a lot with me, so I decided to tell her about me and Reggie. She knew exactly who Reggie was and couldn't believe that we had messed around in high school and no one ever knew. I also told her about seeing him in Applebee's with another woman and the jealousy that came over me.

"Kel, I know you got married young, but I always knew you could handle it because you got a good head on your shoulders. I told you not to do it, but maybe I was a bit jealouse because it wasn't me. I know you're a real friend, too. Terrance told me this morning in the kitchen how Tasha and Bri told you that they hadn't talked to me since they had left me at the bar with those guys, and you took it upon yourself to come to my house to see if I was all right. That's a real friend. So in return, I'm gonna be a real friend and say that you already know what you have at home. Me and everyone else are on the outside looking in. You know how you feel and what your heart is telling you. Just follow your heart. If you have feelings for someone else, I think you should find out for yourself and check it out to see how you really feel." Tif looked at me with sadness in her eyes and said, "Don't lead Terrance on the way my daddy led my momma on." A tear rolled down my face, and I wiped it away with the back of my hand.

I sat there and thought about it for a minute. I thought about what Mike had said about him feeling something special. I felt like there may have been something there, but I wasn't sure. I could tell that Mike was a good guy and I didn't wanna end our friendship the way it just had ended. I just wasn't ready to face him quite yet. Especially after the comment he made about me and Reggie. He apologized for it, but I was still upset about it. Maybe it hurt so badly because it was the truth.

"Everything will be all right, Kel, just like I believe everything will be all right with me. Just know that everything you say to me will stay between me and you."

I was glad to have someone I could talk to. I didn't plan on telling Tif everything, but at least I could vent to someone when I needed to.

Chapter 10

The rest of the week, I avoided seeing Mike. I would look out the window every time I got ready to leave the house to make sure he wasn't outside. I had looked at Reggie's phone number a couple of times but still didn't bring myself to call him. Tif had found herself a new apartment, which made me a little upset because I enjoyed her company when Terrance wasn't home. She would still be living with us for a few weeks until her apartment was completely ready. About a week after Tif found a new apartment, I heard Tif in the living room talking to Tasha on the phone about going out to celebrate. She wanted to celebrate making it through her tragedy and starting over. I just didn't know if she was ready to go out yet. It seemed pretty soon, and what if she saw that crazed maniac out there? The police still hadn't found him, claiming they were still looking, which I felt like was some bullshit.

"Tif."

"Hold on, Tasha."

"Yeah. What's up, Kel?"

I spoke softly so that Tasha couldn't hear me. "Are you sure you're ready for that? I don't know if it's been long enough since the incident for you to be going out partyin'."

"Yeah, I'll be fine. You're gonna come too, right?"

"Now you know Terrance don't like me goin' out."

"Well, ask him to go with us. It's cool."

"I don't know. Maybe I will. We'll see." I walked out the room and Tif continued making plans for the night.

Terrance was in the bedroom, watching a basketball game. I laid next to him and gave him a kiss on the cheek.

He jumped up so fast it scared me. "Where's the foul! They cheatin' like hell."

I said, "Baby. You wanna do somethin' tonight?"

"Do something like what?" he said, still staring at the TV.

"Since it's Saturday, the girls are going out to celebrate Tif getting her life back on track after all she went through, and Tif really wants us to go."

"I don't know, babe."

"Come on."

"Naw. You can go."

"You sure?"

"Yeah. I'll be all right. Just don't be out all night."

I couldn't believe Terrance was gonna let me go out. I didn't know how to act since it had been so long since I really hung out. I just hoped he wouldn't hang this over my head every time I turned around. Tasha and Bri weren't gonna be able to believe it either. They were always trying to jive on somebody, talking about I was on lockdown. I was gonna have fun tonight because there was no telling when the next time would be.

Terrance laid in the bed, watching me as I got ready to go out with the girls. I knew he wouldn't feel what I was putting on, but I didn't care. I was gonna be cute. I put on a my black strapless mini-dress that showed a lot of cleavage and these bad ass black-and-fuchsia DKNY shoes with the matching handbag that I had bought when Terrance and I had gone to the mall the week before.

"I thought you were gonna wear that when we went out somewhere together."

"Terrance, I asked if you wanted to go and you said no. Please don't throw a guilt trip on me now."

"I'm not throwing a guilt trip on you. You just look too damn good to be going out without me."

There was a knock on my bedroom door.

"Yeah."

I heard Tif's voice on the other side of the door. "You almost ready. It's already ten o'clock. You know you got curfew."

"Ha! Ha! Really funny!" I said sarcastically."

Terrance said, "It's not meant to be funny. You do got curfew. You a married woman. You can't be out in these streets all night." Terrance made me mad when he made demands, but it turned me on at the same time.

"I climbed on top of him and said, "What's my curfew, daddy?"

"You betta not come back in here past one-thirty, or I will come find you and embarrass your ass."

I gave him a kiss and left my lipgloss smeared across his lips. I went downstairs, and he followed. Tif was standing at the door waiting in a cute cream-colored strapless catsuit. It had gold embroidery and rhinestones going all the way up both pants legs and across the top. Tiffany had a very curvaceous figure, similar to Beyoncé, so she was wearing the hell out of it.

Terrance walked us to the door and said, "Alright now, Kel, remember our agreement."

"Don't worry, baby. I'll see you in a little while."

Tif was already all the way out the door and said, "Bye, Terrance. I'll take care of her." He stood in the door until we got in my car and drove off.

"So what time is your curfew, girl?"

"One-thirty," I reluctantly said.

"Why you say it like that? He gave you more time than I thought he would."

"Yeah. I guess I just miss those days when there was no curfew. When I went home whenever I got there because I didn't have anyone to answer to."

"Yeah, I know what you're sayin', but I had to find out the hard way that there's nothing but trash in these streets. Now I feel kinda nervous about going out. I did learn not to separate from my girls ever again. I never wanna go through what I went through again. I still have dreams."

"What kind of dreams?" I asked.

"Dreams of it happening over and over again. I just hope they go away because I don't wanna have to go to therapy. I had enough of that after my parents died."

"Well, you might still need it. You can't keep going through life having those kinds of dreams."

"I know. I just wish I could go back and change the whole thing."

"We all sometimes wish we could go back and change things, but all we can do is move on and leave the past behind us."

I pulled up to the Regal, and I drove around the parking lot until I saw Tasha's car. There weren't any parking spaces close to hers, so I had to park on the other side of the club. After I parked, I looked in the mirror to make sure my makeup was flawless, and Tif did the same, just like we did before I was married, except it was usually me and Tasha riding together. We got out the car and walked up to the door like we was the shit. There was a long-ass line at the door and as we walked past the crowd of people to get to the end of the line, all we could hear was niggas saying, "Damn, baby!" We didn't stand in line long because most of the people in line were sent back to wherever they came from because they were too young to get in. I had been there and done that, but the majority of the time, I got in. We finally made it inside the club and searched for the rest of our clique.

Tif and I tried to stay together, but there were so many people in the club that we got split up. This had to be a fire hazard. There was no way in hell this many people should've been in this club. I walked around for about ten minutes looking for my girls, and my feet started killing me. I should've known better than to wear four-inch heels to a club, but like my grandma always told me, cuteness will kill you. Men just don't understand what women go through to impress their low-down asses, and half the time they don't even appreciate it. Surprisingly, I found a vacant table, so I sat down hoping that I would see Tif, Tasha, or Bri walk by. I wanted to stay close to Tif just in case we saw the dude that raped her. She said his name was Ray, but he probably didn't even use his real name. I tried to use my cell phone to call them so they could tell me where they were in the club, but I couldn't get no damn signal. I knew I should've switched phone companies. While I was sitting there, I just looked around and wondered what the hell I was doing there. The women up in there looked so skanky and desperate. I tried to remember if I ever looked like that when I was hittin' the clubs all the time. If I did, I couldn't recall it.

About ten minutes after I had sat down, this ugly-ass negro came over trying to holler.

"What's up, baby. You look like you need a little company."

"No. I'm just waiting for my girls to come back from the bathroom." I felt like I was screaming cuz the music was playing so loud. They were playing that jam, "Climax" by Usher.

"Well, can I sit down and keep you company until they come back?"

Damn. I did not want this ugly-ass dude sitting with me, but I couldn't think of anything else to say without sounding rude.

"Kellie!" I heard someone screaming from the crowd so I looked past Mr. Ugly that was standing in front of me with his dingy jeans and baby shirt and saw Tasha. *Saved by the bell,* I thought.

"Hey, Tasha girl. I am so happy to see you."

Tasha looked at the guy that was hovering over me, then looked at me and said, "I know you are!"

I stood up and politely said, "I would love to sit down and talk to you. You really seem like a good guy, but my friends are waiting, so maybe I'll see you around some other time." Before he even had the chance to ask for my number, like I knew he would, I grabbed Tasha's hand and said, "Come on girl, let's go."

"What the hell was that, Kel? He was horrific!"

"I know. I owe you one. You came right in time. Have you seen Tif?"

"Yeah, she sitting over on the other side with us. We been looking for you, but I see you were preoccupied."

"Oh, ok. You got jokes!"

We got over to the table, and Bri was sitting with some guy she probably had already picked up to pay for her drinks for the night.

I think that was the only girl that I had ever seen that never paid for her own drink. He was kinda cute but not nearly cute enough for me. You had to be fine for me to even give you a second look. I think that's why I got dogged out by men in my past because I always picked the finest ones. I realized the fine ones are the ones that all the women want, so that's a problem right there. I never had a problem with Terrance and other women, though. He wasn't the cheating type, unless he just hid it very well. I knew he didn't have it in him to cheat on me.

"Where you been, girl!" Tif screamed from the table.

"Looking for y'all! I'm surprised y'all ain't out there showing y'all asses on the dance floor."

"Not yet," Bri said. "You know I gotta get some liquor in me first. She looked at the dude next to her and said, "Oh yeah, this is my friend Dre," and finished sipping on whatever she was drinking. Bri was kinda shy, but she turned into somebody else when she got alcohol in her system. She felt like she could do anything and talk to anybody.

"Hi, Dre." He looked at me, gave me the peace sign, and kept bobbing his head to the music. Before I sat down at the table, I told them I would be right back. I was going to the bar to get me something to sip on. "Anybody else want something back?" I don't think anybody was listening because no one responded. Bri and Tif were listening to whatever Tasha was talking about. I shouted, "I'll be back. I'm going to get a drink!"

They all said in unison, "OK, girl," and Tasha kept running her mouth.

When I got to the bar, there was a line, which I shouldn't have been surprised by. There was a girl standing in front of me, and just looking at her made me want to throw up. Her skirt was hiked up so high that I could see the bottom of her ass cheeks. On top of that, she had cottage-cheese thighs. I never grasped the concept of coming out the house looking like a damn fool. She thought she was looking good, so she had to get some attention some type of way. What other way than to start acting ghetto as hell.

"This don't make no muthafuckin' sense how long people gotta wait around here to get some dranks! I need to bring my black ass back there and show y'all slow asses how to make dranks!" she

said in the most annoying voice I had ever heard. I guess she
wasn't the only ghetto chick in line because about ten other women
concurred in the same ghetto manner. I wanted to ask every last
one of them if they knew how ignorant they sounded.

"What's a damn shame is how stupid they makin' themselves
look right now!" someone behind me said, with a deep, baritone
voice.

"I know, right?" I said over my shoulder without looking all
the way back. There was no reply after that, so I just continued to
wait so I could get my drink and head back to the table.

When I finally got to the front of the line, I sat on one of the
stools in front of the bar and ordered a top-shelf Long Island. I
watched the bartender carefully while she made my drink just in
case she thought I was one of the broads giving her a hard time and
decided to spit in it or some shit. I'm real careful when it comes to
stuff like that.

When she brought my drink over to me, I pulled out a ten and
was about to hand it to her, when the guy who was standing in
back of me handed her a fifty and said, "Add a Hennessy on the
rocks to that." I turned around in the bar stool and looked at the
man who had just paid for my drink. He was grimy lookin'. He had
that need-to-shave look, which I usually didn't like, but it looked
kinda nice on him. He was brown-skinned with the most beautiful
eyes. They were dark, but the white of his eyes were so bright, and
his eyelashes were prettier than any woman's I had ever seen. His
hair was cut low, and lined perfectly.

"You know, I could've handled that," I said.

"I know, but I didn't want you to have to."

I stood up and said, "Thank you . . . what's your name?"

"Ty. Ty Wesley."

"Thank you, Ty Wesley." I got up, grabbed my drink, and
walked away. I decided to play the hard-to-get role. I refused to let
any man get the impression that all they had to do was buy me a
drink to get a chance with someone like me.

By the time I got back over to the table, Bri and Tasha were on
the dance floor looking like some freaks. Bri was dancing with
Dre, and Tasha was dancing with some goofy-lookin' dude. I

looked around for Tif, but I didn't see her. I sat down and started sippin' on my long-awaited Long Island.

I was sitting there drinking and laughing at Bri and Tasha's crazy asses when I heard someone say, "I didn't get yo name. I did buy your drink. I think I at least deserve to know your name."

I looked up at Ty and started to make up a name like I usually did when I didn't feel like being bothered, but I considered myself to be in a good mood, so I said, "Kel. My name is Kel." He didn't need to know my whole name. Kel was good enough.

He looked down at my hand. "Oh, well, I see you married, or are you just flossin' that big rock on your wedding finger?"

"No, I'm married."

"Well, can you have a friend?"

"Do you think you could really be my friend?"

"What you mean by that?" he said, frowning and squinting his dark eyes.

"I don't believe a man can be friends with any woman that he's interested in."

Ty sat down and crossed his arms. "Who said I was interested in you?"

"It's obvious, or you wouldn't have bought me a drink or took the time to come all the way over here to ask my name."

"I guess you got a point, but is it a crime to approach a sexy-ass woman like yourself and try to get acquainted? I've had female friends before, and things do work out."

I looked out on the dance floor to make sure Tasha and Bri weren't paying attention to me talking to Ty, then I continued my conversation. I sucked my teeth and said, "So what does being my friend consist of?"

"Just chillin'. You know, having somebody to talk to when you going through hard times with your husband, maybe going to dinner sometimes, catchin' a movie. Does that sound aight with you?"

"Yeah, but me and my husband rarely go through hard times. Being your friend might cause more hard times than necessary."

Ty lightly tapped on the table with his finger and said, "Well, you think about it. I'm going back to my table to chill with my boys. You'll be able to find me if you need me." His chair made a horrible shrieking noise as he scooted away from the table. I didn't say a word. I smirked as I watched him get up and walk away.

Right after he walked off, Tif came back to the table and plopped down in the booth. "Where you been, Tif?"

"I went outside to get a little air. It's stuffy and funky up in here!"

"You need to be careful, girl. Don't be going outside by yourself. I would've gone with you."

"You need to stop acting like my guardian. I am ok!," Tif said defensively. She obviously had been drinking and the liquor was getting to her.

"I'm just concerned about you. I would hate for anything else to happen to you, but I'll leave you alone." Tif was being real funky. I had never known her to go outside a club to get some air, but I just left it at that. I knew something wasn't right. I got up and left her sitting there so I could get a few dances in before my "night of freedom" was over.

Tasha was still dancing, but I didn't see Bri. Tasha could dance all night long. That's what she loved to do, and she was good at it. She taught all of us how to dance when we were in high school. I would never go to any of the dances or sock hops because I couldn't dance a lick. My mama was kinda strict, so she didn't even let me watch music videos to even get an idea of how to dance. Even though she was strict and tried to keep her eye on me, I still got away with a whole lot of dirt.

I went over by Tasha and started dancing. She continued dancing and started laughing and said, "Girl, didn't I teach you better than that? Yo ass still can't dance!"

"Girl, shut up. I don't get any complaints!"

"Yeah, cuz don't nobody wanna hurt your feelings." I flicked Tasha off and kept on dancing. I looked over at our table at Tif. She was sitting over there looking like she had an attitude. I had no idea what was wrong with her. It escaped me what changed her mood from the time we entered the club 'til now. After I danced to a couple of fast songs, the DJ decided to play my song "Dance for You" by Beyoncé. Tasha grabbed somebody real quick to dance with, and as I started walking back to my seat, I saw Ty walking towards me. He grabbed my left hand and walked me back to the floor. He pulled my body close to his and put one arm around my waist.

I started pulling away from him and said, "Ty . . ." He put his index finger up to my lips, silencing me while he gazed in my eyes. He grabbed both of my arms and put them around him. Tasha couldn't concentrate on what she was doing, stepping all on her dance partner's feet because she was trying to be all up in my business. That's exactly what I didn't want. I had told Tiffany enough shit. I didn't need Tasha to be asking any questions. This was just a dance anyway. Nothing serious.

Ty rocked me gently on the dance floor without saying a word. I could feel his breath right next to my ear. I could smell the Hennessy on his skin mixed with his cologne, but he still smelled good as hell. He was about six feet, but I was close to his height with my tall-ass heels on. Usually I would feel uncomfortable dancing with someone and not saying a word, but it felt normal. The next couple of songs were slow jams. After the last one went off, I felt Ty loosen his grip from my hips. I looked around, and we were the only two on the dance floor.

"See you later, Kel," Ty said and walked the other way. I went back to our table and Tasha had to start some shit.

"Un huh. So who was that fly-ass nigga?"

"I don't know. He asked me to dance so I danced with him. Is that a crime?"

"It is if you not gon' tell yo husband that you was dancing with somebody at the club. He pulled you out there like he knew you."

"Well no, I don't know him."

"Well then, I might need to get to know him." Tasha loved to test me. She always had. We were always close, so she always knew how to get to me. I knew she was just trying to see if I responded to her, so I didn't. Tif and Bri were having their own little conversation. While I was dancing with Ty, I had seen them talking, and they looked like they were having a deep conversation. It had to be deep for Bri to be interested in listening. She was sitting there engaged in whatever Tif was talking about. The first thing I thought was maybe I made Tif mad in some way, and she was telling Bri everything I had told her, but then again, I didn't think she would do that. I would get it out of Bri later. That's why

I never told Bri anything. She was the big mouth of the group. She couldn't hold water.

I looked at my gold diamond watch and it was almost one o'clock. I remembered my deal with Terrance that as long as he was letting me go, I would be home by one-thirty.

"Hey, y'all," I said.

Tif responded, "What's up, Kel?" Whatever Bri and Tif talked about, helped Tif's attitude. All of a sudden, she was acting herself again.

I raised my arm and tapped on my watch. "I gotta go. Y'all know Terrance is at home waiting for me. You ready to go, Tif?"

"Naw. Tasha, can you drop me off at Kel's house?"

Tasha took a deep breath as if she was irritated by the question and said, "Y'all know gas ain't cheap."

"Don't even worry about it. I'll just leave now with Kel."

That was some bull. My house was on the way to Tasha's house, and she acted like she couldn't bring Tif home.

Tasha said, "Girl, I'll take you. Calm your ass down. You know I was just playing."

I cut my eye at her and grabbed my purse. "I'll talk to y'all later and be careful." I made my way through the crowd that had cleared a whole lot since we had first gotten to the club. I didn't know if I felt real comfortable leaving Tif with them, but she was getting tired of me so I had to leave it alone and let her do her. I didn't see Ty in the club. I saw his boys he was sitting with, but not him. I stood at the door looking for my keys before I walked outside. I knew it was late, and there were a bunch of drunk fools around, so I knew I needed to be prepared to get in the car. I walked fast, looking around to make sure I wasn't in harm's way.

"You wouldn't have to be so paranoid if you had somebody to walk you to your car." I heard someone say in the distance. I looked around and I saw Ty, leaning up against an old-school silver Cadillac with what looked like twenty-two-inch rims on it. When I looked his way, he stopped leaning and stood straight up. He was smoking a Black & Mild. Smoking was always a turnoff for me. I kept walking to my car. *Damn, why did I have to park so far away!* I thought to myself.

When I finally made it to my car, I dropped my keys, and they slid under my car. "Shit!" I was trying to be cautious, and it backfired. I felt like the stupid white girl in horror movies that always fell while running from the villain and took forever to get back up! I got on my knees to get my keys. I felt someone standing over me, and it scared the shit out of me. When I looked up, I looked right into Terrance's face.

"Terrance. What are you doing here?"

"I knew you would just now be leaving the club trying to hurry your ass up and get home, so I came to make sure you and Tif got to the car safely."

I didn't know if I should've been happy that Terrance was looking out for me, or think that maybe he was spying on me.

He looked around and said, "Where's Tif?"

"She decided to stay longer, so Tasha's gonna bring her home."

"You know you don't need to be walking out here by yourself. They could've walked you to the car or something."

"I know, but I'm ok. Thank you for looking out for me, baby."

"No problem. I'll see you when you get home." Terrance waited for me to get in the car before he got in his and pulled off.

Just when I was about to pull off, someone knocked on my window. Scared again, I slowly looked to see who it was. It was Ty.

I rolled my window down halfway and said, "Yes. Can I help you?"

"So your husband is a stalker, huh?"

"My husband cannot stalk me. He was merely looking out for my safety."

"Yeah, ok. Now I see why you refused to be my friend. You on lockdown."

I tried to jump hard and said, "I am not on lockdown. I do whatever the hell I wanna do! Don't you come over here trying to judge me!"

"Well, since you do whatever you wanna do, then give me your number, cuz I know you want to."

I unlocked my doors and for some strange reason, I trusted him enough to tell him to get in. For all I knew, he could've been another Ray. He walked over to the passenger door and got in.

"You must trust me a little bit if you let me get in your car."

"I wouldn't say that. I just don't want everybody in my business."

"So what's up? You gon' give me your number or what. I know you was feelin' me on the dance floor the same way I was feelin' you." He was so damn arrogant it didn't make no sense. His ruggedness reminded me of Eric Benet. Every time he spoke, I smelled the Black & Mild on his breath. I usually hated that smell, but it smelled good coming from his mouth.

"You give me your number," I said.

"Naw, cuz I don't got time for no other nigga calling my phone acting stupid if he find my number in your purse or somethin'. Just tell me when and when not to call."

I didn't know who I was anymore. I reached over Ty and tore a piece of paper off of something in my glove compartment. I grabbed a pen off of my sun visor and wrote down my cell phone number. Before I gave it to him I said, "Do not call me on the weekends, do not call me before 10:00 a.m., and do not call me after 8:00 p.m.! Do I need to write that down for you?"

Ty looked at me and said, "Woman, whatever." Then he grabbed the number out of my hand. "I'll talk to you later," he said as he grinned and got out of my car. I pulled my car in reverse and headed home. On my way home, my cell phone started ringing. I already knew it was Terrance trying to find out why I wasn't home yet.

"Hello."

"Hey, baby. You almost home?"

"Yeah. I'll be there in a few minutes. I had to stop for gas." I knew I was lying, but he didn't need to know all that. When I got off the phone, I stopped at a red light, put my head on the steering wheel and started crying. I had everything I wanted and needed, but I still felt the need to have someone else. I didn't want it to be like this, but this is how I felt content. I loved the attention other men gave me, and I craved it all the time. I didn't know if this was a phase that would pass, but I guess I would find out.

Chapter 11

It was Tuesday, and the weekend of a hairstylist was officially over. My alarm clock went off at six-thirty. It seemed like I had just gone to bed. I turned the alarm off and threw a pillow over my head to hide from the sun shining through my room. I lay there for about fifteen more minutes. I had to get up because I had a client coming in at seven-thirty. She was one of my regulars, so I couldn't afford to piss her off by being late. When I got up, I threw my pillow on Terrance. Now I knew why I felt like I had just gone to bed. I had to put up with his snoring all night. I rushed through the house trying to hurry up and get dressed when all of a sudden, the doorbell rang. I ran down the stairs and looked out of the peephole to see who the hell was at my door this early in the morning. Mike was standing there looking around with his hands in his pockets. He wasn't dressed like he was going to work. He had on jeans and a polo shirt. I didn't want to open the door because I hadn't seen him since our last incident, but I knew if I didn't answer it, Terrance would. I opened the door, and it felt like his eyes just grabbed me as soon as I looked in them.

Instead of cussing him out for coming to my house so early like I had intended, I said, "Hey, Mike. What's going on?"

I know it's early, but I was just coming by to see if you and Terrance wanted to go to breakfast with me and a friend of mine." He pointed over towards his car when he referred to his friend. I looked over, and there was a woman sitting in the passenger seat waving and smiling at me. I crossed my arms and shook my head.

"Thanks for being considerate," I said sarcastically, "but we're good. We have to go to work."

"Alright then. Well, I guess I'll check y'all out later."

"Yeah." I didn't know if he had anything else to say, but I didn't care. I slammed the door in his face and turned around. Terrance was standing right behind me. When I saw him, I jumped, and my heart started pounding.

"What was that about, Kel?"

"Nothin'. Mike just wanted to know if we wanted to go to breakfast with him and his friend."

"I heard that part, but you were a little rude, don't you think?"

"Oh, was I? If I was, I didn't mean to be. I'm just a little tired."

"Yeah. Me too. I feel like I didn't get any sleep."

"Well, you did. Kept me up all night with your snoring, but I'll survive." I put on my shoes and gave Terrance a kiss.

"I'll see you later, baby. If Tif wakes up before you go to work, tell her I'll be home around five-thirty."

"Alright, Kel."

Since Tif had been staying with us, I didn't think Terrance was too comfortable because he couldn't walk around the house however he wanted to. I was starting to feel the same way, but she would be leaving in a little over a week.

When I pulled up at the shop, it was only seven-twenty, and my client, Daria, was sitting outside in her car, smoking a cigarette. When she saw me pull up, she jumped out of her car with her bag of weave and beat me to the door. No one else had gotten there yet, so she had to wait for me to unlock the door. I was still grabbing my stove and curlers out my car when she finally decided to come over and help. I always took all of my stuff home with me at the end of my work day. I didn't trust those sneaky women up in there.

"You want me to carry some of that, girl?" Daria asked.

"Hey, girl. Yeah. Can you take this for me?" I handed her my bag with my stove. When she grabbed it, I looked at her hair. It looked like a brown matted dog was sitting on top of her head. She came and got her hair done every week, so I didn't understand how she managed to get her hair like that in just a week's time.

She must've noticed how I was looking at her because she said, "I had a long weekend, girl!"

"I can tell. Go over there and hurry up and sit in my chair before anybody else comes in here and see this mess." She started laughing and sat down. That weave was so damn nappy, I had to wet it so I could comb through that mess. It didn't help much that she always bought the cheapest brand of hair she could find. She got to telling me about how she spent the weekend with this guy she had started messing around with and how he put it on her. My job never got boring listening to my client's stories. Everybody always told me their business. I had heard it all.

Daria was twenty-seven with five kids. All five had different daddies. Her oldest was thirteen and her youngest was four, so her thirteen-year-old carried on the responsibility of babysitting so her momma could party and do whatever she wanted to do. I felt sorry for that little girl.

"So how you getting your hair today?" I asked Daria while I was still struggling to get her weave out of her head.

"I want a roller wrap. I got my hair right here."

I pulled the pack of hair out of her bag and said, "That's why your hair gets all matted! You buy this cheap weave that's gonna shed every time you comb it!"

"Girl, that's all right. You know how to hook it up. But anyway, let me finish tellin' you about how this dude made me feel like a lady. I never had a man treat me like he did. First of all, I ain't never had no man that wanted to spend the whole weekend with me. They usually get theirs and gone on about their business, but this one, he different, girl!"

"He sounds nice. I hope he works out."

"He is. I'm gon' make this work. And girl, check this out. He got a job! A legal one!" I started crackin' up! This girl was hilarious. "What's so funny, Kel?"

"Nothing, girl. You gone with your bad self!" I finally finished taking out her weave and headed to the shampoo bowl to wash that nasty shit.

While I was at the shampoo bowl, Phelecia walked in with some white Dolce and Gabbana sunglasses and a cute white summer dress with some bad ass white sandals on. Her hair was short and spiked as usual. Her dress was sexy. It came off the shoulders and the length was a little past her knees with slits going all around. Her long slender legs looks fabulous in it. I barely recognized her. I hadn't seen her look like that since high school. She had taken the whole last week off to go visit her mother who had been sick.

"Hey, Phelecia. What's the special occasion?" I asked.

"Girl, nothing. I just decided it was time for a change." She took off her sunglasses and looked in the mirror like she really admired herself again.

When I finished shampooing Daria, she stood up and walked over to my station and sat down. Phelecia was sitting down in her salon chair waiting on her client. Her station was right next to mine.

"Hey, Daria." Phelecia said.

"Hey, girl. You look nice today."

"Thank you, girl." Phelecia got up and walked to the back.

"I'll be right back, Daria," I said like there was an urgent emergency. Actually, there was. I had to find out what was going on with Phelecia. I didn't want to talk about it in front of Daria, so I went to the back with Phelecia. She was standing at the back door about to light up a cigarette. She hadn't changed her smoking habit.

"So what inspired the change?"

"I woke up a little bit. Or should I say I opened my eyes? When I went to my mom's house, I looked around at all the pictures and started remembering the old me, before I got dogged out by these lowlifes. I used to love myself, and I realized that if I don't love myself, no one will."

"I heard that, girl."

"After I started realizing that, and coming to terms with myself again, a couple of days later, I started cramping real bad. I layed around hoping it would pass, but then I started bleeding real heavy. My sister took me to the hospital, and I ended up miscarrying."

I put my hands up to my mouth and said, "I'm so sorry!."

"Unh uh. Don't do that. I'm ok with it. It just wasn't meant for me to have another one, especially with Duwan." Duwan was the guy Phelecia had been with for a little over a year. He wasn't doing anything with his life. I didn't know if he was a drug dealer or if he was living off of her, but one thing I did know from the few times I had seen him was that he was no good. I was usually good at seeing right through people, especially men, since I had dealt with so many different ones. I wasn't gonna say anything bad about Duwan to Phelecia because I knew from personal experience that love is blind, and you cannot let go of someone no matter how bad they treat you, until you're ready.

Phelecia continued talking about Duwan after she puffed her cigarette a couple of times, saying, "I don't know if he's the man for me, but I do love him, and I do know he loves me, so I'm just gonna wait to see where it goes."

"OK. Well, just keep loving yourself. You and your kids come first no matter what! Now let me go out here and finish this girl's hair."

"I'll be out there in a minute. If my client is out there, tell her I'm coming." When I got back to the front, I had two more clients sitting on the couch, and I saw Phelecia's client reading the bulletin board on the wall. I told her Phelecia was here, and she'd be starting on her hair in a minute. Daria was sitting there patiently, looking at a hair magazine.

"I'm sorry about that, girl. I got an emergency phone call from home." I had to think of a lie real quick. I didn't want Daria to know I had left her sitting there for ten minutes to go and be nosey.

"Is everything ok?" She said in a concerned tone.

"Yeah, everything's ok now."

Phelecia came to the front and turned on the radio. Kelly Price was singing "Not My Daddy." I blow dried Daria's hair and put her new weave in. While she was sitting under the dryer, I started on the next client. The other beauticians started rolling in around nine-thirty. They were too lazy to get their butts up at six or seven o'clock for their clients. That's why Phelecia and I had the largest clienteles in the shop, in addition to the fact that we were the baddest bitches up in there.

Phelecia and the other hairstylist, Cameron, were doing their client's hair, arguing about who was cuter, Boris Kodjoe or Shemar Moore.

I was sick of listening to it, so I put my five cents in and said, "You might as well say they the same man. They're both tall, light-skinned with dark features. One just got fucked-up teeth!" Cameron got mad as hell because she loved Shemar Moore, but she had to admit that brotha needed something done with his grill. In the middle of our discussion, my cell phone started vibrating. I looked at the screen and it said "Private Caller."

"Hello." The person on the other end said "hello" back, but I couldn't hear with all the commotion going on in the shop. "Hello?" I repeated as I told my client I would be back and walked towards the back of the shop.

"Hey, sexy. What's up?"

I tried to decipher the voice, but it wasn't familiar. I tried to play it off, hoping that whoever it was would continue to talk so I could figure out who in the hell it was, so I said, "Hey, what's up?"

"You told me not to call before ten. It's ten on the head, and I couldn't wait no longer to talk to you." By then I had figured out that it was Ty. I looked at the clock and it was one minute past ten. I guess he couldn't wait!

"What were you doing? Waiting by the phone until ten o'clock?"

"I told you I couldn't wait to talk to you. Is something wrong with that?"

"Not at all. Not at all."

I started walking back towards the front of the shop while I continued my conversation with Ty so I could finish my client's hair.

"So what you doin' today?" Ty asked.

"Um. I don't know. My last customer is coming at three, so I'll probably be done around four-thirty or so."

"What do you do?"

"I'm a hairstylist at Hair Haven." That slipped out before I could catch myself. I did not mean to tell his ass where I worked.

After that, I didn't have anything else to do except to ask him where he worked.

He replied, "I own my own business. I have clients who pay a lot for my goods and services. They tell me what they need, or what they need done. I contact my manufacturer or whoever else necessary, and I handle it. They know they can rely on me, so I have a pretty big clientele. I distribute all over the country. "That sounds interesting." That really sounded interesting to me because he had an old-ass Cadillac. By his job description, it seemed like he should've been able to afford a whole lot more than that, but I also knew how people embellished their careers by using big words to describe it. While I was talking, it seemed like the whole shop got quiet so I said, "Let me finish working, and I'll give you a call a little later."

"I would say that's cool, but how you gon' call me and you don't got my number?"

I lowered my voice and said, "Well, maybe I would have your number if you didn't call me private."

"How about I just call you around five?"

"OK. That's cool." I ended the conversation as fast as I could. I didn't need any unnecessary people knowing my business—especially in the beauty shop. Business travels fast when it comes out in the shop.

After I finished my last customer for the morning, it was almost time for Terrance to go to lunch, so I figured I would surprise him by meeting him for lunch. I told the girls I would be back and jumped in my car, trying to make it to the bank before Terrance left. It only took me about four minutes to get there. When I walked in, I looked around and didn't see anything but women. Terrance was the only man that worked in the bank, besides the security guard. At first, I didn't like the fact that he worked with all women, but I learned that I could trust my man. I asked his coworker, Stacy, if she had seen him. She said that I had just missed him. He had already left for lunch. Stacy seemed nice, but she also seemed like one of those sneaky women that would smile in your face and talk about you like a dog behind your back. She was a petite black woman with long thick hair. She kinda reminded me of William's wife, Monica, on the TV show

Girlfriends. She had to have been about thirty. There were very few women that I trusted and she definitely wasn't one of them. When I jumped back in my car, I pulled out my phone to call Terrance. His voice mail picked up, so I left a message. "Hey, baby. It's me. I just left your job. I was trying to surprise you so we could go out to lunch. Um . . . Guess I'll see you tonight. Call me later if you get a chance. I love you. Bye."

I sat in the bank's parking lot for about five minutes trying to decide what I was gonna do for lunch. I wanted to go somewhere and sit down and eat, but I hated eating alone, so I called Tif. I would've liked to spend some time with Tasha, but I knew she had to work the day shift today. Tif's phone rang about four times before she finally picked up.

"Hey, girl. I was just about to hang up. What you up to?"

"Girl, nothing, just doing a little cardio," Tif said, breathing heavily.

I didn't know why Tif was exercising with her perfect body, but I ignored the fact that she was working out and said, "Oh. Good. You wanna go out to lunch?"

"Naw. I can't. I told Theresa I would go to the mall with her in a little while."

"I'll go with y'all then. What time y'all going? I have about two hours before my next client comes in."

"I don't know. I'm waiting on her to call me back. You know how slow she is, so ain't no tellin'. I don't want you to spend your whole lunch waiting for us. We'll get together for lunch before I go back to work next week though."

Tif was still off from work since she had been in the hospital. It wasn't like she needed the money that bad. Her and Theresa's grandmother had left them a lot of money behind when she passed away.

"All right then. I'll see you later." I stopped at KFC and picked up a three-piece dinner and headed to Whitebeach Park. It was a beautiful park right next to the beach where my friends and I used to always hang out during my days when I was single. It was nice being able to see the beach while relaxing under a tree at the park. The water was always so beautiful and crystal clear. The sand on the beach was white, and the one thing I just loved about it was that it was the only beach around that was kept clean!

When I got to the park, I pulled a blanket out of my trunk and found a tree with nice shade to sit under while I ate my lunch. I took my shoes off and laid down after I finished eating and envied the woman sitting under a tree across from me who was having her feet massaged by her male companion. I tried not to be obvious while I watched them together. They seemed like a perfect couple, but so did Terrance and I, to people who were on the outside looking in. I yearned to have a relationship that the two people in my view seemed to have. The romance in my marriage was leaving slowly but surely, and I was sure Terrance could feel it too.

I laid there in the park for about an hour before I headed back to the shop. When I got back, all the other stylists stared at me like they were studying my every move. When I got to my work station, Phelecia came over to me and said, "You have a client in the bathroom." He's been here for almost an hour, sitting in your chair, waiting for you. I told him you were gone to lunch, and you wouldn't be back for a while, but he was persistent."

"He? I'm not a barber!"

"I'm just letting you know." Phelecia walked back to her station and continued working on her client's hair. I was getting nervous because I knew who it was in the bathroom. I had told that fool, Ty that I didn't get off until around four-thirty. I knew I shouldn't have told him where I worked. Now I gotta try to play this shit off.

Phelecia whispered, "Here he comes." I could feel everyone's eyes on me, waiting to see how I reacted. I glanced over and didn't see Ty. Instead, I saw Reggie. I hadn't seen or talked to Reggie since Terrance and I had seen him at Applebee's. He came and sat in my chair.

I had to put on a front. "Sorry I kept you waiting, but I didn't have any more appointments until one-thirty. What did you want done?"

I just want you to tighten up my lining for me and line up my beard and mustache." I only had lined up a few men since I had been doing hair. I guess Reggie wasn't too scared that I would jack his hair up.

While I lined Reggie up, I didn't say a word. I was just trying to figure out how in the hell he knew where I worked. He knew I was a stylist, but I never told him what shop I worked at. After I finished lining his hair, I started working on his beard and mustache. I wished that he would close his eyes, but he just gazed at me as I worked. He made me weak in the knees, but then I started getting pissed off when I started thinking about that beautiful-ass woman he was with at the restaurant. I felt like fucking his shit up, but I didn't. I couldn't mix business with my personal issues.

"Alright. You all set."

"Did you hook a brotha up?"

"You can't expect nothing less from me," I said sarcastically. Reggie stood up to look in the mirror, and all the women's eyes followed him. They were like hounds. You would think they never saw a man before.

He pulled his wallet out his back pocket and said, "How much I owe you?"

I felt like saying, "You owe me a whole lot of explaining!" but I settled for "It's just $15. All I did was line you up."

"Thank you. I appreciate it." He slid the money in my smock pocket.

He looked around at the other women and said, "Thank you for the hospitality, ladies." Then he left out the door. I never saw so many smiling faces in that shop.

"Girrrrrrl. That nigga was fine," Cameron said as she gave a high-five to her client.

Phelecia said, "Girl, you know he was too young for you. Didn't he go to school with us, Kel?"

"Yeah, I think so."

Cameron just had to start some shit. She was a mid-age shit starter. She was the type that if she couldn't be happy, she didn't want anybody else around her to be happy.

"Out of all these barbers in this city, why the hell he want a beautician to do his hair? And out of all the beauticians in the city, why you, Kel?"

"How am I supposed to know, Cameron? Maybe he heard that I was good at everything I do and wanted to give me a try."

"Maybe he already knew how good you were at everything, as you say, and wanted to give you another try. Ain't that right, y'all!" Everybody was nodding their heads and snickering, agreeing with Cameron's crazy ass.

"Girl, whatever. You don't even know what you're talking about. I have a happy home, and I don't need nobody stepping in messing it up."

Phelecia said, "That's right, girl. Cameron, quit hatin' because Kel got a good man. I wish you would find one so you could stay out of everybody else's business."

Cameron replied, "Girl, I'm not even gonna get on you."

Cameron could be cruel sometimes. I'm just glad she didn't put Phelecia out there because all the stylists in the shop knew that she was with a no-good, low-life nigga, but it did not need to be broadcasted and discussed. We knew if we continued, the discussion was gonna get too heated, and somebody was gonna walk out of there with their ass beat, so we all shut up and tended to our clients.

After I finished my last client for the day, I told the girls bye, even Cameron, even though she had pissed me off. It was still early because my last client had called and rescheduled for another day. When I got in the car, I took my money out of my smock, so I could go by the bank and drop it off. I hated having all that money on me because I was more susceptible to spending it, and that gave me a reason to go by and see Terrance for a minute. When I emptied my pockets, I noticed one bill that was rolled up and it seemed like it had been for a long time because every time I tried to unroll it, it would snap back. When I finally got it unrolled, I saw that it was a hundred-dollar bill and a yellow piece of paper fell on my lap. I picked it up and looked at it. Written on it was, "Call me. It could get better than this." Underneath those words was a phone number. Reggie's phone number. He had given me a hundred dollars just to line him up. *I must be a bad bitch!* I thought to myself and finished counting my money. It had been a very good day.

As I was about to pull off, I saw Phelecia coming out of the shop with her purse, but I didn't see her car. I figured Duwan probably had it as usual.

"Phelecia. You got a way home?"

"Yeah, girl. Duwan should be on his way. I'm about to call him right now." As she was pulling out her cell phone, Duwan came pulling up, looking like a damn thug driving her damn Camry. When Phelecia started walking towards her car, some dude that was driving down the street honked his horn at her, almost having an accident while hanging his head out the window, gawking at her.

Phelecia got to the car and before she opened the door, I could hear Duwan snapping, saying, "Who the fuck was that nigga?" He looked pissed off. He never looked like a nice person. He always had an evil look in his eyes that I perceived as nothing but the devil being in him. I sat there and watched them argue. I wanted to make sure Phelecia was ok.

"I don't know who that was, Duwan. I would tell you if I did!"

"Who the hell you talkin' to like that, Phelecia? That was probably the nigga you dressed all up for today. You foul as hell. You can walk yo ass home." Phelecia's car screeched as Duwan pulled off without her.

Phelecia turned, looked at me, and said, "Can you still give me a ride?"

"Come on, girl." I didn't even end up going to the bank like I had intended. Phelecia and I drove around for a while, just talking about high school and everything she had been through with men. I was always cool with Phelecia, but she was never anyone who I would call and talk to on the phone or hang out with. I saw us as being very different. The fact of the matter was that I had a backbone and she didn't. When we finally arrived at Phelecia's house, we didn't see her car anywhere in sight. "How the hell is he gonna run off with your car?"

"I'm not worried about it. He'll be back later. He just needs some time to cool down."

"Girl, I don't know how you do it, but you got a whole lot more patience than me. I probably would've been then reported my car stolen."

"I know, but I also know people can change, and when he finally does, I know it'll be well worth the ride."

I looked at Phelecia like she had serious issues and said, "Well, you got my number, so call me later on and let me know that everything is all right."

"I will. Thanks for the ride."

It was around four o'clock by the time I dropped Phelecia off, so I decided I would just go and deposit my money in the bank tomorrow. I had a short day, but it seemed extra long. When I got in the house, I immediately went upstairs and put on a tank top and my VS Pink lounge pants and laid across my bed watching a re-run of *The Tyra Show*. I must've dozed off for a little while because when my cell phone rang, it scared the mess out of me. I looked at the TV, and Tyra was dancing around in the crowd and clapping like she does at the end of the show. That's how I knew it was five o'clock. I looked at the caller ID on my cell and it said "Private Caller" once again. I knew what that meant. It was Ty calling back at the time he said he would. One thing I could already clearly observe about him was that he was very timely.

Chapter 12

"So did you figure out what you gonna do today?" the voice on the other end said as soon as I picked up and said hello.

"No. Right now I'm just lounging around."

"Why don't you come and chill with me? Let me show you a good time."

Even though Ty really wasn't my type, I was still curious to see what he had to offer. Terrance wouldn't be home for a few hours, so I said, "OK. Where you want me to meet you?"

"Oh. I ain't good enough to pick you up?"

"Ty, you know . . ."

"Girl, I'm just playin' with you. Meet me at my house."

"Oh. You can give me your address, but not your phone number. That makes sense."

"I would give you my phone number. I just don't want yo boy callin' me, actin' a fool. So can I proceed with giving you my address or not? Cuz right now we just wasting valuable time." He had the nerve to try to act like he was runnin' shit, but I was sweet on that shit and got a pen and a piece of paper to write down his address.

I talked to Ty almost the whole way to his house since the drive was longer than expected. I was hoping he lived close, so that if I did happen to have a good time with him, I wouldn't have to leave early to make it home at a decent time. His house was a good forty-five minutes away. He lived way on the other side of Chicago. On the way to his house, I told him a little bit about myself, like how long I had been married, and I also made sure to let him know how much I loved my husband. I didn't want him to expect too much from this. He kept taking deep breaths every time I brought my husband up in the conversation, but he needed to know the truth. I wanted this to be nothing more than a friendship with Ty. He just seemed like a cool and interesting person to hang out with. He didn't seem like anyone else who I had ever been around in my whole life, and that intrigued me even more. Terrance clicked on my other end while I was talking to Ty. I was so deep into my conversation, I almost didn't click over, but I knew that that would make me look a little suspicious.

"Hold on, Ty. I got another call." I clicked over and said, "Hey, baby."

"Hey. I tried to call you at home. You still at the shop?"

"No. I went home and relaxed a little while. Now, I'm about to go pick up Phelecia so we can go hang out."

"You and Phelecia? Since when have you two been cool like that?"

"We've been talking a lot because she's been going through so much, so I told her I'd hang out with her for a little while. Go shopping and out to eat or something. You know how people think I'm their therapist!" Once I mentioned Phelecia's name to Terrance, I thought about the fact that she hadn't called me to let me know everything was cool. Knowing a little about her situation, I figured Duwan probably came home and apologized, telling her everything she desperately wanted and needed to hear, and they made up, like always. I would just wait to see her tomorrow to find out how everything went if she didn't call tonight.

"Alright. Well, I'll see you later. I just pulled up at school."

"OK. Love you."

"Love you too." In the middle of making up that horrible lie, I had completely forgotten that Ty was on the other end. Terrance knew that Phelecia and I had never been "friends". In school we were associates, and now I just considered her a coworker who I felt bad for, and wanted to help as much as I could. I knew that I was digging myself deeper and deeper into a hole, but I didn't know how else to get away with what I was trying to do, which in my mind was completely innocent, but I knew Terrance wouldn't see it that way.

When I clicked over, Ty had hung up. Well, now I knew he was a man with no patience. I was around the corner from his house anyway, and he probably figured as much. When I arrived on his street, I drove slowly, looking at the numbers on the light posts in front of all the most gorgeous homes I had ever seen.. All of the houses were about three times the size of mine, and I didn't have a small house. I thought it was pretty big, until I saw these. All of them were all brick with nice curb appeal. They were so huge, you would've thought celebrities lived there. I wouldn't have been surprised if I saw R. Kelly. I finally reached Ty's house. I didn't see his Cadillac outside. It must've been in his three-car garage. As I walked down the long, spiraled walkway, I thought, *No wonder he has an old ass car. His mortgage has to be a bitch!*

I got to the door and there was a large, arch-shaped window above it, displaying a huge crystal chandelier. I rang the doorbell. It even sounded expensive. I didn't realize how serious his profession really was.

I heard the door opening and got so nervous. I said he wasn't my type, but I got to thinking that maybe he was completely out of my league. I suddenly felt an insecurity that I had never felt before. When Ty opened the door, he looked just like he had looked when I saw him at the club that night, except he wasn't dressed to impress. He was still unshaven, which I suddenly found attractive, but he did have a low hair cut like I liked on every man. He had on a pair of gray sweats, which hung so low I could see the top of his blue boxers, and no shirt. He held out his hand and led me into what seemed to me to be a mansion and gave me a hug.

"I'm glad you could come by. I didn't think I would get to see you for a while, with you bein' married and all."

I stood there looking around in awe of his magnificent home, not hearing a word of what he was saying. "You have a beautiful home."

"Thank you. You seem shocked."

"No, I just wasn't expecting this. You know, most men would boast about something like this."

"Baby, I don't have no reason to boast. All I have to do is show you."

He took me to the den, and we both sat down on his tan leather sectional. If he furnished and decorated all by himself, he had good taste for a man. I knew that that wasn't always a good thing. Women had to be careful of men who had good taste when it came to decorating. There were a lot of down-low brothas out there these days, and they usually were the finest ones. I kept smelling the aroma of food cooking, but I thought it might've been my imagination because I was so hungry. I finally asked, "You cooking something, Ty?"

"Yeah. I'm cooking a little somethin'. I didn't start cooking until you told me you was comin'. I thought I'd show you a little bit of my cookin' skills."

"That was sweet of you."

"Anything for a friend," he said with a smirk. "You look nervous. You scared of me?"

"No! I just can't believe I'm here with you in the middle of nowhere, and I barely know you, that's all."

"Well, let's get to know each other. What you wanna know about me that you don't already know?"

This was my opportunity to ask some more questions about his job. "So tell me a little more about what you do. It has to be something major for you to be able to afford something like this."

"Basically, I told you earlier when we talked on the phone what I do."

"What types of products do you distribute?"

"Whateva a client needs. They call me and tell me what it is they need, and I go through whatever means necessary to find whatever it is they need. Most of my clients are rich because they work all the damn time, and don't have time to do some of the other necessary shit in life, so that's where I come in. That's how I can afford to have what I have. Believe me, I work very hard for it. Nothing has ever just been handed to me."

That was a good enough explanation for me. This man had it going on, and what I liked about him was that he was humble. After we discussed our jobs a little and what we liked to do, he went to the kitchen to check on the food. He was gone for a few minutes, so I got up and managed to find him. When I entered the kitchen, he was pouring us some champagne. Our plates were already on the table.

"I was about to come get you, but since you here, go ahead and sit down, so we can eat." There had to be something wrong with this man. He was too good to be true. He had a good job, nice house, and car . . . well, I'll leave that one alone, and he could cook. I wondered to myself could I really be just friends with a successful black man such as Ty.

I looked at my plate and everything looked so good. Terrance would never be able to fix a meal like this for me. Ty had cooked baked chicken breasts, steamed broccoli, and baked potatoes. The bottle of Moët was sitting in the center of the table. The more I talked to Ty, the more interested I became in him. There was just something different about him that distinguished him from all the other men I had ever talked to. He was so mysterious. I kept looking at my watch while we were eating. It was already going on eight o'clock. I knew that I would have to be leaving soon, even though I didn't want to. There was so much more I wanted to get to know about Ty.

"You don't have to head home already, do you?"

"Yeah, it's almost . . ." Before I could finish, my cell phone rang. The call was from my house, but it was a little early for Terrance to be home. "One second, Ty. Let me answer this." I opened my phone and said, Hello?"

"Hey, Kel. Where you at, girl?"

It was Tif. I didn't know if I should tell her the truth about where I was or not.

"Oh. I'm at the mall right now."

"Oh, so you did make it to the mall today anyway. How long before you're gonna be home?"

"Probably in an hour or so. Why?"

"I was just wondering. I was really just checking up on you. I know you're usually not out this late."

Was it that obvious even my friend noticed something different about my routine? If she noticed, I was sure Terrance would too. I had to get home.

"I'll be there in a little bit," I said before I hung up the phone. I grabbed my napkin and wiped my mouth. "I hate to eat and run, but I'm gonna have to go, Ty." He looked a little annoyed when I said that, but he knew what he was getting into when he asked to be my friend.

I drank a little more of my Moët and stood up from the table. Ty remained seated and stared at me with his dark eyes. "So when am I gon' see you again?"

"Ty, you know I can't make any promises, but I did enjoy tonight. Thank you for dinner. It was wonderful." I walked around in circles trying to find my way back to the den so I could grab my purse and shoes. Ty finally decided to get up and put me out of my misery by showing me the way.

He stood in front of me when I sat down to put my shoes on. When I stood back up, he looked like he was gonna kiss me, so I turned my head and said, "Well, I guess I'll talk to you later." He grabbed my chin and turned my face towards his and took his index finger on his other hand and rubbed it across my lips, then rubbed it across his. I picked up my purse, and we walked to the front door. Before I walked out the door, I said, "Call me tomorrow?"

"No, you call me," he said.

I looked at him with a confused expression because he knew that I didn't have his phone number. He grabbed his cell phone out of his pocket and started dialing numbers. My cell phone rang, and I pulled it off my hip and looked at it.

"That's my number. I abide by your rules of what time I can call you. The only rule I have is don't let that nigga get a hold of my number, or it's gonna be real ugly." That sounded a little to me like a threat, but it turned me on even more. I rubbed my finger down his bare chest, turned around, walked to my car, and drove back to my side of town.

I pulled up next to Terrance's car. He had actually beaten me home for once. When I walked up to the door, I heard a whole lot of laughing coming from inside. I walked in, and Tif and Terrance were on the couch with wine glasses in their hands, watching Mike Epps's comedy show on HBO.

In the middle of a laugh, Tif looked towards the doorway where I was standing and said, "Hey, Kel. What you buy?"

"Girl, not a damn thang. They didn't have anything that caught my eye."

Terrance said, "What's wrong, baby? You look like you had a rough day."

"Yeah. It was pretty long." I walked towards the staircase. It wasn't my day that was bothering me. Something else was bothering me that shouldn't have been. The fact that my friend and my husband were on the couch having drinks and laughing together like Terrance and I used to was tearing me apart, and I didn't know why. I knew better than to think he was interested in anyone else. He always put me on a pedestal and I never had anything to worry about. My own guilt was eating at me and it didn't feel good. I was the one doing wrong and wanted to make it seem like Terrance was doing something wrong.

I went in my room, shut the bedroom door, and tried to relax my mind. I pulled out my cell phone to make a quick call. I went to my received call list and pressed the call button. As soon as the phone started ringing, I hung up because I thought I heard someone coming up the stairs. I got up and peeked out my door. I still heard Terrance downstairs laughing. I didn't hear Tif, but I wasn't worried about her. I closed the door again, and as soon as I was about to pick my phone back up, it rang.

"Hello," I said in a whispering voice.

"You already playin' on my phone?" Ty asked.

"No. I'm sorry about hanging up. I got distracted, but I was just about to call you back."

"What's up? Why you talkin' so low?"

"My husband's downstairs, so I was just calling to let you know I was home and tell you again that I had a wonderful time."

"Aiight. I'm glad you had a good time. I just hope it don't stop there."

"No, it won't. I'll talk to you tomorrow."

"Good night, beautiful."

"Good night."

After I hung up, I hugged my pillow for a few minutes, thinking about where this thing with Ty could possibly go. I wanted so badly to go back to his house at that moment and strip him down to nothing but his bare brown skin. My mind kept telling me no, but my body obviously spoke a different language. I wondered why God kept putting these men in my life who I would find attractive in some way. The funny thing was that they all were attractive to me in different ways. Was He intentionally tempting me? Maybe He was testing me. If so, I was failing horribly. After I finished contemplating, I put my pajamas on and went downstairs to enjoy some time with Terrance, which is where all of my attention needed to be focused anyway. I went and sat on his lap and wrapped my arms around him like I never wanted to let him go. He held me tight and gave me a kiss. I just wished that it could always be like this, so I wouldn't have to go elsewhere to get the love and attention that I desired. After the comedy show went off, Terrance and I left Tif asleep on the couch, and we went upstairs and made love. Terrance had gained some endurance from somewhere, but I wasn't asking any questions. I was just enjoying it while it lasted. He actually lasted long enough for me to cum. The whole time, it was hard for me to think about anyone else but Ty. I imagined that it was him, and not Terrance making love to me. That night, I came harder than I had ever come in my life.

The next morning, I got a call at six o'clock. My hair was all over the place from the night before. I brushed my hair out of my face with my hand and answered, never even opening my eyes. It was Phelecia sounding oh so pitiful.

"Kel. Sorry for calling you so early, but I know you go in early and I need a ride."

"Duwan didn't come home with your car?"

"Nope. Didn't even call. I tried to call him and he won't answer."

I felt like telling her about herself. If she was trying to be herself again, she needed to get a backbone.

I was too tired to talk anymore. "Alright. I'll be there in about an hour."

"Thank you so much."

"Yeah," I said in a tired and irritated tone, and I closed my phone. When I finally did get up out the bed, Terrance didn't budge. I had worn his ass out. That's one thing I did remember on Mike Epps's comedy show. How he talked about women and the power of their pussies. He was right. Pussy has a lot of power, and some women, like Phelecia, didn't realize exactly how much power it had.

When I got ready to go to work, Terrance was still asleep. I bent over and gave him a kiss on the forehead. He squirmed a little but still didn't wake up. He had to work, but I didn't bother waking him because I knew the alarm clock would go off soon. I found a pen and a piece of paper in my nightstand drawer and wrote him a note, letting him know that I was gonna meet him for lunch since it didn't work out yesterday when I tried to surprise him. I left the note on top of his clothes that he had laid out for work, then I looked in the living room, and Tif was still on the couch, balled up. I found a blanket in the closet and threw it on top of her before I left. I was a little pissed because I had to leave out early just to pick up Phelecia, but I knew she would do it for me. I didn't even have time to fix a little breakfast. I just hoped Duwan brought his ass home with her car because I couldn't be doing this shit every day.

I pulled up to Phelecia's house and honked my horn. She opened the door and put up one finger, telling me to wait a second. While I waited on her, I listened to Cousin Tommy and one of his prank calls on the *Steve Harvey Morning Show*. He always had me cracking up!

"This is ridiculous," I said. I had been sitting there waiting on Phelecia for almost ten minutes. I picked up my phone and tried to call Ty. His voice mail picked up on the first ring, which meant he either turned his phone off or someone was trying to call at the same time I was. I tried to call again, and the same thing happened. I was gonna leave a message, but I preferred to leave it a mystery for him to know whether or not I had called.

I saw a girl with pajama pants, a tank top, and house shoes on walk up to Phelecia's door. Phelecia finally came out a few minutes afer the girl walked in. I didn't know what took her so long to get ready, but I could've gotten ready twenty times faster than the time that it took her. She had on another cute outfit today. I was surprised since I knew she probably felt like shit. I was expecting her to look like shit, too. When she got in, the first thing I noticed was the scent of her perfume. It was a very different scent, but it was sweet and subtle.

"Girl, I'm sorry I took so long." I looked at her eyes and they were puffy like she had been crying all night. That's the only reason I gave her the benefit of the doubt. I felt sorry for her dumb ass.

"That's all right. We still got time to get to the shop before my first appointment. What kind of perfume you got on?"

"Flower Bomb."

"That smells good. I'm gonna have to get me some of that. But it seems like every time I smell something nice on somebody, it never smells like that on me."

"Yeah, that's how it is. Different body chemistry."

"Who was that who just came to your house?"

"Oh. That was Misty. She babysits for me sometimes. She graduated from high school in June, and she's not doing anything right now so I pay her a little somethin' when I can." Phelecia stared out the window during the whole drive, looking like she was hoping to see Duwan on the way. I kept trying to make conversation with her to try to keep her mind off that dumb muthafucker.

"I'm about to stop at McDonald's to get some breakfast. Did you eat?"

"Naw. I'm not hungry, though."

Phelecia was making me depressed. I stopped at McDonald's and pulled in the drive-thru. I happened to look in the window on the inside and saw Ty sitting right next to the window with a woman that looked like she was mixed and in her early thirties.

While I was over Ty's house, he had mentioned to me that he was usually into older women. This woman wasn't much older than he was, if I had presumed correctly about her age. Ty was twenty-nine.

"Ain't that some shit!" I said in disgust.

Phelecia looked at me and said, "What's wrong?"

I had forgot she was in the car with me for a second so I had to play it off. "They went up on their prices, like they wasn't high enough already!" I ordered my food and pulled up behind the blue van that was in front of me, waiting to get to the window to pay and get my food. While I was waiting, I decided to mess with Ty. I could still see him from where my car was, so I tried calling him again. It started ringing, and I watched him as he reached down to grab his phone. He looked at it and hit a button. As soon as he hit that button, the voice mail picked up. His ass had hit ignore on me!

I watched the movement of his mouth and if I wasn't mistaken, he said, "It can wait," and he continued his conversation with that broad.

I put my phone away and said, "Will they hurry their asses up!" I was very POed at this point, and I just wanted to get out of line and go to work. I wasn't even hungry anymore. I didn't even know that man well enough to be getting pissed off cuz I saw him with another woman, but the shit pissed me off like he was my man! What kind of spell did he put on me?

Chapter 13

Ty began calling my cell phone a few hours later. I had decided that I wasn't gonna answer any of his calls because of the way he had disrespected me earlier by not answering his phone and pressing the ignore button. Even though I wasn't answering, I was curious about what kind of excuse he would have for not answering when I called. I didn't know why I even became upset, as many men as I had chasing after me. It was just something about Ty, though. He captivated me, even before I knew he was ballin', and I knew deep in my heart that I could never have only a friendship with this man. Maybe it was for the best that I left it alone right now before it got any more serious. I had already done enough to destroy my marriage, but that hadn't succeeded. I knew that I should stop while I was ahead.

After I finished all my clients for the morning, I swung around in my salon chair, watching Phelecia and Cameron work on their clients. We were the only three stylists who came in on a regular basis. The other stylist, Sabrina, hadn't been to the shop in about a week. Rumor on the streets was that she had gone to another salon.

She usually left her styling tools at the shop, but the last time she was there, she took everything.

Rhonda was pissed because Sabrina hadn't even paid what she owed in booth rent. I just knew one thing. Sabrina better not had let Rhonda find out which shop she was at because Rhonda wasn't the youngest woman, but she didn't play when it came to her money. I remembered the last stylist who tried to pull that shit. Rhonda went to the salon where the girl had started working, walked in, grabbed her by her ponytail, and pulled it harder and harder until she emptied her pockets of all the money she had made for the day. Rhonda politely picked the money up off the floor and walked out. That's how she rolled.

Phelecia was trying to look like everything was all good. She may have been fooling everyone else, but I knew what was going on. I had to give it to her. With everything she was going through, she didn't let it affect her work. I was just hoping that she got her car back soon. It had to be hard to not have any transportation and have three kids. Duwan's ass didn't care. None of the kids were his anyway. They were all by three different men who Phelecia couldn't even find. She got pregnant with her first baby right after graduation. That baby was four now and the other two were three and one. I don't like to sound cruel, but it was probably for the best that she miscarried with the last one. That would've made the situation with her and Duwan even worse. At least right now she could walk away with no ties.

I was tired and bored of sitting there, but I didn't like to leave Phelecia alone with Cameron. Now, that was a bitch that could be cruel. She was a lot older than us, but she acted very immature sometimes. She was a real live bitch, but she could still be cool at times. That was just one person who you didn't want to know your business. I picked up the shop's phone and dialed Tasha's number. I hadn't talked to her in a couple of days. I needed to find out what was going on in her life. Surprisingly, she picked up on the first ring. "Hey, Tasha girl. What's goin' on?"

"Ain't shit goin' on over here. What's goin' on with you?"

"Nothing. Sitting here at this shop bored out my mind."

"It's slow today, huh?"

"Yeah. A little bit."

"I was gonna call you last night to ask you what's been up lately. We don't talk the way we used to. I know you married and all, but you know you still my girl, right?"

"Of course, but you know our schedules conflict so much now, and it's not like I can still go to the clubs with you every other night, but I did have fun the other weekend."

"Yeah. I did too. Well, I'm off today. What you doing when you get off?"

"I don't know." At that moment my cell phone started ringing. I picked it up and looked at the screen. It was Ty calling again. I continued my conversation with Tasha. "I might just chill at home today."

"Since I'm off, maybe we can get together later on, but I'll call you back later. I got company right now."

"OK. Well, I'll go ahead and let your fast ass entertain your company!"

"Bye, girl!"

Tasha always had a man up her sleeve somewhere. After Tasha dissed me for a man, I got up out my chair and went over to Phelecia and said, "I'm about to go sit out in my car and enjoy the weather. I lowered my voice when I said, "You gonna be ok if I leave you in here with you-know-who?"

"Yeah, girl. I'm cool."

I grabbed my purse and keys and went outside to my car. I let my top down, took my shoes off and let my seat back a little bit. I went out to my car because I just needed some privacy. I felt like I needed a cigarette even though I didn't smoke. I opened my phone and started to dial Ty's number and then closed it. I had other options, so I decided to use them. I grabbed my smock and stuck my hand in the pocket, feeling for the piece of paper Reggie had rolled up in the $100 bill he had given me. I kept pulling money out that I hadn't taken to the bank yet. I finally found the piece of paper, so I slowly dialed the number. I think I was only calling because I had gotten upset with the person I really wanted to talk to. Ty. Reggie was currently the rebound guy. I was really hoping that Reggie didn't even answer.

After the first ring, I almost hung up, but I let it continue to ring. Suddenly, I heard Reggie's voice. He sounded like he was asleep.

"Hey, Reggie. How you doin'?"

I heard Reggie take a deep breath and say, "Oh. You finally decided to call?"

"I've been real busy the past couple of days, and I know you don't got no attitude about me calling after I saw you in Applebee's with your woman!"

Reggie started laughing hysterically. "You are so funny, Kel. How you gon' get mad at me for going out to eat with somebody else and you don't even wanna call a brotha?"

"You acted like you wanted me so bad. I didn't expect to see you with anyone else so soon."

"Oh. So you just expected me to sit around and wait for you?" He had the nerve to ask me a dumb-ass question like that. Hell yeah, I expected him to sit around and wait for me even though I wasn't even thinkin' about him anymore. Of course I wasn't about to tell him that. Reggie was just a toy to me right now. He was someone I knew I could have whenever I felt like being bothered.

"I guess that was your woman since you didn't deny it."

"I don't have anything to hide from you, Kel. Who are you to question me about who I see?"

"I thought that I was someone you were pursuing."

There was a long pause. I figured Reggie didn't have a comeback, but then he said, "Kel, you know how I feel about you. The same way I've felt about you since high school. I don't think I need to keep repeating myself, but until you're ready to accept me, there's nothing else I can do. I tried showing you. I know you not happily married. You can't be, especially after what happened between us. I know you den thought about it because I have . . . Several times, over and over again. It's on you."

That's when I didn't have anything else to say. What could I have said after all that?

"Kel. You still there?"

"Yeah, I'm here."

"I was hoping I didn't just express my feelings to dead air."

"No. I heard everything you said."

This is the first time ever that I think I didn't have anything to say. I always had a comeback for everything. That's why no one ever liked to argue with me. I always won, but I was about to lose this one.

"I know you in a bad position right now, Kel, so this is what I'm gon' do. I'm just gon' leave you alone, and I know you'll decide the right thing." What Reggie didn't know was that Terrance wasn't the only one he was competing with right now. He didn't know anything about Ty, and I planned to keep it that way.

I felt so unnecessarily stressed, and I say "unnecessarily" because I didn't have to be going through any of this if I didn't want to be, but I felt like when successful, nice-looking men approached me, I needed to act on it in order to see if I was missing out on something good. Maybe I needed to be agoraphobic to be cured of whatever I was going through. People who are afraid to leave house can't get into the type of trouble I find.

"Yeah, Reggie. I'll decide the right thing."

"Oh yeah. You know you fucked up my lining, right?" We both started laughing because we both knew that I didn't know what I was doing when I put those clippers to his head.

"Shut up, boy. You paid good money for that fucked-up lining!"

"Yeah, a little too much." Reggie finally had broken the ice, and we talked a little while longer, having a few more laughs. I felt like I was talking to my old friend again. Reggie did mean a lot to me. I just didn't think I wanted to break up my marriage to be with him. He was always a good friend, and I think that was the way it would always be.

I finally got off the phone with Reggie, and I was glad it was on good terms. It was almost time for Terrance's lunch hour, so I went back inside the shop to tell Phelecia and Cameron that I was about to go to lunch. They were in there laughing about something, so I figured I didn't have to worry about Phelecia. I guess Cameron was having a good day. I headed to the bank to have lunch with the man who I still felt was the love of my life. I just wished I yearned for only him.

When I walked in the bank, Terrance was closing his window. He looked up at me and winked. I smiled back at him and grinned at Stacy as she watched. I went and stood by the door, waiting on Terrance. While waiting on him, my phone rang. I looked at it and quickly turned my phone off. Ty wasn't giving up easily. The thought passed through my mind that the woman he was with at McDonald's couldn't have been that special for him to be blowing up my phone the way he was. Terrance finally met me at the front door, and we walked out to his car. When we got in the car, I rubbed his smooth jawline with the back of my hand and kissed his cheek.

He looked at me and said, "What was that for?"

"I just want you to know that I love you."

"I love you too. Where you wanna go eat?"

It was such a nice day outside that I wanted to sit outside somewhere and eat.

"I'm not that hungry. Why don't we just go to Dairy Queen and have some Chili Cheese Dogs. That way we can sit outside and enjoy the weather and eat at the same time." Terrance agreed.

Everyone must've had the same idea today. Dairy Queen was packed. It was so packed, after we ordered our food, we almost didn't find a table to sit at outside. When we finally sat down, I took a bite of my chili dog and stared at Terrance as he devoured one of three of his. He was so fine. His skin was so dark and smooth, and his muscles bulged through his dress shirt. He was all that I needed and what most women wanted in a man. I just needed to convince myself of that.

I took a sip of my strawberry milkshake and said, "Tif's gonna be leaving in a couple of days. It's gonna be kinda nice to have our privacy back, won't it?" I was waiting to see how Terrance responded because I honestly felt that he and Tif were becoming too comfortable around each other, even though I knew they weren't thinkin' about each other. I would just feel more comfortable once she moved out. I never thought of myself to be the jealous type, but I was starting to become this woman that I didn't know. If they were in the kitchen together, I became jealous. It was a feeling that I didn't enjoy.

Terrance looked away from his food for a moment to look up at me and say, "Yeah. It'll be nice." He didn't sound as excited as I would've liked him to be, but as long as we were on the same page, it was cool. Terrance started talking about how he remembered when we first met we used to always go on picnics, and he had never known anyone until he met me who brought full-course meals on picnics.

"That's what I love about you, Kel. You are so unique. I would never be able to find anyone else like you because there is no one else out there like you."

I got goose bumps from his words and a tear built up in my eye, but I fought to hold it back. "That's what I love about you, Terrance. You always know the right thing to say." At that moment, the sun disappeared. I looked up at the sky and the clouds were suddenly gray. "We better get ready to go, Terrance. It looks like it's about to pour down."

Terrance finished his last chili dog, and as soon as we stood up, it started raining hard as hell. We grabbed our drinks and ran to the car. My hair was soaked. I wasn't even thinking about my clothes.

Terrance got in the car laughing. "Girl, I never saw you run so fast."

"That ain't even funny. You know I'm too sweet to get rained on. I might melt."

"You right about that. You are sweet. Maybe I'll get a taste of that tonight. I got a sweet tooth."

I had to squeeze my legs together as tight as I could after that statement. "Yeah. We'll see if you're a good boy."

After I left Terrance and got back to the shop, I turned my cell phone back on and went in. Phelecia was the only one there. "Hey, where's everybody?

"We had a lot of cancellations. Two of your clients cancelled," Phelecia said.

I guess I was done for the day. I only had two clients left. Women always cancel their hair appointments when we get a little rain, but I guess I couldn't blame them. I wouldn't wanna pay all that money to get my hair done, just for it to get wet as soon as I walked out the shop either. That was exactly why my hair looked a hot mess and Phelecia just had to point that out.

"What happened to your hair?"

"Terrance and I went to Dairy Queen and sat outside to eat lunch, then it wants to start raining on us!"

"Come on and sit down in my chair." Phelecia started blow drying my hair and then used some hair pins to put it in a cute updo.

"You still haven't heard anything from Duwan?"

"Girl, no, but he's done this before. I know that sometimes everybody needs some time to themselves so I'm respecting that."

In my mind I said, *You a damn fool,* but out loud I said, "Yeah, everyone does need that time to themselves sometimes, but you should still let the one that you supposedly love know that you need that time." Phelecia didn't say anything. She looked like she didn't wanna talk about it anymore, so I shut up. We waited around for about another hour to see if we were gonna get any walk-ins. When we didn't, I told Phelecia, "Let's get out of here."

I looked out of the door. It had stopped raining, but it was still gloomy. As soon as we closed up the shop and walked to the parking lot, I said, "Look what the wind blew in. Phelecia hadn't looked up to see what I saw yet, but as soon as she did, the biggest smile appeared on her face. Duwan was just sitting outside the shop. How long he had been out there was a mystery.

He rolled down the window and said, "Come on, girl."

She looked at me and said, "I told you he just needed a little time." She ran to the car and got in. Duwan looked at me like he was saying "Bitch" with his eyes. He knew that I didn't care for him, but who did? They drove off and I got in my car just thinking how a woman could be so stupid over a nigga. I guess that I would never find out because I vowed that I would never be that woman.

Chapter 14

I went straight home after work. Whenever the sun wasn't out, I wasn't in the mood to do anything but sit at home. When I pulled up, I saw Mike standing in his door. I had still been avoiding him, but I couldn't today. He waved at me and I waved back. I could hear his screen door opening as I was walking to my door.

"Come here for a minute, Kel." I stopped in my tracks and began walking towards him. He held his screen door open and said, "You look nice today, but you always do."

"Thanks."

"Come in for a minute. I won't bite."

"I don't think that's a good idea. I'm tired and I just wanna go in and lay down."

"Just for a minute. I think we need to talk."

I looked around to make sure no one was watching, and I stepped into Mike's house.

He walked in front of me and led me into his living room. He had a very nice house. I didn't know what was up with these men having houses decorated better than mine. I sat down on his maroon-and-tan couch and he sat right next to me, thigh to thigh.

"How you been, Kel?"

"I've been fabulous," I said, unable to look him in his eyes.

"It seems like you been trying to avoid me. I haven't seen you in a while. I'm sorry if I made you uncomfortable, but I thought you were feelin' me the way that I was feelin' you."

I tried to look at Mike while he was talking to me, but I couldn't. Every time I looked at him in his face, my stomach started fluttering.

"Mike, I thought I was feelin' you, but honestly, I don't know what I was feeling at the time."

"You are just so beautiful to me. I feel like I need someone like you in my life."

"Yeah, maybe someone like me, but not me." At that moment I realized how chaotic my life had become. I was living a double life, and I didn't even know how it had evolved. I felt like I was addicted to men or some shit like that, but I didn't even know if there was a name for that. I felt like I had feelings for Reggie, Mike, and Ty, but I loved Terrance. It was confusing, but it was the way I felt. When I was with those other men, it felt like Terrance didn't even exist.

"Didn't you enjoy the little time we spent together on your patio?"

"Yeah. It was nice . . . I guess."

"If you would give me a chance, I could show you a whole lot more."

"Mike, you know I'm not right. You saw partially of what I already did to Terrance, and he's my husband. Do you really think it would be different with you? Terrance never did a thing to me. He's nothing but good to me, and I can't continue to do him wrong."

"It would be different with me because I believe that I'm the person you're supposed to be with. He has done something wrong for you to want to look elsewhere. You wouldn't be sitting here right now if everything was ok. Terrance isn't innocent either."

That's when my insecurities hit me. I started wondering if Terrance was innocent.

"What do you mean? Do you know something?"

"All I know is that something between y'all is not right." I looked up at Mike, and I just started crying. I couldn't hold it back any longer. I wanted myself to believe that everything between me and Terrance was picture perfect, but I knew something wasn't right. I just tried to wait for it to fix itself. I blamed myself for being impatient with Terrance. I knew he had a lot going on with work and school, and I just needed to wait it out, but it was so hard. I wasn't getting the attention that I yearned for, and I couldn't really tell anyone how I felt because I didn't want them to think I was selfish.

Mike held me close while I cried on his shoulder. I rarely ever cried in front of anyone. Maybe this was a breakthrough for me.

He rubbed my back as he held me, then he got up and said, "I'll be right back." I sat there with my elbows on my knees and my hands over my face while I waited for him to come back. When he finally returned, he laid me back. He laid a warm towel over my eyes.

"I don't want you to leave here all puffy-eyed. I hate to see a woman cry."

"I'm sorry. I guess everything just built up inside. I think that's what I've been needing."

"I would tell you what you need, but I know you don't wanna hear that."

My cell phone started ringing. I wasn't gonna answer it, but Mike opened it and handed it to me while I was still lying there with the towel over my eyes.

"Hello."

"I been trying to call you all day. What the hell you been doing?" I sat up as soon as I heard Ty's voice.

When I took the towel off my eyes, I saw Mike sitting in the chair across from me. "I've been busy," I said, lowering my voice from my previous tone.

"I wanna see you."

"Now's not a good time."

"I'm playing by your rules. It's not past 8:00 and I know you're not still at work cuz your car is gone, so what you doin'?"

"I'll call you back."

"Kellie, if you hang up, don't bother callin' me back."

I couldn't believe that this negro had been up to the shop. I looked up at Mike, and he whispered, "You cool?" I nodded and continued talking to Ty.

I hadn't been knowing Ty for long at all, but he was already acting possessive. For some strange reason, it was kind of a turn-on. Everything Ty did was beginning to be a turn-on to me.

"You already know the deal." I got up and walked from out of the room with Mike. "Anyway, where's your McDonald's breakfast date?"

Ty got quiet.

"Oh. You don't have anything to say now. You wanna talk all that shit, but can't back it up."

"You never said you didn't want me to see anybody else. But since you really wanna know, she was one of my clients. I had an appointment with her this morning. You know I'm a busy man. We talked about that the other night. I can't answer every phone call."

"Right, and I can't see you every time you wanna see me!"

"Didn't we agree on a friendship, Kellie?"

"Yeah."

"So why are you getting' mad at me for seeing me with another woman anyway?"

I couldn't even answer that, so I said, "Why are you getting mad at me because I can't see you right now?"

"This is real stupid, Kel. I don't got time for this shit. You hit me up when you decide what you want." Before I could say anything else, Ty hung up. I didn't even know where I was in Mike's house. I looked up, and I had roamed into the kitchen. I turned around and jumped. Mike was right behind me.

"You sure you all right?"

"Yeah, I'm fine." I was lying. I was so confused!

"Mike, it was nice talking to you, but I gotta go."

"You don't have to hurry, unless you just have something important you have to do." I sat there thinking. I didn't have anything important to do. It was just something I thought I needed to do. Ty sounded like he was pissed, and I didn't want to leave things that way between us. I felt like he had put some kind of spell on me, and I hadn't even fucked him and didn't have any intentions on it.

"Kel, it's not that important is it?"

"Me being over here is just not a good idea."

"Alright. Well, maybe we can still get together somewhere else sometime. Maybe go to lunch or something."

"Yeah. Maybe so." I said just to get him to shut up. Mike walked me to the door and gave me a friendly hug and kiss on the forehead.

"If you need anything, Kel, I'm right next door."

"Thanks, Mike. I truly appreciate it."

I went in the house to freshen up and make sure my eyes had gone down from crying. I was just glad that Tif wasn't there because I definitely would not want her to see me like this. I felt like I was in charge of my life, but I felt weak at the same time. Weak for a man I barely knew. I decided to change clothes in case I smelled like the Issey Miyake that Mike was wearing. I always knew my colognes, and Issey was one of my favorites.

As soon as I left the house and got in the car, I pulled out my cell phone and dialed Ty's number. When I put the phone up to my ear, I looked up and saw Mike looking at me through his oversized picture window in his living room. Ty's phone rang and rang until the voice mail answered. I didn't leave a message. Even though he didn't answer, I still headed to his house while I still had time before Terrance was due back at home. On my way to Ty's house, I kept dialing his number because I knew I was gonna feel like an ass if I drove the whole way there and he wasn't home. I thought maybe he was just being ornery because I wouldn't come see him when he wanted me to. I knew that if I got there and he was home, he wouldn't be able to turn me away, even if he was a little upset. I kept driving, hoping he was home.

When I got about fifteen minutes away from Ty's house, my cell phone rang. I knew he would call me back sooner or later. He was trying to act all hard and shit, but I knew he couldn't resist me. I was so confident that it was Ty calling, that I didn't even bother to look at the caller ID. I cleared my voice so I could sound sexy when I answered. "Hello," I said in the voice I only used when I was trying to seduce a man.. All I heard was crying in the phone. There was always some drama going on somewhere.

"Hello? Who is this?"

They tried talking, but I still couldn't understand what they were saying. I looked at the number on my phone's screen, but I didn't recognize it. I started getting nervous, so I pulled over on the side of the road.

"I can't understand you. Calm down."

The woman on the other end took a few deep breaths and I could hear a man's voice in the background cussing and shouting. She tried to speak clearer and I finally understood what she was saying.

"Help me, Kel. Please come get me."

"Phelecia?" Then I realized whose number it was. I hadn't called Phelecia enough to know her number by heart, but that's who it was. Duwan was over there beating on her ass, and she called me.

"Did you call the police?"

Phelecia didn't answer. I heard shit breaking in the background and I could hear her screaming something at Duwan, but I couldn't tell what it was. I started driving again, still holding the phone up to my ear, trying to hear as much as I possibly could. I made a U-turn and started heading towards Phelecia's house. I wanted to call the police, but I didn't know if I had three-way on my cell and I didn't want to lose Phelecia's call.

I kept screaming Phelecia's name through the phone, but I still didn't get an answer. The background was still loud, but I did notice that I didn't hear any kids. Hopefully they weren't there. I knew it was gonna take me at least a half hour to get to Phelecia's, but I kept holding the phone. I was hoping someone would click on my other end, so I could tell them to call the police for me to go to Phelecia's house, but I didn't even know Phelecia's address. I only knew how to get there. All of a sudden, I didn't hear anything. There was dead silence on the other end. I felt more comfortable when I was hearing all the commotion going on. Silence was not a good sign. After a couple of minutes, I heard crying again, but not like it was before.

"Phelecia?" I said. The crying sounded far away from the phone. Like it was coming from another room. "Hang in there, girl. I'm almost there," I said, hoping she was listening.

When I pulled up in front of Phelecia's house, I noticed that her car was gone, which wasn't much of a surprise. I closed my phone and ran up to the front door. It was closed, but I twisted the knob and it was unlocked. I slowly walked in. The only light in the house was the sunlight shining in through the windows. I heard the same crying I heard in the phone coming from one of the back rooms. As I was walking to Phelecia's bedroom, I almost tripped over her legs. I looked down and saw Phelecia lying there and her four-year-old daughter, Candace, lying on top of her, crying. That was the crying that I had heard. I started shaking Phelecia, saying, "Phelecia! Phelecia! Come on girl. Wake up. I felt her neck to see if she had a pulse. I was trying to remember what I had learned in CPR class in high school. I felt a pulse. "Thank God." I turned Phelecia over and looked at her face. She had two black eyes, and her nose was bleeding. She had on the same clothes she had left work in, but they were all ripped up. Candace sat there on her knees with tears in her eyes. I went in the kitchen and got some ice water for Phelecia and grabbed a towel from the bathroom and put it under cold water. When I got back to the hallway where Phelecia was lying, she was trying to open her eyes.

"It's me—Kel. You don't have to try to open your eyes. I know they hurt." I put the cold towel over her eyes and then cleaned the blood from her face.

"Mommy's bleeding." Candace said in the most innocent, precious voice.

"Yeah, but she's gonna be ok, all right?" Candace looked at me with hope in her big, bright eyes. I felt so sorry for her because she had to be put in this situation.

"Where's your brother and sister, Candace?"

"At Misty's," she said.

"Phelecia. Are you strong enough to sit up? We need to take you to the hospital." She tried to shake her head. "You have to go. Your nose might be broken." She sat up slowly. She looked horrible. Nothing like she looked when she left the shop with Duwan earlier. "Look what that ignorant muthafucker did to you!"

I helped Phelecia stand up and walked her to her room and sat her on the bed. I looked in her closet to find her something else to put on. While I was looking, I heard her whisper, "Thank you." I put her clothes on the bed, and Candace watched while someone else had to help her mommy put on her clothes because a stupid-ass nigga had whooped her ass.

Before I took Phelecia to the hospital, I took Candace around the corner to the babysitter's house with her brother and sister. Phelecia didn't say anything the whole way to the hospital. When we got to the emergency room, the nurse took her to the back right away after she looked at her. When they put her in a bed, the nurse asked a lot of questions, including of course, what happened. It wasn't like Phelecia could've made up a lie, like she fell, or something stupid like that.

"My boyfriend was a little upset and we got into a fight." As Phelecia spoke, the nurse was writing on the paper that was on her clipboard.

"Your boyfriend did a job on you. Does this happen frequently?"

"No. We argue sometimes, but this time, I really made him mad." Phelecia looked at me as though she was embarrassed, and she should've been. It was like she was taking the blame for him whooping on her ass. The nurse said she would be right back and walked through the curtain.

"Phelecia. Why are you acting like this is your fault?"

"I knew Duwan didn't want me dressed that way, and I did it anyway. He just got mad, and I understand. I should've respected him more."

"What? He didn't want you to look nice? That's all you did. It wasn't like you was dressed like a hoe. You looked nice, and obviously he don't want you to look that way because he knows that there are a whole lot of better men out there who are looking for a woman like you. What kind of way is that to live? You can't go out looking homely just because your man is too insecure to let you out the house lookin' good. You're supposed to look good. You're a professional."

"You just don't understand Duwan the way I do." The nurse walked back in with a police officer right behind her. He was an older black man with a bald head.

"Hello ma'am. I understand you were the victim of domestic violence. I just need you to tell me what happened, so I can write out a report."

"No. It was just a little fight. That's all. Everything's fine now." Phelecia said like she didn't have bruises all over her face and body.

That's when I butted in and said, "Everything is not all right. You cannot let this man beat you and then let it ride. You are supposed to be making a change for yourself, and you can't do it if you let him run over you like that."

The officer began to speak again and said, "I can't force you to, but I recommend that you press charges against your partner. By the bruises you have, it looks more serious than you say it is."

"I don't want to press charges."

I said, "Phelecia. You have to."

"He just said I didn't have to, and I don't want to." Phelecia said, raising her voice.

I saw that I wasn't gonna change her mind, so I said, "Well, at least get a restraining order against him so he can't get close enough to do this again."

She looked iffy about that too, but she said, "OK, I'll do that. I just don't want him to go to jail."

The officer said, "Well, we can't do the paperwork here, but here's my card. Come to the station, and tell the lady at the front desk that you want a form for a restraining order and show her my card. I should be there all day tomorrow, but if I'm not there when you get there, someone else will be able to help you."

After the officer and nurse left, the doctor came in and bandaged Phelecia up. Her nose wasn't broken, but he packed it to stop the bleeding. He gave her some ice packs and prescribed some pain medicine and told her she was free to go home. On the way to the car, I asked Phelecia what she was gonna do for the night. I didn't think it was safe for her and her kids to be in the house without having the restraining order yet. She said she just wanted to get her kids and go home.

"Are you sure you'll be ok at home by yourself?"

"We'll be fine."

I went to the sitter's house and went in to get the kids for Phelecia. She didn't want Misty or Misty's mother to see her like that. After we got the kids, I took them home and helped them get in the house. I made sure I went in with them to make sure the coast was clear.

Chapter 15

I was glad I was able to help Phelecia, even though she interrupted my plans. Through all that drama, Ty still hadn't called me back. It was almost eight o'clock, which meant it was too late to head back over there. I tried to call him again, and he still didn't answer, so I just went home. When I got there, Tif was there, but she was getting ready to go somewhere. She was dressed all up with her makeup looking flawless, like always.

"Hey, girl. Where you goin'?"

"I'm going out with this guy I met a few days ago. We're probably just gonna go out to dinner somewhere. The apartment complex called today too. My apartment is ready, so I'm gonna start moving tomorrow instead of Monday."

I sat down on the couch and took a deep breath.

"What's wrong, Kel? You look tired."

"Yeah, I am. This day was so full of drama. You just don't know."

Tif still didn't know a thing about Ty, so when I told her about my day, I made sure I left the part about me going over Mike's house and anything about Ty out of the conversation.

"Wow, girl! You did have an eventful day! Is Phelecia gonna be all right?"

"Besides being stupid, yeah, I think she'll be all right." Tif started laughing, and I cracked a small smile.

"Well. I'm going upstairs to take a shower so I'll be fresh when my man gets home."

"Gone, girl! I can't wait 'til I have somebody to come home to every day. That has to feel good."

"Now you know you not ready to settle down!"

"I'm gettin' there! Don't hate!"

I couldn't be faithful, so I knew Tif couldn't! I didn't know who she was trying to fool, but it sure wasn't me.

"I'll see you later. Have a good time and tell me all about it tomorrow." I walked upstairs and went in my room. The light on my phone was blinking, which meant I had messages.

I sat down at the bottom of my bed to check my messages before I got in the shower. The first message was from Tasha. Between everything that had been going on, I had forgotten all about the fact that we were supposed to be trying to get together today. I wanted to be nosey and see who the hell her company was when I had talked to her earlier. She said in the message that she had tried my cell phone, and the call wouldn't go through. I wondered how many other calls I had missed. Maybe Ty had called me back.

My next message was from Terrance. "Hey, baby. I just found out that my deadline for my portfolio was moved up by the firm, so me and Carl are gonna be working late trying to finish this up. Love you. I'll see you later."

Carl was an attorney that Terrance was interning with at Mercet Law Firm. Terrance worked with Carl on some of his cases to give him the experience that he needed. Well, I guess I had to change my next set of plans too. There was no telling what time Terrance would be home, so that meant that actually, I did have time to go to Ty's house, but I guess it just wasn't meant to be. I took a shower, popped some popcorn, and pulled out the DVD of *A Family That Preys*.

I couldn't really concentrate on watching the movie because I was waiting for my phone to ring. I picked up my house phone and dialed my cell phone to make sure my calls were coming through, and they were. Ty just wasn't calling. During the movie, I ended up calling Tasha. I knew she was gonna be mad at me for not telling her what was up for today.

As soon as she answered the phone, she said, "It's too late to do something now. I know you haven't been busy all day."

"Girl, you wouldn't believe the day I had. I had good intentions on calling you."

I went on to tell Tasha about my day with Phelecia. I just extended the time it took at the hospital with Phelecia so I would have an excuse for just now calling Tasha. She felt stupid after I finished the story.

"So who was the company when I called you earlier?"

"You know you nosey as hell."

"Damn right! We supposed to be best friends, so I think I have the right to be all in your business!"

"Girl, whateva. Anyway, we're just friends . . . for now. He's a real cool dude."

I had heard Tasha say that about many a men, and they all ended up being a waste of sperm.

"What's so spectacular about this one?"

"We got a lot in common, and guess what, girl!"

"What?"

"He ain't even tried to fuck me. I don't know if I should take that as a sign of a down-low brotha or he just likes me for me."

"Just cuz a man ain't tried to sleep with you, you can't always assume he's gay. Maybe he just wants to get to know you first to see if it's gonna go anywhere."

"Yeah. That could be true. Anyway, we been doin' a lot of stuff lately. That's why I haven't talked to you in a minute. He been takin' me on real dates, girl! Not just to his house or my house. He took me to Red Lobster and the movies. Not just the dollar show either, like these other cheap-ass Negros do. He took me to the Cineplex Theater! You know they charge $10 a ticket."

"He sounds good so far. What's goin' on with Malik?" I knew that Tasha loved her some Malik, but they couldn't last longer than a week without getting into it over something stupid.

"Girl, fuck Malik! I'm tired of this on-and-off-again shit!"

"What's the new guy's name?"

"Oh. I didn't tell you his name, did I? His name is Reg. Short for Reggie. You might know him. He went to school with us, but he messed around with some skanks back then."

My heart dropped. I couldn't believe Reggie had stooped so low. I was trying to remember if there was another Reggie that went to school with us, but I couldn't think of one. Reggie was using my best friend to get back at me. Wasn't that some shit! I didn't know what to say next. I didn't want to burst Tasha's bubble, but I didn't want Reggie to make a fool out of Tasha either. I knew Tasha wasn't Reggie's type. She was my best friend, but we were total opposites. She was way too ghetto for Reggie.

"I don't think I remember any Reggies, Tasha." She started describing him. She went on and on, so I finally said, "Yeah, I think I do remember him. Him and Sherice Carlson used to go together."

"Yeah that's him. I can't believe he used to go with that bougie-ass bitch." Sherice was the girl Reggie was with when we used to mess around. He would've dumped her without a second thought if I would've told him I wanted to be with him. I never thought of Sherice as being bougie, though. She just wasn't ghetto.

I didn't feel like talking to Tasha anymore because I knew if I had, I was gonna come out with the truth. I knew how Tasha was. If I did try to tell her the truth, she probably would think I was trying to hate on her, and everybody knew I had no reason to hate on anybody. The other reason I didn't want to say anything was because I didn't want my business to get out there about me and Reggie, and Reggie knew that. That was exactly why his slick ass was doing this shit. He was trying to get my attention, and he got it. I was dumb to think Reggie and I truly had an understanding after our talk.

"Well, girl, I'll talk to you tomorrow. I think I'm just about to go to bed since I'm here all alone."

"Where is everybody?"

"Tif went out on a date, and Terrance had to work on something for the firm."

"Well, I'm about to see if I can get a hold of Reg. If not, I'll probably be goin' to bed too." I couldn't believe she called him

'Reg.' He always hated that, and the sound of it coming out of Tasha's mouth made me cringe.

"Alright then. Bye."

After I hung up the phone, I was about to call Reggie to cuss him out, but I needed to think about exactly what I was about to say to him, so I decided to wait until tomorrow. At least I thought that I could wait. I turned the lamp off next to my nightstand and grabbed the TV remote and pushed the power button to turn it off. I laid there staring at the bright red numbers on my clock. Then I briskly sat up and grabbed my phone off the night stand and dialed Terrance's number.

"Hey, baby," he said as soon as he picked up the phone.

"Hey. You still got a lot to do?"

"Yeah. Quite a bit and I'm tired as hell. I wish I was there with you."

"That' so sweet. Well, I'm probably about to go to bed, so I'll just see you when you get here, or in the morning when I wake up."

"OK, baby. Good night."

"Good night."

It was probably gonna be a while before Terrance made it home, so I had clearance to do what I needed to do. Most likely, Tif wouldn't be back until the morning. I turned my light back on and got up looking through my purse, trying to remember what I did with Reggie's phone number. Then I remembered the time he came to the house, I put it under the mattress on my side of the bed. I stuck my hand underneath, feeling around for it, but I didn't feel a thing. Then I got down on my knees, so that I could see what I was actually feeling around for. I lifted up the mattress with one arm and looked around. There was nothing there. I sat there thinking what I could've done with it. I knew that sometimes I would put things one place and then put them somewhere else, but I couldn't remember moving it. It crossed my mind that maybe Terrance found it, but I knew he would've asked me about it, and he had no reason to look under the mattress anyway. It wasn't like he actually ever made up the bed.

After I finished looking on my side of the bed, I thought that maybe I accidentally put it on Terrance's side. My heart started pounding because I was panicking. I climbed across the bed to the other side and got on the floor and lifted that side. There was nothing there. "What the hell?" I said out loud. I looked under the bed to make sure it hadn't fallen on the floor. There was still nothing there. I didn't know what to think. I kept telling myself that I put it in a safer place, and I just couldn't remember where. I remembered that he had given it to me again when he paid me for his haircut, and I left it in my smock pocket. My smock was out in the car, so I put on my house shoes and walked outside. It was such a nice night. It was warm with a nice breeze. I looked in the sky and noticed that there was a full moon. It was so beautiful outside, I felt like lighting a couple of candles and sitting outside on my patio.

Mike's lights were still on throughout his house. I wondered what he was doing in there all alone. Or maybe he wasn't alone. He might've even been watching me. I sat in the driver's seat of my car, and grabbed my smock from the passenger's side. I rambled through my pockets and didn't find anything except a piece of Doublemint gum and a lunch receipt. I didn't know what I had done with that number after the last time I used it. I wasn't about to stress over it anymore. It would come up sooner or later, but hopefully not in the wrong hands. That wouldn't be nice.

After I slammed my car door and as I walked up to my door, I noticed Mike looking through his vertical blinds. Neither one of us waved. We just stared until we could no longer see each other. Nothing could ever be between me and Mike because he already knew too much about me. There are certain things I wouldn't want him to know about me if I did start a relationship with him, and one of those things would be that I had already cheated on my husband once. The fact that Mike knew that ended any possibility of anything every happening between us. He already had a preconception of me and he would judge me based on that, and that is something I definitely didn't want.

Since I couldn't find Reggie's number to call him and I was done calling Ty since he didn't wanna answer the phone, I went in the house, turned everything off, crawled into my bed, and went to sleep.

I woke up the next morning to the sun shining through my mini-blinds. I had forgotten to close them before I went to bed. I looked at the clock and it was six-twenty. I rolled over to look behind me, and Terrance wasn't there. I jumped up ready to beat somebody's ass.

I started talking to myself. "I know this negro betta had brought his ass home last night!" I grabbed my robe off the back of my bathroom door and ran downstairs. I looked in the living room first and didn't see anyone, then I looked in the den. I was relieved when I saw Terrance asleep on the sofa bed, but I was still curious as to why he didn't just get in the bed with me when he got home.

I went in the den, got on the bed and straddled Terrance. He still didn't wake up, so I gave him a kiss on the jaw. He opened one eye and put his arms around my waist.

"Good morning," I said as he struggled to get the other eye open.

"Good morning," he said.

"What you doing down here?"

"You looked like you were sleeping so good all over the bed when I came in, I just came up and grabbed my pajamas so I wouldn't wake you up when I got in the bed."

Terrance was so considerate, even though I wouldn't have cared if he woke me up.

"What time did you get home?" I asked curiously.

"Not until around one-thirty or two o'clock, but we got everything done, so it was well worth my time. I'm just glad I only have about a month of this intern shit left, and then I can get out there and make some real money. Hopefully I can get a job with Mercet. Carl and I work pretty well together."

"That's good, baby. Maybe you will since you're such a hard worker, and they can see that. Speaking of work, I gotta start getting ready to go. Come get in the bed until it's time for you to get up."

"Yeah. I think I will. My back is killing me. All this damn money we spent on this couch, the sofa bed could at least be comfortable."

I got up and went back upstairs. Terrance followed behind shortly. After I finished getting dressed, I peeked in Tif's room.

She was in the bed so far under the covers I could barely see her. I was surprised she was even home. I knew how she did when she went on dates. They were usually all-nighters, especially if it was someone she was supposedly taking serious. I went downstairs in the kitchen to get on the phone and called Phelecia to see if I was supposed to be picking her up for work. I didn't know since she hadn't called me.

When she answered the phone, she was talking to her kids in the background, then she finally said, "I'm sorry. Hello?"

"Hey, girl. I didn't know if you were going to work today, or if you needed a ride."

"Naw. Thank you though. I'm not going in today. I canceled my appointments last night. I don't wanna go in there all bruised up like this."

"Ok, girl. So everything's all right?"

"Yeah. It's cool."

"Did Duwan call?" Phelecia paused after I asked her that question and then told that bold-faced lie.

"Unh-uh. He didn't call."

"What time you going to get the restraining order?"

"I'm gonna go this morning sometime. Misty's momma is gonna take me."

Yesterday, Phelecia didn't want Misty or her mom to see her like that. Now all of a sudden she didn't care. I wasn't gonna try to figure her out as long as she got that restraining order because that negro, Duwan, was ill!

"OK. Well, I'll talk to you later. Call me at the shop if you need anything."

"I will. Thanks."

As soon as I hung up the phone, I heard Terrance say, "Who you talking to about getting a restraining order?"

I turned around and said, "I thought you were trying to get some more rest before you had to get up."

"I was, but I got hungry, so I came down to get a bowl of cereal."

"If I had time, I would fix you some breakfast."

"You know I don't mind eating cereal, but who was that on the phone?"

"Phelecia."

"Duwan still beatin' on that ass, huh?"

"Oh yeah. I didn't get a chance to talk to you yesterday about what happened. He brutally beat her yesterday. She come calling me, so I go over there . . ."

"You did what. Don't do that shit. He dangerous, and he'll do anything to whoever gets in his way."

"Yeah. I know, but anyway, I took her to the hospital, and she wouldn't even press charges. She's going to get a restraining order today, though."

"That's some crazy shit. I don't know how a man could ever lay his hands on a woman. That's some punk-ass shit. But, like I was saying, just don't go over there when they having problems like that. Just call the police and let them handle it. I would hate to have to go kill a nigga for putting his hands on you." Terrance finished pouring his milk in a big-ass bowl of Frosted Flakes he had made, and sat at the island.

I grabbed my purse and said, "I'll see you later. Are you gonna be home on time tonight?"

"Yeah, I should be. We won't be able to meet for lunch today, though. Carl and I got some loose ends to tie up, so I'm gonna meet with him for a minute."

"Man! You need to hurry up and finish this internship. I miss our lunch dates." I poked out my lips and folded my arms like I always did to try to get my way, but I knew there was nothing Terrance could do about this. He stood up and gave me a hug and a kiss before we departed until the day's end.

Chapter 16

I had thirteen clients total today, so by the time I got home, it was almost six o'clock. When I pulled up I saw Tif, Mike, and Theresa lugging suitcases to Tif's car. They were blocking the driveway, so I parked on the street. I thought she would've been done by now, but I guessed she probably got a late start. Mike had on a white T-shirt with the sleeves torn off, so you could see how cut he was. While I was walking up to the house, he stopped what he was doing and acted as though he was my bodyguard. I had my case with all my hair styling equipment in one hand and my bag of hair products in another hand. I never left any of my stuff in my car overnight. We lived in a nice neighborhood, but I spent a whole lot of money on that stuff, and I would be pissed off if I walked out to my car one day and everything was gone.

Mike left Tif and Theresa struggling and walked over to me and grabbed the case out of my hand. "Let me take that in the house for you." He started walking towards the door before I could even tell him no.

"Hey, Tif. Hey, Theresa."

"Hey, Kel." Theresa responded.

Tif walked over to me and softly said, "I hope you don't mind Mike helping us. I watched him every time he went in the house. I was right behind him making sure he didn't slip anything in his pockets."

"Girl. He's cool." Tif didn't know that the last thing I was worried about was Mike stealing something. He had a whole lot more than what we had. When I walked in the house, Mike was standing in the living room, still holding my equipment.

"Where do you want me to set this?"

I pointed to where the den was and said, "You can put it in there on the floor.

Thanks."

"No problem," He said as he walked in the den. When he walked back into the living room, he said, "You got a nice house, Kel."

"Thank you, but it's not as nice as yours." I looked around to make sure no one heard me.

"What are you doing the rest of the day?" he asked.

"I'm about to rest a little. I had a busy day at work. I did thirteen clients."

"I guess you did have a long day. Well, I think they're done, so I'm gonna go on home. If you get bored, that's where I'll be."

I looked at Mike and smiled and said, "OK, Mike. I'll be sure to remember that."

As Mike was walking out, Tif thanked him and walked in. "Well, Kel. That's about it. Thank you so much for your hospitality."

"You're welcome, girl. Did you get your furniture out of storage?"

"Yeah. We did that earlier. I found some movers to pick everything up for me and take it to the apartment, so I'm all set up. I just need to go grocery shopping, but a bitch gon' be hungry tonight or eat some fast food cuz I'm tired as hell!"

"I know exactly what you mean."

"I'll call you when I get my phone turned on to give you the number."

"You better! I walked Tif outside and waved goodbye to
Theresa. Mike was still standing outside on his porch. I walked
back in the house and closed the front door.

I took a shower to get all that hair and hairspray off of me, and
I threw on my peach Victoria's Secret sweats and a peach tank top.
I combed my hair back into a ponytail and lounged in the den on
the couch. While I was watching *Are We There Yet?* with Ice
Cube, Nia Long, and those bad ass kids, I heard my cell phone
ringing. It was coming from upstairs. I flew up the stairs and slid
onto the bed.

"Hello," I said, breathing heavily.

"You sound like you was busy."

"Who is this?"

"Oh. So it's like that? You got that many niggas callin' your
phone, you can't tell one from the other? Yo man gotta be a pussy
to put up with that shit cuz if you was my woman, wouldn't none
of that shit be goin' on."

"Ty?" I finally said after I listened to his voice long enough to
know who it was.

"What's up with you, boo?"

I sat up on the bed and said, "Oh. You over your little childish
episodes?

"Girl. Ain't nothin' about me childish."

"You are childish. You gonna sit up there and get an attitude
because I wouldn't come see you when you wanted me to. Then on
top of that, you wouldn't even answer my phone calls." I didn't
tell him that I was actually on my way to his house the other night
before Phelecia had called me needing my help. I didn't want him
to know he was on my mind like that.

"I been busy taking care of business, or did you forget I was a
businessman? Like I told you before, I can't pick up the phone
every time somebody calls. As much as I like you, not even for
you."

I was so happy to hear Ty's voice, but I was trying my best not
to show it. Maybe he was too busy to answer my phone calls. I
guess he did have to work hard to pay for all those nice things he
had.

"You busy right now?" Ty asked.

"No. I'm just lying down. I was at work all day."

"You didn't sound like you was lying down when you answered."

"I had to run upstairs to grab my phone."

"Oh. Yeah. I saw that you was busy today. I was gonna stop by, but the parking lot was packed," Ty said.

"What you doing? Stalking me?"

"Hell naw! I ain't got no reason to stalk nobody."

"What you call it then?"

"Checking on a friend."

I laughed and said, "Oh. OK."

"So can you get out?"

I thought about it for a minute. Terrance told me he would probably be home on time tonight. That was gonna be in a couple of hours, but I was willing to take that chance. I would just have to come up with a lie later or suffer the consequences.

I continued talking to Ty and said, "What you got in mind?"

"Before I go into all of that, first answer my question. Can you get out?"

"I wouldn't have asked you what you got in mind if I couldn't get out!"

"Aight. You betta watch who you talkin' to, woman. But anyway, I was just gonna take you out for a minute. I ain't even gonna front. I wanna see you bad as hell."

I got goosebumps all over when he said that. That's when he suckered me right in to say, "I wanna see you, too. I've been thinking about you so much." I could hear him laugh softly and then clear his throat. "What's so funny, Ty?"

"Nothin'. So you wanna come here or you want me to pick you up from somewhere else?"

I did not wanna ride in that old-ass Cadillac, so I said, "I'll come to your house."

"I'll be waitin'."

"I'll be there in about an hour."

I looked at the clock, and I knew I didn't have enough time to enjoy myself with Ty, but I was ready to deal with the consequences with Terrance. I got up and got cute. I forgot that I was even tired ten minutes ago. I put on some denim capris and a white and gold top that hung off one shoulder. I touched up my ponytail, and instead of letting it hang down, I pinned it up and put on my gold hoop earrings. I was a certified D-I-V-A. I had no idea where Ty and I were going, but I hoped I wasn't underdressed.

By the time I left the house, it was almost seven-thirty, which meant I probably wouldn't get to Ty's house til almost eight-thirty. I bumped my radio all the way there. I didn't listen to the radio a whole lot cuz they have so many damn commercials, but they were jammin' tonight. When I pulled up in front of Ty's house, the first thing I saw was Ty's raggedy-ass Cadillac sittin' there on them damn rims. I made my journey to the door and rang the doorbell. I saw the light come on inside, and Ty opened the door. As soon as he saw me, he grabbed me and pulled me in.

He scared me. "What's wrong, Ty?"

"Nothing. I told you how bad I wanted to see you." He put his arms around me and hugged me tighter than I had ever been hugged before. He let me go and looked at me from head to toe. "You are fine as hell!"

"Thank you."

"How did I get so lucky to have a friend like you?"

"Now you tryin' to be funny." When I saw how Ty was dressed, I knew we weren't going anywhere formal. He looked nice. He had on a pair of loose fitting Levis and a striped brown, tan, and white polo shirt. The casual shoes he wore matched his shirt perfectly. He still had the grimy look goin' on with his facial hair. One thing I liked about his was that he didn't let it get all wild and out of control. I think the only people who could get away with it was Ty and Eric Benet.

After Ty and I got done scrutinizing each other, he gave me another hug and said, "Let me go get my keys, then we can roll." I stood by the door and waited for him. I felt so nervous. It felt like a first date. Ty came back and grabbed my hand. We walked out together and I stood there as he locked up.

I started walking towards the dreaded Cadillac, and I heard Ty say, "Where you going?"

"Oh, are we taking my car?" He pushed a button on his keys, and I heard his garage opening. I felt like a fool when the garage opened and there sat a black Hummer H2 with thirty-inch rims on it and a silver hard-top convertible Mercedes Benz with what had to be twenty-twos.

"You choose which one you wanna go in." Ty said, with a smirk on his face. I felt like picking my face up off the ground. Well, at least I found out why he had a three-car garage.

We walked over to the garage and I walked to the passenger side of the Benz.

"Good choice." Ty said as he came and opened the door. I got in and looked around while Ty was walking to the driver's side. There was wood grain everywhere, cream leather interior, and a navigation system. The car even talked to him like Knight Rider! I was in the wrong business! When Ty got in, he said, "You like it?"

"Yeah, it's nice. What kind is it?"

"A 2013 S-Class. They not supposed to come out until November, but I got a hook-up through one of my clients."

"That must be nice. Why didn't you tell me you had two other vehicles?"

"Because like I told you before, I don't have a reason to boast. Did you really think that the Caddy was my only ride?"

"Yeah. I did." Ty laughed hard as hell. I didn't think it was funny. "Where are we going?"

"Well, first I was gonna take you out to eat, if that's all right with you, then I wanna show you something."

"Sounds good." Ty turned on the radio and rap was playing. I didn't mind listening to some rap music, but whoever we were listening to, I couldn't understand a word that was coming out of his mouth.

Finally, Ty asked, "Do you like rap?"

"Not really, but it's cool." I was lying my ass off about it being cool. I just didn't wanna be a brat.

"If you don't like it, turn to something you do like. I reached towards the dashboard and Ty pointed towards my door. He had a radio tuner on each door panel and on the steering wheel. I started tuning through stations and didn't know what they were because he had XM Satellite radio. Something that I was only accustomed to when I got the free week's preview. I finally found an R&B station and I figured out how to let my seat back a little and enjoy the ride.

Ty put his hand on my thigh about five minutes into the ride, and he kept it there the whole way, moving it back and forth. I could see him in the corner of my eye every time he looked over at me, and it was too many times to count. We finally pulled up to this place called Thornton Steak House. I had heard about how good it was, but I had never been there. The parking lot was packed. I was hoping that it didn't take forever to get our food because I was running very low on time.

When we walked into the restaurant, there were three other couples standing in front of us. While we were standing there, my phone rang, and I looked at the screen. It was Terrance calling from his phone.

"Oh shit!"

Ty looked at me and said, "What's up?"

"Terrance is calling."

"Tell that nigga you out with your friend. You are allowed to do that right?" I didn't answer Ty. He just didn't understand my end of the situation at all.

"Hello," I said, trying to sound calm.

"What's goin' on?"

"Nothing. I'm just hanging out with Phelecia. Are you home yet?"

"No. I was calling to tell you I was gonna be a little late tonight, but not as late as I was last night. Some things in my portfolio were rejected by the boss, so it's gonna take a couple of hours to fix them." While I was talking to Terrance, the hostess came over to show us to our table. Ty grabbed my hand, and we started following behind her. I continued talking while I walked.

"So what time do you think you'll be home?"

"No later than midnight. I promise. But it doesn't sound like it should matter to you anyway. You out hangin' with your girl."

"Yeah, but I still miss you." By then, Ty and I were sitting in a booth across from one another, and when Ty heard the "miss you" statement, he looked away from his menu and looked at me. I shrugged my shoulders and smiled.

"You gonna stay up and wait for me?" Terrance asked.

"Yeah, but you better be there by midnight."

"I will. I love you, baby."

"Love you, too."

After I hung up the phone, I looked at Ty, and he looked upset. "What's wrong, babe??"

"I just find it rude for you to carry on a conversation with somebody else, husband or not, while you're out with me."

"What was I supposed to do? Tell my husband that I'm too busy to talk right now, but I'll call him back at my earliest convenience?"

"That would be nice." I was waiting for Ty to laugh, but he was dead serious.

"Ty, we're friends. You know I'm married. If you can't deal with this, we need to back off right now because it'll never work." The waitress came over and asked us if we were ready to order. I hadn't even looked at the menu.

"Can you give us a few more minutes?" I politely asked. She nodded and told us she would be back.

There was dead silence at the table, which was very uncomfortable, until the waitress came back. I ordered steak and shrimp and Ty ordered the same.

After we ordered, Ty said, "So how much time you got left?"

"I need to be home by midnight." Ty looked at his gold Movado watch. He picked up the alcoholic beverage menu and looked at it as if he was concentrating hard on what he wanted. Without lifting up his head, he said, "Kellie, what do you really want out of this?" It took me a minute to answer because I was wondering what this conversation was gonna lead to.

"Um. I guess I'm looking for companionship. What do you want?"

"It started off as me wanting a female companion who I could just chill with, like we're doing now. Even though I don't know you that well, I think I know you enough to know that I'm gonna want more than that out of you. I realized that it's more serious than I thought it was when I just got mad as hell cuz you had a conversation with your own husband. That ain't cool."

"Well, I don't know what you want me to do." The waitress walked by and asked if we needed anything, and Ty ordered a Hennessy on the rocks. I ordered a margarita.

"Honestly, I don't know what I want you to do either. I know what I would like you to do, but I know you would need more time before you made a drastic decision like that."

"What's that?"

"Leave him," Ty said without hesitation.

"Just like that? Are you crazy? Then what?"

"Then I'll take care of you. You wouldn't have to worry about nothin'."

"It's not that simple. Like you said, we don't know each other that well, and I love Terrance."

"We'll see how you feel after I wine and dine you for a little while." Our drinks and meals came at the same time. Ty gulped down his Hennessy so fast, you would've thought it was a shot. The whole way through my meal, I wondered what Ty had to show me.

When we finished eating, Ty left a twenty on the table for a tip. I still had about two and a half hours before I needed to be home. Ty and I conversed during our whole ride. He never brought up my husband or home life again. We just talked like there was nothing or no one else in the world but the two of us. I was glad that he had calmed down and gotten over my conversation with Terrance in the restaurant. I told him about my friends and their different personalities and how I'm the sanest one out of the group. I hadn't been paying attention to where we were going, but when I stopped talking, we were pulling into Ty's garage.

"I thought you had something to show me."

"I do, but I think I should wait."

"Wait for what?"

"For us to get to know each other better." I didn't ask any more questions. I had no idea what he wanted to show me, but whatever it was, he must didn't trust me enough to show me right now.

We walked to the door, and Ty started unlocking it. I heard the click as he turned the key, then he turned around, looked at me and pressed his lips against mine. I stood there and didn't move. He then turned back around and opened the door.

"Go ahead and sit in the den. I gotta go make a phone call. Don't go nowhere."

"I won't." I watched Ty as he walked towards the stairway. I grabbed the remote and turned on the television. I flicked through the channels for a few minutes until my patience ran out. I was trying not to be rude by just walking through Ty's house, but he left me no choice. He was rude by leaving me to go make a phone call.

I got up and walked towards the stairs. I could hear Ty talking while I stood at the bottom of the stairs. I slowly crept up the stairs and when I reached the top, I looked around. There were so many doors to different rooms. I walked towards the one in the direction of Ty's voice.

"I don't care how you get there, but the product needs to get there by the morning," Ty said in a calm but strong voice. He didn't see me enter the room. It had to have been his bedroom. There was a king-size bed that was full of pillows. The whole color scheme was black, tan, and leopard print. I walked up behind him, put my hands underneath his shirt, and started massaging his broad shoulders. I didn't know what had come over me, but I knew I was getting myself into something that wasn't gonna be easy to get out of. "Look, man. I gotta go. Don't make me or my clients unhappy." Ty slammed down the phone and said, "You give people everything they need to get a job done, and they still find a way to fuck it up." He turned around, grabbed by plump ass, and started kissing me aggressively.

"Ty. Stop. We can't do this."

He stopped, looked at me, and said, "What? You came up here rubbin' all on me for a reason. Now you telling me you don't want this?"

"I do. It just feels wrong."

"Here you go again. OK, Whatever. I don't have to beg for ass."

I put my hands on my hips and said, "What you mean by that? So I'm just another piece of ass to you?"

"Naw. I just mean I'm not about to beg you for nothing. I got everything I need. I would like to have you, but if you don't want me, what can I do?"

Ty pulled off his shirt and sat on the bed. I didn't want Ty to think it was like that. I really did want him. I was horny as hell, and as much as I wanted to believe I didn't know what was gonna happen when I went up those stairs, I knew. I went and stood in between Ty's legs. I kneeled down and started unbuttoning his pants.

"I don't want you to be regrettin' nothin' later, so don't do it if you really don't want to, and definitely don't start nothin' you can't finish. I remained quiet while I finished undressing Ty. He lifted his body as I slid his jeans down and pulled them off. I could see his dick sticking straight up through his red-and-black plaid boxers. He was well-endowed. Out of all the dicks I had ever been acquainted with, I don't think I had ever seen one so long and thick. Well, not in real life.

After I got his pants and boxers off, I stroked his dick a little and laid on top of him, kissing his neck and his chest. He moaned like he was already getting ready to cum. I was saying in my head, *Please Lord, not another one of these!* While I kissed him, he started unbuckling my belt with his eyes squeezed tightly together. He sat up and stood me up, pulling my capris down to my ankles and revealing my cream lace thong. He then stood up and pulled my shirt over my head and stared at my breasts that were partially hidden underneath my bra that matched my thong. He lifted me up by my thighs, and I wrapped my legs around his waist. Ty made me feel so good. He put his face in my cleavage and sucked so hard that it started stinging. I didn't care though. I was in the heat of the moment, and I didn't want it to end. I wanted Ty to know how much I did want him.

After Ty put me down, I gently pushed him back on the bed and straddled him. I began to perform my famous talent on him, but gagged for the first time in years. His dick was too long to make it down my throat, but I took it as far as I could. Ty grabbed my hair so hard, I thought he was pulling it out by the roots. I felt all my hair pins falling out and heard my rubber band pop.

"Baby, I'm about to cum!" Ty said and started moaning. I sucked faster until I could feel the cum at the tip of his dick, and I let the rest of his cum run down my chest. After that, Ty sat up and rolled over on top of me, giving me every last inch of his manhood.

Chapter 17

I woke up with my hair over my eyes once again. I could barely see a thing. I could feel Terrance's arms around my waist. I tried to look up at the clock to see what time it was, but the clock wasn't there. My nightstand wasn't even there. I rolled over and saw Ty lying there with his mouth wide open. I had fallen asleep at his house after having the best sex of my life.

"Ty! Ty!" I was shaking him vigorously, but obviously he was a hard sleeper.

"What up, baby?" Ty finally said in slurred voice.

"How did you let me fall asleep? What time is it?"

"Calm down, woman!" Ty sat up and grabbed his cell phone off the dresser.

"It's two o'clock."

"Two o'clock? What am I supposed to tell Terrance!" I was out of control. There was no way out of this lie, no matter how hard I tried. I thought I would be willing to suffer the consequences if it came to that, but now I felt quite differently. I hurried up and put my clothes on and found a brush to brush my hair. Ty followed behind me, every step I took.

"Just tell him you and yo friend was having so much fun, you lost track of time." I could've said that, but my phone was downstairs, and I knew Terrance had probably been blowing it up. I ran downstairs to where my purse was with my phone. I looked at the screen which said that I had fifteen missed calls. All of them were from the house, Terrance's cell phone, Tif, Bri, Tasha, and my momma. I knew then that Terrance had called everybody looking for me.

"Shit! This is real fucked up." I was so upset, that I didn't even tell Ty bye. I ran out the house, jumped in my car, and sped off. I saw him standing in the door as I drove down the street.

I started dialing my home phone, but then realized that was the dumbest thing I could do. I tried to think of a lie the whole way home. I was so freaked out I almost started crying. This double life shit was stressful, and it may not even be worth it. While I was driving, Lyfe came on the radio, singing "Let's Stay Together." I definitely didn't wanna hear that shit. My cell phone rang when I was almost home. I wasn't even trying to answer it if it was Terrance. I had come up with a lie that I believed would work. It wasn't Terrance calling. It was Ty.

When I answered, he said, "Oh, you just not gon' tell a nigga bye after all that good lovin' I gave you?"

"You know how paranoid I am right now? You not feelin' what I'm going through. This is not a good situation I'm in right now."

"It's gon' be aiight. Just calm yo ass down. He don't got proof of nothin'. Just make some shit up and gon' ahead about your business." Ty made me feel worse than I already felt. He wasn't making things any better. He couldn't possibly know how I felt since he didn't have shit to lose! He was pissing me off, so I rushed off the phone.

"Well, I'm around the corner from my house, so I'll talk to you later."

"Call me tomorrow."

I hung up the phone and turned onto my street. I was nervous as hell. Not because of what I had done, but because I didn't know what to expect when I got home.

When I pulled into the driveway, I saw my living room light on, so I knew Terrance was still awake. I threw my cell phone underneath the seat of my car before I got out and started walking to the door.

Before I made it all the way there, Terrance opened the door and said, "You know you got some explainin' to do. Where the fuck you been, Kel!"

When I stepped into the foyer, I looked in Terrance's eyes and convincingly said, "I am so sorry! Me and Phelecia lost track of time, and when I went to grab my cell phone I couldn't find it. I don't know where I lost it, but I most definitely gotta stop by the Sprint store in the morning to get a replacement. Phelecia's broke ass don't even have a cell phone."

"I was just about to call the police. I didn't know what could've happened to you. I called everybody."

"Please tell me you didn't call my momma." I knew if Terrance had called and told her, she would be all in my business the next day, asking all kinds of questions.

"Of course I called her. I thought maybe you had gone by her house."

"Damn, Terrance!"

"That's not my fault. You should've called or something." That explained why my momma had called my cell phone. She rarely ever called it. If she wanted to get in touch with me, the majority of the time she would call the house and leave a message. This was all a big mess.

"I'm really sorry. You accept my apology?"

"I gotta think about it. You gotta make it up to me. You ready?"

I couldn't do nothing with Terrance knowing Ty's scent was all over me, but I knew I had to do something to get Terrance off my back. I wouldn't even let him get close to me.

"Let me go take a shower and you just lay here and be ready for me." Terrance wanted to smile, but he was trying to act hard and hold it back.

I went in the bathroom and closed the door behind me. While I was in the shower, I scrubbed hard as hell to get Ty off of me. I looked down at my breasts to make sure I didn't have any hickeys.

I just knew I probably did, the way Ty was sucking all over them. When I got done with my shower, I dried off and walked into the room butt naked. Terrance was lying there with his eyes closed.

I leaned over and whispered in his ear. "Wake up."

He opened his eyes and said, "Damn, baby, you look good." He grabbed me and laid me down on top of him and started kissing me. When I reached under the cover, Terrance's dick was limp as hell. I started kissing his neck and sucking on his nipples to get him erect. I knew his nipples were always sensitive. I kept playing with his dick and massaging his balls, but nothing was changing.

"What's wrong, baby?"

"I don't know. Maybe I'm just tired. Can I take a rain check?"

"A rain check?" I paused and said, Alrighty."

What man asks if they can have a rain check when it comes to ass? I knew Terrance was a minuteman, but he never ever rejected my pussy. Maybe he was just still upset about me not calling. He seemed to have taken it well. I crawled over to my side of the bed and went to sleep. I had gotten mine anyway, and it was good.

The next morning while I was getting ready for work, my momma called. I started not to answer the phone, but I knew she would just keep calling until she got me, so I just prepared myself to listen to some bullshit.

"Kellie!"

"Yeah, Ma."

"Why didn't you answer the phone when I called you last night? It could've been an emergency."

"I lost my cell phone last night. I didn't get any calls."

"Well, if you wasn't out with Phelecia's ass, you wouldn't have lost your phone. You should've been at home with your man." I left the room, away from Terrance. He was still asleep, and I felt like I was about to snap, so I tried to avoid waking him up.

"Look, I barely ever go anywhere, Momma. If I wanna go out and hang with my friends every now and then, I think I have the right. I'm still young, and I'm tired of feeling like an old grandma."

"You gon' learn girl, and you gon' learn the hard way. You got everything you need at home."

"OK, Ma. Now that you know I'm all right, I gotta let you go so I can get ready for work."

"Just remember what I said. I only say the things I say because I love you."

I just hung up the phone. I didn't feel like hearing anything else my nosey-ass momma had to say. She needed to find her a man, then maybe she could stay out of my business.

After I hung up the phone, I realized I didn't have any clients coming in until later on in the morning, so I decided to go in the guest room to clean up whatever Tif didn't. When I walked in and looked around, everything seemed to be in its place. I looked in the mirror, admiring myself, and that's when I realized how dusty it was, so I got the Windex and dusted almost everything in the room. I didn't like my visitors to have to sleep on the same linen as my previous guests, so I started pulling the cover off so that I could throw everything in the washing machine before I left. I looked at the sheets and noticed white stains everywhere. They were very noticeable because the sheets were navy blue. I pulled the sheets all the way off the bed and put it up to my nose. All it took was a small sniff to smell sex. Those were cum stains all over my sheets and Tif's ass was too triflin' to wash them before she left. I didn't even know she was having men at my house when Terrance and I weren't home. I shook my head in disbelief and dragged the linen down the hall to the laundry room.

After I put the sheets in the washer with extra detergent, I went to my bedroom to grab everything so I could get ready and go. I sat on the bed for a second and thought about what my momma said about me having everything I needed at home. I wasn't trying to hear everything my momma ever tried to tell me, but I still listened to what she said. I knew she had a valid point. It just wasn't what I wanted to hear. I knew that if she knew what I was doing, I wouldn't hear the last of it. While I was sitting there, Terrance's cell phone started vibrating. I quietly got off of the bed so that I could reach on the other side of Terrance to get it before he woke up. I looked to see who it was first. It was a number I didn't recognize, but I answered it anyway.

"Hello," I said softly so that Terrance wouldn't hear me. "Hello?" I said again. No one answered and then I heard nothing on the other end. I was gonna call the number back, but I didn't want Terrance to think I was spying on him, so I grabbed the pen that was sitting on his nightstand and tore a small piece of paper off the envelope from the previous day's mail and quickly jotted the number down. I looked through his record of calls, and I saw the same number several more times. I grabbed my purse off the back of the door, and I stuck the number deep down inside, gave Terrance a kiss on the forehead and left.

I still had a few hours before I needed to be at work, so I called Ty while I was just riding around.

"Hello," Ty said when he answered after the first ring.

"Oh. You're answering the phone today, huh?"

"Whateva, woman. What's up with you?"

"Nothing. I got a few hours before work. I was just seeing if you wanted to go to breakfast or something."

"Uh . . ."

"Just forget it if you gotta think that hard about it."

"Calm down! I was trying to think when I had to see my next client. Where you wanna go?"

"I don't know. How about Jimmy's Pancake House?"

"That's cool. I'm not too far from that side of town. I'll meet you in about fifteen to twenty minutes."

I headed to Jimmy's and got me and Ty a table. I made sure it wasn't near a window because I saw how easily it is to spot someone in a restaurant after the incident with Ty and his female client. I definitely didn't need anyone I knew to see me with Ty.

I sat at the table waiting for Ty for about five minutes and saw him walk in, dressed in an all-black suit and dark sunglasses. I watched as the waitress showed him over to the table where I was, and I stood up and gave him a hug when he made it over. He smelled and felt so good. I didn't wanna let him go. To be honest, I wanted him to wear me out right there on that table.

Ty sat down and said, "I guess last night went ok after you got home."

"And what makes you say that."

"Cuz you livin' to tell me about it."

"Yeah. Everything's cool. I guess."

"What you mean, you guess?" I wanted to tell Ty about the phone call Terrance had gotten this morning and how I had a strange feeling something wasn't right, but I didn't want him to think I was insecure, and I knew how he got when I gave any insinuation that I cared about Terrance just the least bit, even though he knew that I did. He just didn't want to hear about it, so I left it at that.

"So when can we see each other again?" Ty asked.

With sarcasm, I said, "We're seeing each other right now."

"Yo ass know what I mean. I enjoyed myself with you last night. I want to have some more of those nights. I wish it could be every night without you having to rush home to another man."

"Let me ask you something, Ty. Since we've gone beyond what friends do, what should I consider us now?"

"You tell me. It's not like I can call you my woman. You belong to somebody else." Ty always had to bring that up, and he wasn't slick. He was trying to throw a guilt trip on me and for some reason it worked. I wanted him to call me his woman. That's what I wanted to be, but I wanted to be Terrance's wife at the same time. I knew I couldn't have my cake and eat it too, because Ty wasn't the type to stick around and go for that kind of shit for too long. I figured if he couldn't, I would just have to leave him alone and make him a part of my past.

After Ty and I finished our breakfast, I decided to go ahead and go to the shop since Ty had an appointment with a client. When we walked out the restaurant, I saw his Mercedes parked a couple of cars down from mine. I told him to call me later. Maybe we would be able to get together. Then I blew him a kiss, got in my car, and drove away. When I pulled up at the shop, there were two police cars there. The first thing that came to mind was that Phelecia came to work and Duwan came up there trying to start some shit. I knew Rhonda wasn't going for that mess.

I ran in the shop without getting any of my equipment out of the car. I didn't see Phelecia, but all the other stylists were there. There were two officers at the desk talking to Cameron and Rhonda. Rhonda looked up at me as I walked towards them. I could see tears in her eyes. I got worried, trying to figure out what could've happened.

"What's going on?" I looked back and forth at Cameron and Rhonda, waiting on one of them to say something. One of the officers was holding a notepad and pen. He was a tall, slender white man with a military haircut. The other was a short, stout white man with a bald spot at the top of his head. They both were dressed in suits. Not ordinary cop uniforms.

The one holding the notepad asked, "Ma'am, who are you?"

In a cracking voice, Rhonda said, "This is Kellie."

"You are exactly who we need to speak with."

"About what?" I asked, as my eyes widened in fear.

"I'm Detective Ron Spears. I'm a homicide detective. We were informed that you were the last person to see the deceased, besides her murderer."

I began stuttering as I tried to get my words out. "The deceased? Murderer? What are you talking about?"

"We just called your residence and your husband, Mr. Moore, told us that you were out with Phelecia Sanders last night." My heart dropped. I had this horrible feeling in my stomach. I didn't know if I felt that way because my lie was about to kick me in the ass or because I just had found out my girl had been murdered.

I started crying uncontrollably and Cameron put her arm around me.

I stopped to think for a minute and I said, "Where's the kids? Are they ok?"

The detective started harassing me again by saying, "The kids are fine. We can talk about that later, but right now, I need to know what time you were with Ms. Sanders last night." I looked at the other women in the shop and then looked at the detective. Everyone's eyes were on me, waiting for my explanation of events.

"Detective, can I please speak with you privately?" The detective and his cop buddy walked me outside to one of their police cars. I was shaking out of control. I couldn't believe that Terrance didn't call me and tell me what was going on, but then I realized that I had turned my ringer off when I was at breakfast with Ty because I didn't wanna upset him by receiving any unnecessary phone calls. I hadn't looked at my phone since. I also thought about the fact that Terrance probably didn't think I had made it to the Sprint store to get a replacement phone yet, since I had told that bold-faced lie and said I lost it the night before. After I sat in the back seat of the police car, I pulled my phone out and looked at it. Terrance had called me about ten times and left me a message that I didn't have time to listen to at the moment. It would've been nice to have had a heads up to what was already said, but that was my fault.

Both cops got in the front seat of the car and waited for me to begin. I dug for a piece of tissue out of my purse to wipe my eyes and blow my nose.

"Now, Mrs. Moore, can you tell us everything you know about last night?" They had no sympathy nor compassion. They saw that I was suffering, but they didn't seem to care.

"Can I start from the beginning of what I know?" I knew that if I started by telling the truth about not being with Phelecia last night, they would look at me like I was crazy and immediately prejudge me.

"Go ahead. Tell us everything you know." I started by telling the detectives about Duwan's history of abuse towards Phelecia. I also told them about the incident between the two of them that occurred a couple of days ago and how she had just gone and filed a restraining order on him the day before. I showed them the card of the officer who filed the report when I had taken Phelecia to the hospital.

After giving them all that information, the fat cop said, "So how did you two spend the evening last night?"

I started stuttering again because I had no idea how this was about to turn out. They both looked at me as though I was guilty. I began to speak and they watched me like they were about to study every word that was coming out of my mouth.

"Well, that's the thing, Detectives. I wasn't with Phelecia last night."

The taller of the two said, "Why would your husband make the story up of you being with her, or assume that you were?"

"I told him I was with her because . . ." There was complete silence in the car. They were awaiting my next statement. "Because I was out with a male companion who I don't wish for my husband to know about."

The taller detective began writing again as he shook his head and said, "So what you're telling me is that you had no communication whatsoever with Ms. Sanders yesterday?"

"None whatsoever."

"Well, you're free to go for now. We'll investigate the information you gave us about the restraining order and try to contact Duwan Greene. We'll be keeping in touch, so don't go too far."

"I won't, but one more thing. Where are the kids?"

"Like I told you, the kids are fine, but I can't give any information on their whereabouts."

I was content just knowing the kids weren't hurt and were out of harm's way. I got out the car and folded my arms, holding my head down. I stood against the building and began crying again. I couldn't believe this had happened. If I would've forced her to press charges on Duwan the other day, this would've never happened. He would be locked up somewhere. After I regained my composure, I slowly walked in the shop and everyone watched me as I walked over to my station and sat down.

Cameron came over and said, "You ok, girl?"

"Yeah. As ok as I'm gonna be right now. I don't think I can handle doing anybody's hair today. I only have a few clients. Can you cover for me, or are you booked?"

"I'll do their hair if they let me. You know your clients don't like anybody in their heads but you."

"Well, I'm gonna head out cuz I can't stay here right now. They'll just have to reschedule if they want to." I looked over at Phelecia's station and almost started crying again, but walked out the shop and held it in until I got to the car. I was so hurt by this tragedy. Phelecia was no longer just an associate, or a co-worker. She had become, what I considered, a friend and it was always hard to lose a friend.

Terrance had called my phone a few more times. I was hoping that the truth wouldn't get back to him. I sat in my car until I figured out what I was gonna say to him. I was supposedly with Phelecia until almost two o' clock that morning. I didn't know how I was gonna clean that up, but I would figure something out. I've had to do so much lying in so little time just because of Ty. I needed to get away from all this confusion for a while. Maybe that way, I would be able to find myself again. Phelecia and I were supposed to go to a hair show in Atlanta together in a few weeks. Maybe I would go by myself, just so I could clear my head. Too much had been going on in the past couple of months, and I felt like I couldn't handle much more.

When I got home, Terrance was already gone to work. He had left me a note on the refrigerator to call him as soon as possible. I sat in the kitchen staring at the wall. I don't know how long I was sitting there, but all of a sudden, I was taken out of my trance by the doorbell. I almost didn't answer it because I didn't feel like being bothered by anyone. I didn't even feel like talking.

I walked to the front door and looked through the peephole. Mike was standing on my porch dressed in a suit and tie. I took a deep breath and opened the door.

"Hey, Kel. I just came by to check on you. I know you're usually not home this time of day. I wanted to make sure everything was ok." I tried to say that I was fine, but it just couldn't come out. I broke down right in front of him, worse than I did the first time. He made his way in and walked me over to the couch and sat me down.

"What's wrong, sweetie?"

"Everything!" I screamed out. Mike gave me a hug and continued holding me. If we weren't anything else, we were becoming good friends. I felt like I could talk to him about anything. I just didn't want to because I felt like I might later on regret opening up too much.

Mike got up and walked towards the kitchen like he was at home. When he returned, he brought me a glass of ice water. "Now tell me what's wrong. I don't like seeing you like this. I started crying again. That's all I felt like doing because so much had built up inside of me and all my emotions were taking over.

After I finished that episode of crying, I said, "My whole life is fucked up!"

"It can't be that bad. You're beautiful, you got a career, friends, and a lot of people who love you."

"You just don't understand. My friend was murdered last night!"

"Who?" Mike asked in a concerned voice.

"My coworker Phelecia." I told Mike the whole story about Phelecia and Duwan and paused when I got to the part about me lying and saying I was with her last night. He told me that I did all I could do by helping her when she needed me. He also helped me to realize that love is blind, and Phelecia had to want to leave Duwan and no one could've made her.

Mike still couldn't understand how I felt because he didn't know the whole story. I just didn't want him to think I was some kind of hoe. I ended up telling him about Ty anyway and how I felt about him. I didn't know if it was gonna be a mistake in the long run, but I needed somebody to listen and understand me. After I finished telling him everything, he put his fist under his chin, stared at me, and shook his head. I knew that what I told him had hurt him because I knew how Mike felt about me.

"How does a woman like you get in so much trouble. I'm gonna be honest. You might need a lawyer, and you might need to go ahead and tell Terrance the truth because it's probably gonna come out. I'll help you however I can because I care about you." Mike looked and sounded so sincere. That's why I liked talking to him. "You need to lay down and get some rest and figure out what you're gonna tell Terrance. I gotta go to work, but call me if you need anything." Mike picked up my cell phone off the table and stored his number. Before he stood up, he moved closer to me and gave me a peck on the lips. The next thing I heard was the door closing behind him.

I tried closing my eyes, but every time I closed them, I saw Phelecia's face. I wondered how Duwan killed her and if she suffered long. I couldn't believe she was gone, and the part I hated most about it was that she was really trying to love herself. I decided to get up and call Terrance. The longer I waited, the worse the situation was probably gonna be. When I called the bank, a woman answered the phone. It sounded like Stacy. She sounded pleasant until she heard my voice.

She said, "I think he's busy, but hold on and let me check." She sounded as if she was irritated because I was calling my husband. Fortunate for her, Terrance came to the phone.

"Hi, Terrance," I said in a dispirited tone.

"Hey, baby. Are you ok?" He sounded so concerned about me. There was no way I could tell him the truth about where I was last night. I didn't like hurting people's feelings, and I knew that it would tear him up inside and things would never be the same between us.

"I'm not good, bae. I just can't get Phelecia out my mind. I left work early to just come home and relax."

"Well, I'll try to make it home as early as possible and bring you something to eat.

"Thank you. I'll see you later." That was easier than I thought it would be. I rested the rest of the day and didn't answer any more phone calls. My phone was ringing off the hook. All my girls called, and I knew exactly what they wanted. I knew how fast news spread in this area.

I did make one phone call though. I called Mike to tell him I appreciated him looking out for me and how I felt so much better. He always had to make it known how he felt about me and this time wasn't any different.

"Kel, I'm trying to prove to you that I'm a good man, and I'll always have your back. No matter how many stupid things you do!" He laughed after he said that and continued to say, "Maybe you just have to do all those stupid things to realize where you're supposed to be. Just maybe God is preparing you for me."

I ended that conversation by saying, "Thank again, Mike. I'll talk to you later."

"You always trying to cut me off when I'm being real with you, but you'll see one day. Hopefully sooner and not later. I'll let you go right now though. Get some rest."

Chapter 18

The next day, I got a call from Detective Spears bright and early.

"Hello. Is this Mrs. Moore?"

"Yes. This is she."

"This is Detective Ron Spears. How are you this morning?"

"I guess I'm as good as expected. Did you find Duwan?"

"No, we haven't spoken with him, but we did look into the restraining order Ms. Sanders was supposed to have against Mr. Greene, and there was nothing on file. We even spoke with the detective that made the report at the hospital, and he said that she never came in to file the order against Mr. Greene."

I couldn't believe that Phelecia had lied about the restraining order. She had assured me that she was going to get it, and Misty's momma was gonna take her.

"She told me she was gonna get it done the next day. Maybe she didn't get around to it."

"Obviously not," The detective said in a sarcastic, unprofessional tone.

"We will still be keeping in contact so we can get this case solved. We wouldn't want a murderer walking around on the streets."

After I hung up, I laid back down and started biting my bottom lip. Terrance rolled over and wrapped his arm around me. I could feel his hot breath against my neck.

"Who was that, baby?"

"The detective, just giving me an update on what's going on. They still haven't found Duwan." I got up and went downstairs to fix some breakfast. It felt so good not having to get up and go to work. Especially under the circumstances. I got ready to go outside to get the newspaper. I had forgotten to put my house shoes on upstairs, so I walked outside barefooted. The ground was already hot. I tiptoed to the paper and tiptoed back to the house. As soon as I got to my door, I heard a horn honk. I looked back and I think my heart jumped out of my chest and hit the concrete. I saw Reggie's car pulling up. I could see Tasha's bright blonde weave before she even opened the passenger-side door. She jumped out as soon as the car stopped moving and ran and gave me a hug.

"Girl, I heard what happened to Phelecia. I am so sorry. I didn't know her that well, but as far as I knew, she was cool."

"Yeah. She was."

Reggie came walking slowly up the driveway. I was trying to pay him no attention, but it was hard. I wanted to go off on him so bad. I never got a chance to since I had lost his number.

When Reggie finally made it up the driveway, Tasha said, "This my boo, Reg. But y'all kinda know each other, right?"

"Yeah, just a little bit, I said." Reggie had this smirk on his face that made me just wanna smack him, and I made it obvious to him by rolling my eyes every chance I got.

"Come on y'all. Let's go in. My feet are burning the hell up." Tasha started laughing and hooked her arm inside of Reggie's as they walked inside. I led them to the den and ran upstairs to wash up and throw some clothes on. They could've at least let me know they were coming.

"Terrance. Tasha and Reggie are downstairs." I said Reggie's name as if Terrance knew him. "Who is Reggie?"

"Oh. That's Tasha's boyfriend."

"Tasha has a real boyfriend?"

"Yeah. Ain't that a trip? That don't even feel right coming out my mouth." Terrance laughed as he got up to put some clothes on. I told him he didn't have to come down. To be honest, I didn't really want him to.

When I got back downstairs, Tasha was sitting on Reggie's lap with her arm wrapped around his neck. He was trying to look like he was happy, but I knew differently. He wanted me so bad, it led him to this. What he failed to realize was that this made me not want him even more.

"Kel, me and Reg was talkin' about maybe going to dinner tonight. Y'all should go with us to help you get your mind off things." The thought of sitting at the same dinner table with Reggie and Terrance made me cringe, but I had to act as if it didn't bother me.

"Yeah, that sounds nice," I said as I gave Reggie an evil look. "How did you find out about Phelecia anyway?"

"Girl, I saw Cameron's cousin, Krystal, at the grocery store yesterday, and she told me that Cameron had called and told her everything."

I turned on the TV, and Reggie tried to stay fixated on that. I think that initially, Reggie thought that this would be funny, but he started looking more uncomfortable than I was. All I could think was, *That's what his ass gets! Trying to play somebody!*

"Tif and Bri gon' be here in a minute. They said they was gonna meet us here. So I heard that you and Phelecia was together that night," Tasha said.

"Yeah," I said, and right before I got ready to finish my lie, the doorbell rang.

Tif and Bri both came in and gave me a hug.

Before I could get a word in, Tif said, "Did you see the article in the newspaper?" "No. I didn't even read it yet. Tasha and her man Reggie pulled up as soon as I went out and got it." I emphasized Reggie's name to let Tif know what was up, but obviously she already knew.

She walked in the den and said, "Hey, Tasha! What's up, Reggie?" and gave them both a hug.

"Oh. You remember Reggie from high school, Tif?" I asked, trying to see what was going on. It seemed like I was being left out on a lot of things lately.

Before Tif could answer, Tasha said, "Girl, we was out one night, and Tif got Reg to come over and talk to me."

"Mmm." I said. Tif knew I was pissed, so she looked at me and shrugged her shoulders.

After everything I had told Tif about me and Reggie, and how I felt when I saw him in

Applebee's with another woman, she had gone and hooked him up with Tasha!

Terrance came downstairs a couple of minutes later, in the middle of me making up more lies, telling everybody what Phelecia and I had supposedly done the night before. They were all so damn nosey, they kept on asking questions. I told them we had gone to this club on Seventy-Ninth and Burlowe, had a few drinks, and just sat around talking the rest of the night.

"What's up, y'all?" Terrance interrupted.

"Reg, this is Kel's hubby, Terrance. Terrance, this is Reg," Tasha said proudly.

Terrance walked over and shook hands with the loser and said, Hey, man. Don't I know you from somewhere?

"Yeah, Kel introduced us at Applebee's."

"That's right! Kel, you didn't tell me this was the same dude." I had completely forgotten that Terrance was with me when I ran into Reggie that day.

Tasha was sitting there looking confused, and then finally said, "Kel, I thought you didn't remember Reg all that well when I tried to tell you about him."

"I didn't think that he was the same Reggie you were talking about."

By then, Reggie and Terrance had started having their own conversation about basketball. I couldn't watch any longer, so I went in the kitchen to get a glass of orange juice. The next thing I knew, Bri was walking in right behind me.

She had on a white mini skirt and a black-and-white halter. Her black wedges were so high, she looked like she was about to tip over.

"What's up, Bri girl?" I said, trying to hide my anger.

"Girl, nothing, but I do need to talk to you." I walked closer to her with my glass in my hand. Bri looked back to make sure no one was coming. "Kel, I know I haven't been around or talked to you lately, but I just didn't wanna get in the middle of anything."

"In the middle of what?"

"Please promise you won't say anything if I tell you."

"I won't. I promise. Just tell me!"

"Tif told me that you had been talking about me behind my back, calling me all kinds of hoes and bitches. If that's the case, I don't think that's cool if we're supposed to be friends."

I started thinking back to all the conversations Tif and I had had and never once did I remember talking about Bri.

"Bri, you know me better than that. I didn't say no shit like that."

"I didn't think so. That's why I came to you myself. I know a lot of shit I do is crazy, but it's my life and I don't need nobody judging me.

In the middle of our conversation, Tif walked in with a big smile on her face. "What y'all doin' in here?" Bri looked at me with a look in her eyes telling me not to do it because she knew I was ready to snap.

"Nothing, girl. I hadn't seen Bri in so long, we were just in here catching up. You want some juice?"

"No thank you." She better had been glad she said no because I probably would've spit in it while she wasn't looking. "I do need to use your bathroom, though. I'll be right back."

"That stupid bitch!" I snarled when Tif left the room. Why would she lie on me like that after what I did for her?"

"I don't know, but I just thought I'd let you know."

"Thanks, girl."

Bri and I walked back in the living room after I finally calmed down. Between Reggie and Tif, I didn't know who I was more upset with. Tasha was still sitting on Reggie's lap. I knew his knee had to be sleep or something. Terrance was reading the paper.

"Hey, Kel, the paper says that the police have a couple of suspects under investigation for the murder," Terrance said.

I snatched the paper and said, "Let me see this." Terrance sat there with his hands in the same position as if he were still holding the paper. I didn't mean to be rude. I just had to make sure they didn't have any of the information I told them about not being with Phelecia that night in the article. The article stated that they still didn't have anyone in custody, but they did have suspects. It also said she was beaten in the head with a blunt object. That's what caused her death. I dropped the paper and put my hands over my face. I couldn't control my tears.

I felt Terrance rubbing me on my back, and Tif came and knelt down and said, "Everything's gonna be all right, Kel." I felt like slapping that phony-ass bitch. I couldn't believe she was trying to comfort me. As far as I was concerned, Phelecia was a better friend to me than Tif was.

I was so glad when everyone left. I needed some time to think. I still couldn't figure out why Tif would betray me the way she did. I even talked about it with Terrance, and he couldn't understand it either. I had promised Bri that I wouldn't say anything to Tif, but it was eating me up inside. After Terrance went to run some errands, I called Tif and began the conversation like everything was all right. Then I said, "Tif, I was given some information today that really bothered me."

"What?" She said sounding like she was eager to hear what I was about to say.

"Bri told me that you told her I was talking about her behind her back, calling her bitches and hoes."

"She said what!"

"You heard me."

"Why would I say that shit?"

"That's what I would like to know," I said in an agitated tone.

Tif took a deep breath and said, "Look. This is how it was. Bri and I were talking one day, and she was saying how you didn't talk to her very often anymore. I just told her how you two had different lifestyles now since you're married, and she's still out there. Maybe she took it the wrong way. You know how Bri is. She's always trying to blow things out of proportion. She's just seeking attention."

I thought about what Tif was saying, and she was speaking the truth. Bri wasn't all that bright, and knowing her, she was probably drunk when she and Tif were having that conversation.

"Thanks for clarifying that, Tif. But I got another bone to pick with you."

Before I could even finish, Tif said, "Don't tell me. You wanna know why I hooked Tasha up with Reggie."

"Uh, yeah!" I said sarcastically.

"We were at the club one night and Reggie happened to be there. You know how Tasha is when she drunk. She approached him the wrong way, stumbling all over the place, so I had to go over there and apologize and walk her back over to our table."

"So how the hell did they end up hooking up?" I said impatiently.

"Let me finish. Reggie came over to the table trying to holler at me, but I rejected him and told him he better move on. Then he started pushing up on Tasha."

"You knew what he was doing, right?"

"Yeah. Trying to get to you, but wasn't shit I could do. I did my part by rejecting him. I can't control what Tasha does." Tif had pleaded her case and she was right, so I apologized for believing somebody else before talking to her myself.

After I got off the phone with Tif, I thought about Reggie and how fine his ass was when he was sitting there with Tasha. I didn't want to see them together anymore, but I didn't think I would have to worry about seeing it too much longer. I knew Reggie like the back of my hand. Well, almost like the back of my hand. I sure as hell didn't know that he would ever pull some shit like talking to my girl to get at me, especially after the last conversation we had went so well. I knew that I might just snap if I went to dinner with them tonight, so I called Tasha and told her I wasn't feeling well. She told me that there was a change of plans anyway because Reg ended up having to go to work on short notice. I knew the truth though. He was trying to let her off easy because he was done using her ass. I felt sorry for her, but she didn't realize what I had gone through today watching her sitting on his lap and kissing all on him. I had to give it to myself though. I held my shit together. Sign of a true diva.

Chapter 19

It was hard, but I went back to work the next week, trying not to look at Phelecia's station and her possessions. The funeral wasn't gonna be until the weekend because it was taking a while to get money together for the expenses. I couldn't believe that Phelecia didn't have life insurance, especially with her having kids. I had found out that one of Phelecia's older sisters decided to take in her children. The police were still harassing me because obviously they didn't believe my story. In fact, I was one of the couple of suspects they were investigating. I just played it cool even though I always knew I was being followed. The detectives had spoken to Duwan, but of course, he acted as though he didn't know what was going on. He told them he was gone out of town and came back to find out that she had been killed. I knew that was some bullshit because I knew Duwan. I didn't know how he could live with himself knowing what he did.

I began seeing Ty almost every day, either in the mornings before work, or in the evenings when I got off. I met him for lunch a couple of times when Terrance wasn't available. Ty and I were becoming attached, but I just took it day by day. I knew the shit was getting serious the day Terrance and I were sitting around watching TV and the doorbell rang. Terrance was lying on the couch on his back, and I was lying on top of him watching *Takers*. I watched that movie over and over because I love me some TI!

When the doorbell rang we both looked at each other and Terrance said, "You expecting company?"

"No. You?" I asked. He shook his head. The doorbell rang again, so I jumped up and ran to the door and looked out the peephole. It was a white woman with long blonde hair pulled back in a ponytail.

When I opened the door she asked, "Are you Ms. Kellie Moore?"

"Yes I am." I looked in the driveway and saw that she was driving a white van that said "Shar's Florist" in big, green letters.

"One second. I have quite a few things for you," she said in an animated voice.

She started walking towards her van and gave a hand signal to someone else sitting in the passenger seat. It was another woman, but she had short brown hair. They opened the back of the van and each grabbed a plant. They were beautiful, but I had no idea what they were for.

"Do you want us to bring these in or do you want to take them?"

"Who are they from?"

"We'll let you know when we're done," the lady with the brown hair smiled and said. During their third trip to my door, Terrance came to see what was going on.

"Where did all these flowers come from?"

"I have no idea. I was beginning to think they were from you."

"Noooo. I know better than to waste money on flowers that are gonna die." I saw the blonde woman coming back to the door with one more thing, and the other one sat back in the van.

"OK, Ms. Moore. This is it. Have a good day." She handed me a beautiful vase with roses of every color in it. There was a card inside, but before I could grab it, Terrance did.

I said, "Who is it from?" As he continued to read, his eyes became bigger and bigger. That was the first time I looked at Terrance and became afraid. Very afraid.

"Who the fuck is Ty, Kel?"

"Ty?" I asked, trying to sound confused.

"I have no idea. I don't know no Ty!"

"Obviously he knows you. If he don't know you, how did he get my address?"

"I don't know, Terrance!" I yelled. "I am listed. The phone number is under my name. Maybe it's someone who knows me from the shop and has a crush on me."

Terrance threw the card down and started walking up the stairs. I picked the card up and read it to myself. It read:

Hey, baby.
I didn't know what you liked, so I got you everything they had.
I hope you like it. Talk to you later.
Ty

No wonder it was hard for Terrance to believe me. Ty made the card so personal. I couldn't believe he had sent flowers to my house. Now I had to go upstairs and try to explain to Terrance why another man was sending me flowers.

When I got upstairs, I didn't see Terrance at first and then I saw the master bathroom's door closed. I walked in and Terrance was in the shower. I quickly took off my clothes and slid in behind him.

I grabbed his arms from behind and was about to kiss his back until he turned around and said, "Don't fuckin' touch me, Kel. Who you been fuckin'?"

"Nobody, baby. I told you, I don't know a Ty. You know I love you, and I only want you. There's nobody else." I started kissing his chest while he stood there staring at me. He wouldn't even touch me. I knew I had to make this one good. I licked the water off of his body as it ran from his chest all the way down to his balls. Water ran down my face as I sucked Terrance's dick better than I had ever sucked any dick in my life. Even better than I sucked Ty's big-ass dick. I closed my eyes and imagined that it was Ty. Terrance rubbed his hands through my soaking wet hair and grabbed it all in one hand, pushing my head back and forth, forcing his dick down my throat. He started moaning until he came in my mouth.

After Terrance came, surprisingly his dick was still hard. He lifted me up and put me up against the shower wall and started bangin' the shit out of me. He was rough, exactly how I had started liking it, after experiencing it with Ty.

"Whose pussy is it?" Terrance said in a commanding tone. All I could do was moan. "Whose is it?" he said again in the same manner.

"This pussy is yours, baby." He let me down and put his hand on top of my head and said, "Get down there and suck it, baby." I got down on my knees and sucked his dick some more until I could no longer feel my jaw. He grabbed my hair and yanked me up and started kissing me. Kissing me fast and hard. He began to slow down. I opened my eyes, and he was staring at me. He gave me a peck on the lips and left me in the shower. Terrance and I had never fucked like that since we had been together. Maybe I needed to tell Ty to send me flowers more often.

A few days passed and Terrance never asked anything else about Ty, but he did make me dispose of all the flowers. When I asked Ty why he would send flowers to my house and, on top of that, make out a personalized card with his name on it, he told me he was testing Terrance's love for me, to see if he would just walk out on me. He was actually hoping that he would. That way, he could have me to himself. Ty had already made it clear that he wanted me to leave Terrance and move in with him. I didn't know what the future held for me and Ty, but that was just not about to happen right now, if ever. I had strong feelings for Ty, but I still didn't know him well enough to just get up one day and tell Terrance I was leaving him for another man.

The day of Phelecia's funeral was a sad occasion. When I walked into the church, everyone looked so sad. Police officers were standing all around. I saw Tif, Tasha, and Bri sitting in the row right behind Phelecia's family. They had made it there before me and Terrance. It took us longer because Terrance had to make me get out of bed and get dressed because I didn't wanna go. I couldn't stand the thought of seeing Phelecia in a casket because of a stupid-ass nigga. Terrance and I walked slowly to the front to where Phelecia's lifeless body was. We stood in line to see her, even though I just wanted to sit down. An older woman and Phelecia's children were standing at the casket. I figured that the woman must've been Phelecia's mother. I could hear her saying, "My baby. Why my baby, Lord?" All three of Phelecia's children were crying as if they really knew what was happening.

A girl who looked like an older version of Phelecia with long, thick black hair came up and helped Phelecia's momma and kids to their seats. Terrance and I walked up, and I instantaneously started crying as soon as I saw her. Her hair looked like she had done it herself. It was always so perfect, never a strand out of place. Whoever had picked her clothes had done a good job. She looked like she was just gonna open her eyes and start talking to me, telling me how much Duwan loved her. What I couldn't believe was that she had on a little diamond ring on her wedding finger. Duwan had given it to her about a year ago, promising to marry her. I felt like snatching that shit right off.

When we turned around to go find a seat, Duwan was standing behind us and had the nerve to have tears in his eyes. Terrance got a tight grip on me, knowing I was ready to kick Duwan's ass. We found a seat near my girls and everyone watched as Duwan kneeled down and gave Phelecia a kiss. He started mumbling, but it was too low for anyone to know what he was saying.

Then he burst out crying loudly and then he said, "I didn't mean to, baby! I'm sorry. I'm so sorry! You shouldn't be here." Everyone's eyes widened. "Please wake up!" Duwan began to get out of control, shaking the casket. I could see the officers talking through their walkie-talkies and signaling each other. Two officers walked up behind him. One cop cuffing him and the other reading his rights, right there where Phelecia lay. I knew that if Phelecia could've said anything, she still would've stopped them because she loved Duwan more than anything in the world. She would've even forgiven him for killing her.

I was so happy that Duwan was finally getting what he deserved, even though it was really too late. It wasn't gonna bring Phelecia back, but I wished that it could. I was also glad because it cleared my name. I didn't have to worry about detectives following me around all the time asking me questions or the truth getting back to Terrance. I knew Ty would be glad too. He wouldn't even let me come to his house while the police were following me around. He said he didn't want the neighbors looking at him crazy since he was the only black person on the block. He didn't want them to think he was causing trouble. We would always have to meet somewhere.

After the funeral, Bri and Tasha came and asked me was I going to the repast because they were gonna go with me if I was. I started looking around for Terrance to ask him if he wanted to go. If not, I was just gonna ride with my girls.

"Is Tif going?" I asked. Bri looked at me funny, I guess trying to figure out why I was concerned with Tif after what Bri had told me.

"I don't know. She went to the bathroom," Tasha said. I kept looking around for Terrance. I had lost him when everyone in the church started getting up moving around. He always knew someone, so I figured he was somewhere running his mouth. I never knew so many people knew Phelecia. I finally saw Terrance coming through the doorway. Tif was a few people behind him.

"Here they both come right now," I said. When they got near, I said, "What happened to you, baby?"

"I went looking for the bathroom after I lost you and ran into one of my guys."

"Are you gonna go to the repast?"

"Uh. I really got a lot of work to do at home to get ready for next week, and I need to do some studying for my bar exam in a few weeks."

"Ok then. Well, I'll ride with the girls."

I rode with Tasha and Bri, and Tif told us she'd meet us at the pavilion where the repast was being held.

"Bri, when yo ass gonna start running up your own gas?" I said jokingly.

She thought she was slick. She would always ride with someone else so she wouldn't have to buy any gas. I didn't even blame her though. Gas was high as hell.

"If I'm going to the same place as everybody else, what sense does it make for everybody to drive separate cars? That's just the way I look at it," Bri said, sounding as if she had an attitude.

"You know I'm just messing with you! Don't be so defensive." Everyone got quiet, including Tasha. That wasn't like her.

"How are you and Reg doing, Tasha?" I asked, trying to spark up a new conversation.

"Girl, I left him alone."

"What happened?" I asked, trying my best to sound shocked.

"Nothing. He just wasn't my type, and the negro had the nerve to call me ghetto when we got into an argument the other day. You know I'd been then kicked that nigga's ass. I'm not trying to catch a case."

Bri said, "Girl, he wasn't cute anyway!" I didn't know if Bri was just trying to make Tasha feel good, or she just had bad taste in men cuz Reggie may have pissed me off, but he was fine as hell. Always had been.

When we got to the repast, there weren't many people there yet. Probably because they went to the burial first. I hated going to cemeteries, and so did Bri and Tasha, so we decided to just go straight to the pavilion. The girl who looked just like Phelecia, who I had seen at the church, was already there. Tasha and Bri sat down while I walked over to the girl. Her eyes were puffy just like Phelecia's would get when she would cry over Duwan. She tried to crack a smile when she saw me walking towards her. I gave her a hug because she looked like she needed one.

She started crying. "I'm sorry. It's just so hard," she said. She put her hand in her pocket and pulled out a Kleenex. "Do I know you, or are you a friend of the family?"

"I'm Kellie. I work at the shop where Phelecia works . . . I mean worked. We went to school together too. We had recently become kind of close."

"Oh. I'm Phelecia's sister, Pamela. I went to the same high school, but I'm six years older than y'all, so that's probably why I don't know you."

"Are you the sister that's taking the kids?"

"Yeah, me and Phelecia used to be real close, but I didn't agree with a lot of things she did. I especially didn't agree with her dealing with Duwan, so she had stopped speaking to me, but I feel it's only right to raise her kids."

Pamela was so sweet. She reminded me so much of Phelecia. She sat down and talked to me, Tasha, and Bri until the crowd started coming in. She told us she couldn't stand to go to the cemetery either. I met Phelecia's entire family, including her mom. I remembered when Phelecia had gone out of town to visit her momma because she had been sick. She was an older woman, older than my momma. Phelecia was the youngest of nine kids. Her oldest sibling was forty.

We stayed at the pavilion for a couple of hours. As soon as we got ready to leave, Tif came walking her late ass in the door.

"I am so sorry, y'all. I went home to get out of those uncomfortable clothes and made the mistake of laying down for a couple of minutes."

"That was a long couple of minutes!" I said.

"My butt ended up dozing off. I was more tired than I thought I was." While we were standing there talking, I saw my rival, Stacy.

In the middle of Tif talking to me, I said, "What the hell is she doing here?" Tif, Bri, and Tasha started looking around trying to see who I was talking about.

Tasha said, "Who?"

"I'll be right back," I said.

I walked up to Stacy and said, "Hey, girl!" like we were actually friends.

"Hey! Are you part of the family?

"No. I'm a friend. Phelecia and I worked at the same salon."

"Oh yeah. I forgot you were a beautician."

"I prefer to be called a stylist," I said, trying to sound bougie.

"Yeah. OK." Stacy said, like she had disregarded my last statement. "But anyway, Kellie, I've been needing to talk to you. I guess I ran into you for a reason. Too bad it had to be under the circumstances of my friend's sister's funeral."

"You're friends with Pamela?" I asked.

"I'm friends with the entire family. Have been for years, but I'm best friends with Phelecia's other sister, Patrice."

"So what did you need to talk to me about?"

I had nothing to talk to Stacy about. I had no idea what she possibly had to say to me. It must've been something serious because she started digging for a pen and a piece of paper in her purse. She wrote her number down on a withdrawal slip from the bank.

"Call me as soon as you get a chance. Do me a favor, and don't tell Terrance."

"What, is everyone at the bank planning a surprise party for his birthday or something?" Stacy grinned, which told me that that was exactly what it was about. I had already decided I wasn't calling her ass back. I wasn't doing anything to help her out. Especially so she could try and have a birthday party for my man. He was probably gonna wanna come to Atlanta with me when I went to the hair show anyway. His birthday was during that same week.

After we left, the girls were all in my business asking me who Stacy was. I just told them she was an old client of mine. I didn't want them to know another woman was being flirtatious with my man. I never even addressed it to Terrance because I knew he didn't have any interest in her or anybody else.

Chapter 20

"**M**eet me at Sergio's, Kel. I got somethin' I wanna give you."

Sergio's was a Mexican restaurant where Ty and I would often meet.

"Why don't I just come to your house, Ty?" I asked.

"That's cool. I just didn't want you to have to make that long drive." The whole way to Ty's house, I wondered what he wanted to give me. He always gave me little gifts, like lingerie and perfume, but he never made a specific call just to tell me he wanted to see me because he needed to give me something.

When I finally made it to his house, all anxious and shit, there were two other cars parked in his driveway. One was a cream-colored Cadillac Escalade, and the other was a black BMW that was chromed out. I had been learning a lot about cars lately because Ty would take me to car dealerships at least once a week, showing me what he would put me in if I was all his. That was his way of bribing me, even though he wouldn't admit it. He always told me he didn't have to bribe a woman to do anything, and I believed it. If I had everything he had, I wouldn't ever have to bribe anybody either.

I walked up to his door and rang the doorbell. When he opened the door, I said, "I didn't know you had company."

"Can I get some of those luscious lips first?" I gave him a kiss, then he said, "I didn't have company, but right now I'm having a last-minute business meeting. We'll be done in a few minutes." I sat in the den waiting on Ty. I walked around looking at everything as if I didn't know his house like I knew my own. I could hear Ty and whoever else was in the kitchen with him get louder and louder. They sounded as if they were arguing. I crept towards the kitchen and peeked inside. There were four other men in there with him. They didn't look very professional. They were all in jeans, and two of them wore baseball caps. Ty talked to them like they weren't shit.

"I want y'all to know I don't need y'all. I can easily find some new niggas that would love to have half the money I'm paying y'all. Tell me if y'all don't wanna do the job. If you don't, leave my shit here and gon' about y'all business, but don't come back." Ty paced the floor back and forth like he was a teacher, lecturing to his students. They sat there listening and did not interrupt once.

I revealed myself from around the corner.

"What's up baby?" Ty asked in a completely different tone from the one he was using with the other men. They all looked at me and Ty said, "This is my woman, Mrs. Ty." They all laughed, and I didn't know if I was supposed to laugh after I heard how he had just been talking to them before I walked in the room. "So," Ty continued, "do any of y'all need to leave me anything, besides my money?"

"Naw, man," one of the darker men said. The others just shook their heads.

"Kel, go wait for me in the den. I'll be there in a minute." As I was walking out the kitchen, I heard Ty say, "Give me my cheese." I continued towards the den and sat down and waited.

I finally heard Ty let his guests out. He walked in the den with a black briefcase.

"Were those clients of yours?" I asked.

"Hell naw! My clients got a whole lot more class than those niggas. I hired them to work for me, so I don't have to work so much. They on the verge of gettin' fired." Ty opened the briefcase, and it was full of money. Ty really did have it goin' on. He had people working for him, so he didn't have to work, and he was still paid. He sat there counting out some money and handed it to me.

"What's this for?" I asked.

"This is just one of the many benefits of being with somebody of my stature." I counted it out and it was five thousand dollars.

"Ty, this is way too much. Is this what you called me over here for?"

"Nope. I called you over here to give you this." He pulled a black box out of his pocket.

"You are too sweet. What you want?"

"You know what I want. Don't act stupid. Are you willing to do it?"

"If you're trying to buy me, you can take all of this back." I tried handing him the money and the box, but he pushed it back.

"I'm not tryin' to buy you. I just wanted to give you somethin' nice. Now open it." I opened the box and I was almost blinded by all of the diamonds. Bling was everywhere. There was a diamond tennis bracelet and diamond hoop earrings inside.

"You still wanna give it back? With yo stubborn ass."

"Thank you, Ty."

"I just wanna let you know how much you mean to me. Ain't too many times when I buy a woman shit. Most of the time they don't deserve nothin'. Remember that first night we went out to dinner and I told you I had to show you something, but never did?" I remembered that night quite clearly because since that day I kept wondering what it was he had to show me.

He continued after I acknowledged that I remembered. "Well, this isn't the only black briefcase that I have, and I was gonna show you where I keep all my valuables in case somethin' ever happened to me. I just decided that I wanted to make sure you was loyal and trustworthy first. You've about proven that to me and soon you'll reap all the benefits." Ty made me blush and feel so good all the time. That's why he was so addicting. I wanted to feel the high that he gave me all the time.

After I chilled with Ty for a while and we had wild sex, I had to leave to make sure I made it home before Terrance. I learned my lesson after the first time I almost got caught up. I decided to stop by Tasha's house on my way home to see what my girl was up to. At least then I would have a real alibi.

While I was standing at Tasha's door, knocking, I heard her inside talking to somebody. I figured she was probably on the phone running her big-ass mouth. When she opened the door, the phone wasn't to her ear.

"Hey, Kel!" She stood at the door as if she didn't want me to come in. I pushed her out the way and let myself in. Malik was sitting in her living room half-naked. I just looked at Tasha and shook my head. I didn't understand my friends. They just could not be alone. Tasha had just ended her phony relationship with Reggie, now Malik was right back in the door.

"Hey, Malik," I said in a dry tone. He nodded his head. I hadn't been too fond of Malik since the time he tried to fuck me while Tasha was in her room, passed-out drunk. That was when I was still with my ex-fiancé, Jaleel. Bri, Tif, a couple of other dudes whose names I fail to remember, Malik, and I were chillin' at Tasha's house one night playing spades for shots of Patron. Everybody got fucked up that night, except me and Tif. After the other dudes left, Tif drove Bri home, and I just said I would spend the night with Tasha to make sure she was ok. Malik stayed too, of course. My real reason for staying was to make sure that nigga didn't take advantage of my girl. I found a blanket and laid on the couch. I dozed off for what couldn't have been longer than ten minutes, and this negro is standing over me butt-ass naked and my pants were unzipped. All I remember were his nasty, hairy-ass balls in my face.

"What the fuck!" I said.

"Come on, baby. I saw the way you was lookin' at me while we was playin' spades. I know you feelin' me, so come on," he said, like he honestly believed that I wanted his ugly ass. I kicked his ass out, just the way he was. I didn't care if he had to drive home naked. The next morning, I told Tasha that he was drunk as hell and took all his clothes off. She cracked up when I told her I threw him out with no clothes on.

There was a lot of reason behind me not telling her about Malik trying to fuck me, just like there was reason I didn't tell her that Reggie was only with her to get back at me. I didn't want her to know about me and Reggie, but there was also another reason. Every boyfriend Tasha had ever had, and every dude that she had ever even liked, had always tried to holla' at me. It started from junior high school, and it continued until we got grown. I never meant for any of it to happen, but they were always more interested in me than her. I just didn't want her to feel like it was intentional and mess up our friendship. Tasha was one ghetto-ass chick, but she was my girl for life.

I walked into Tasha's kitchen and said, "What you got to eat in here?"

At the same time as I opened her refrigerator and saw that nothing was in there, she said, "I ain't got shit in there. I don't got nobody to cook for, so I eat out all the time."

"I see that," I said, still looking through her cabinets. Tasha followed me in the kitchen.

"Didn't I tell you I don't got nothing, girl!"

I whispered, "That was quick."

"What?"

"You sure got over Reggie fast."

"That nigga wasn't shit. If he was, he would've realized what he had."

"I heard that." Tasha walked back in the living room and I fixed me a glass of Pepsi. While I was drinking my pop and looking at the pictures on the refrigerator of our crazy asses, I noticed a piece of paper that was underneath one of the magnets. It had Reggie's name and number on it in Reggie's handwriting. I kept opening drawers until I found a pen, and I wrote the number on the inside of my hand.

After I finished drinking my Pepsi, I grabbed my keys off the kitchen counter and told Tasha I'd talk to her later.

"That's all you came over here for was to drink up my Pepsi?"

"Girl, naw. I also came to get some food, but you don't have none!" I laughed and walked out the door.

Tasha screamed after me, "I'm gon' beat yo ass hoe!" Tasha and I used to always talk to each other like that. It seemed like that's when we were closest. If we weren't calling each other bitches, hoes, or sluts, people knew something wasn't right with us.

On my way from Tasha's house, I opened my phone and dialed the number from Tasha's refrigerator. I had a mouth full for Reggie's ass.

"Hello," Reggie said.

"Well, what's up, negro!"

"Oh, you finally decided to call."

I decided to play it out like the shit he did didn't bother me at first, so I lied and said, "Yeah, I didn't call before because you didn't even deserve to hear my voice for the shit you did," knowing I didn't call because I couldn't find that muthafucker's phone number. "How you gon' sit up there and use my girl like that?"

"You ain't much of a friend to let your girl be played like a fool just so you don't have to bust yourself out."

"Don't talk to me about friends. I thought we were supposed to be friends, but apparently not. I have gone through so much with you, and you sit there and do me like that."

"Kel, I'll never get over the fact that you rejected me after knowing how much I loved you. I still love you. If I didn't, I wouldn't have gone to the extremes I did to get your attention. You should be flattered, if anything. After getting rid of my baby, I still wanted to be with you."

I was ready to finish snapping on Reggie, until he mentioned the part about me getting rid of his baby. That hurt bad as hell. I just didn't think he realized how bad.

A couple of months before graduation, Reggie and I partied together a lot and most of the time, we would be so drunk, we would have sex without even thinking to use a rubber. The next month, I didn't get a period. I didn't think much of it. I just thought that maybe I was late because I was so excited about graduation. In other words, I was in denial. Within a couple of weeks, I started getting flu-like symptoms. I couldn't eat anything. Reality hit, and I told Reggie, so he went and got me a pregnancy test and brought it to my house while my momma was at work. Reggie followed me in the bathroom like he was gonna help.

"I know how to pee on a stick by myself! What! . . . You wanna hold it for me?" I asked. I slammed the door in his face, and he waited outside, constantly asking me stupid ass questions during an uncomfortable moment. Finally, I let out a long, high-pitched scream that let him know what those dreadful results were.

I came out the bathroom, and Reggie wrapped his arms around me, and I remember him saying, "Everything is gonna be fine. We can do this." I wasn't feeling what he was talking about. I wasn't ready to be a momma. I was too young and had way too many things I wanted to do, like party.

I told Reggie that I planned on having an abortion, and he refused to have any part in it. He begged me not to, but I told him I would, with or without him. I told him it wasn't up to him because it was my body. I had to come up with the four hundred dollars by myself since he wouldn't give me half. I was so pissed at him. I couldn't understand why he wanted to bring that baby into this world, but that last night when we were together, and he asked me to be his woman, I realized that we could've made it work and I was depressed about aborting the baby for a long time. It amazed me back then how he still could've wanted to be with me after I did something so hurtful to him without even being considerate of his feelings. Who knows where life would've taken us if we parented that child together. That's why I had such strong ties with Reggie that would probably never go away.

"Kel, you still there?" Reggie asked.

"Yeah. I'm here. Look Reggie, like I told you before, If I would've run into you before I decided to get married, we might've had another chance, but this is really bad timing." I knew I was full of shit because I met Ty after I ran into Reggie at the license branch, but I gave Ty a chance. I felt bad for having to keep on rejecting Reggie because I truly did love him, but only like a good friend. Our phone conversation turned completely around from how it was meant to go. I was supposed to go off on him, hang up, and never talk to him again, but I couldn't do that. Not to Reggie. He was really a good guy. He just didn't handle rejection well.

Reggie and I ended our conversation by promising that we'll forever be friends, and nothing would ever come between that. I told him that I still better not ever see him out anywhere with another woman, or next time I was gonna kick his ass, no matter where we were! By the time we got off the phone, I was pulling up at home.

Chapter 21

I had a week to finalize my reservations and everything else for my trip to Atlanta. I asked Terrance if he wanted to go, especially since his birthday was that week. I thought it would be nice to celebrate it in the "A". He said no because he knew that he wouldn't get any work or studying done. I hated to go by myself, but Tif and Tasha had to work, and Bri didn't have the money. During the week before I left, I had to really stretch and divide my time between Terrance and Ty. Terrance and I went out to dinner a few times that week. How he got the time off, I had no idea, but I wasn't complaining. The only time I did complain was when Terrance wanted to go out during Ty's time. Unfortunately, Ty had to wait until next time, but he wasn't that patient. He would find out where Terrance and I were going and he would "coincidentally" show up at the same place and watch me and Terrance the whole night.

One day, before I left on my trip, I took the time to go see my mother. My life had been so hectic lately that I hadn't made time for her.

"Look what the wind blew in!" she said when she opened the door.

"Hey, Momma," I said and gave her a hug.

"Did you gain some weight, girl? Your face look a little round."

"No. I don't think so. I look fat?"

"No, you look good. You needed some meat on them bones." I was never skinny. I just wasn't thick like Tif. She had a nice shape that I envied. She could make anything she wore look good.

Out of nowhere, my momma said, "Y'all about to give me a grandbaby or what? 'Cause that's sure what it's lookin' like."

"No ma'am. Not right now."

"What y'all waitin' on?"

"Until Terrance finishes law school and gets a permanent job with this law firm. It's looking good so far."

"That's good." I sat and talked to my momma for a few hours. I helped her cook dinner. It felt good to spend some time with her, and she was excited to see me. I was her only child. That's why I meant so much to her.

After I left my momma's house, I went to the mall to see if I could find a couple of new outfits and some new shoes for my trip. Every year, everyone showed out at the hair shows. Everyone looked their best and all you saw was Gucci, Prada, Fendi, Coach, and every other brand name all around. The hair show was one place you couldn't go wearing something without a name because somebody was gonna ask who you were wearing. I still had the money Ty had given me, but I didn't want to spend all of it on clothes. I wanted to save some of it for when I got there.

As soon as I walked in the mall, I saw a bad ass strapless jumpsuit in the window of this store called Lady Style. I went in, found it in my size and bought it without even looking at the price tag. I think that was the first time I ever bought something without doing that. I was so cheap a lot of times that I checked the price on a pack of gum! I guess I could shop like that when I was spending somebody else's money. I walked around and shopped some more. I was about to be hot in Hotlanta. When I was getting ready to leave the mall, I walked past a men's clothing store, which reminded me I needed to buy Terrance something for his birthday.

I decided that when I got back from Atlanta, I was gonna get
Terrance to go out to a couple of clubs with me and dance like we
used to, so I started looking for him some club gear. I found him a
nice, casual Rocawear outfit that I knew would look good on him.
While I was looking for a thirty-six in the pants, I heard a familiar
voice talking to one of the salesclerks. I looked between the racks
trying to see who is was, and it was who I thought it was.

"Tif." Tif looked my way and told the clerk she'd be right
back.

"What you doin' in here, girl?" I asked, wondering if that new
man of hers already had her buying him clothes.

"Girrrrl. My man bought me this gorgeous necklace, and I feel
guilty for not buying him anything. That's the only reason I'm
buying him a goddamn thing. Oh yeah, isn't Terrance's birthday
coming up?"

"Yeah. I picked this up for him. You like it?" I showed her the
outfit I had picked out for Terrance.

"Uh," she said, sounding like she didn't really care for it, "It's
ok, but I think you could find something nicer."

I looked at it again and said, "Yeah. You right. I'm gonna go to
a couple of more stores before I leave this mall to see if I can find
something that suites him perfectly. You about to stay in here or
you gon' come look with me?"

"I'm about to look around in here a little longer, but I'll talk to
you later, girl."

I ended up finding a way better outfit and shoes for Terrance in
another store. It looked more like his style. I took it to the mall's
customer service center to get it gift-wrapped. While I was waiting,
I called Ty to see what he was doing.

"Hey, baby. I'm in the middle of a meeting right now. I'll call
you later," he said softly and quickly. I could remember when Ty
wouldn't even answer the phone when he was in a meeting, but
since I had become so important in his life, he answered the phone
almost every time I called.

Ty called me back about five minutes later.

"That was quick," I said as soon as I picked up the phone.

"Yeah. I was at the end of my meeting. What's up?"

"Nothing. I was just calling to tell you I was thinking about you."

"I'm always thinkin' about you, and I can't wait 'til you get home from Atlanta."

I frowned in confusion and said, "I haven't even gone to Atlanta yet."

"I know. I want you to go and hurry back. I'm gon' miss yo fine ass."

I started my blushing again and said, "I'm gonna miss you too, baby."

The morning I was set to leave for Atlanta, I handed Terrance his birthday gift to make sure he had it on his birthday.

"Make sure to wait to open it on your birthday. I'm not playing!"

"Don't worry about me. You just hurry up and finish gettin' packed. You are gonna be late for your own funeral."

Terrance was right. I was late for everything. It was already nine-thirty, and my flight was due to leave at noon. I knew I was gonna need my iPod on the plane, so I started lookin' all over the house for it. I was going through drawers and everything else like a mad woman.

"What you lookin' for, Kel?"

I stopped in my tracks and said, "My iPod. You seen it?"

"Nope. You just better hurry up and get ready. You know how that traffic is on the way to the airport."

"OK. Let me just look one more place." I went and looked in the washer and dryer, and there it was, at the bottom of the washer. My poor pink iPod. I went back in the room all frowned up.

"What now?"

"Terrance, can you do me a tiny favor?" I asked

"What you need?" I paused before telling him because I knew he was gonna be mad since he bought me that iPod.

"Can you please go to Wal-Mart real quick and get me another iPod? I accidentally washed mine."

"Unh-uh. Hell naw. You really wanna spend two hundred dollars on another Ipod today, when you're about to go out of town. Where you just get all this money to blow?"

"Please, baby. I need something to listen to on the plane. Tips at work have been good." Terrance jumped up, grabbed his keys, and walked out the door.

I ran to the screen door and said, "Thank you, baby!"

I ran upstairs and finished packing my clothes. When I made sure I had everything, I started dragging my luggage down the stairs, and when I made it to the front door, Mike was standing there in some khaki shorts and a wife beater. He opened the screen door for me as I pulled one bag outside.

"Where you going?" he asked.

"I'm goin' to Hotlanta, baby."

"That sounds nice. Why didn't you ask me?"

"Yeah. Very funny."

"I'm being very serious. I would've liked to be able to spend some time alone with you, away from everything." I let go of my bag and looked in Mike's eyes. He was dead serious. "Kellie, I came over here when I saw Terrance leave because something has been on my mind, and I just had to get it off my chest as soon as I had the opportunity."

"Is something wrong?" I asked with a concerned look on my face. Mike really did look like something had been troubling him.

"I know we haven't spent any real time together. I would really like to take you out one day to show you how good of a time we could have. Let me get to the point, because I think I've told you everything I can besides one thing." There was a moment of silence. Mike looked at me and shook his head. "I love you, Kel."

I didn't know why I did at the moment, and Lord knows I tried to stop myself, but I started crying. Not boo-hoo crying, but my tear ducts immediately filled up, and tears just started streaming down my face. I guess because I could tell Mike was really sincere when it came out of his mouth.

"I love everything about you. I love the way you dress, the way you wear your hair, the perfume you wear, your smile, the little dimple in your chin, your laugh, everything. I know you're married, but you're always on my mind. While you're gone, just think about giving me a chance. I promise I'll make you happy."

I gave Mike a hug. Not just an ordinary hug. It was long and heartfelt, just like the words he had said to me.

When the moment ended, Mike finished helping me put my bags in my car.

"You driving yourself to the airport?"

"No, Terrance is gonna drive me." As soon as I said that, Terrance pulled up. He got out the car and handed me my bag. "Thank you. I appreciate it!" I said. Terrance brought out the last bag and waited outside, talking to Mike while I went back in to get my purse and everything else I needed. After my talk with Mike, I started feeling like I shouldn't leave, but I knew that I needed some time to myself.

On the way to the airport, Terrance and I talked and laughed all the way through all that hectic traffic. Terrance talked to me about how nervous and excited he was to take the bar exam in a couple of weeks. I let him know that he didn't have anything to worry about, especially with all the studying and hard work he had put into becoming an attorney. He told me that he was gonna use the time while I was away to prepare himself for everything, so I felt like this short absence from each other would be a good thing for the both of us.

Terrance and I had been having such a good time talking, we barely realized it when we made it to the airport. We were really cutting it close. It was already eleven-thirty, and I still had to go through the whole routine of checking in my luggage, being searched, and everything else airports take you through since the September 11th terrorist attacks. I just knew I was gonna miss my flight and have to wait on another one, but I made it. I gave Terrance a kiss and a hug.

While I hugged him, he whispered in my ear and said, "Keep it warm for me, baby."

"Don't worry, I will," I replied. I told Terrance I would call him as soon as I got there and that I loved him.

My flight seemed long and rough. My ears kept popping and I had forgotten to bring some gum. I was usually comfortable flying because I flew so often, but I began feeling so many turbulences that I got a little scared. I tried to listen to my music to relax my mind, but I kept turning it off to make sure I could hear everything the pilot and the flight attendants were saying.

At the end of the flight, I couldn't wait to get off that plane. I vowed to myself that I would never fly alone again, even if I had to drag somebody with me next time. I had rented a car from Enterprise Car Rental, so I walked over to pick my car up and drove myself to the hotel. I was anxious to see the hotel where I had chosen to stay because it was one of the more expensive ones, so I knew it had to be nice.

The people at the front desk were very courteous, unlike the people around where I was from. People had to be so ignorant and ghetto all the time. The front desk clerk gave me my key to my room and told me that she hoped I would enjoy my stay. She signaled a young black guy to come over and help me with my luggage. I asked him his name and he told me it was David and didn't say another word. The hotel was twelve stories, and my room was on the eleventh floor. I always thought that the suites were on the upper levels, and I knew I had reserved a standard single room because that's all that I could afford, and I didn't' plan on spending that much time in my room anyway. I began thinking that maybe the hotels in Atlanta were different, and had standard rooms, as well as suites on the upper levels. David and I got on the elevator and headed to my room.

When I finally reached my floor, we stepped off of the elevator and saw that there was a game room, pool and Jacuzzi, and a large picture window with a beautiful view. All of the rooms had double doors. I looked at my key and it said room 1127. I walked down the long hall until I finally found my room. I stuck in the keycard and opened the double doors.

"What the hell?" I said under my breath, with confusion evident in my voice. I walked around the room. There was a living room almost larger than my own, a bedroom with a king-sized bed, and what had to be an eighty-inch plasma TV. There was also a kitchen with appliances and a snack bar. I had only seen this in the movies. I told David thank you and gave him a tip. He then left me alone with my luggage.

I thought of not saying anything to the desk clerk, but I knew they had made a mistake, and I didn't want to have to end up paying for it later. I left my luggage in the room and went back downstairs to the front desk.

The same lady who had previously helped me said with her country accent, "Back so soon? Is there something wrong with your room, ma'am?"

"I think you made a mistake. I'm on the eleventh floor in a suite."

She started tapping the keys on her computer and said, "What was your name again?"

"Moore. Kellie Moore."

"Let's see Ms. Moore," she said as she stared at the screen. "Yes. That's correct. You upgraded your room from a single to a deluxe suite."

"No. That's impossible. I lowered my voice so that everyone couldn't hear my business. "I don't have the money for that room. You have to have something else." "Well, it's already paid for. It was paid for under a credit card with the name T. Wesley on it. Do you know him or her?"

Ty had upgraded my room. He just didn't stop. He kept telling me he wanted me to have the best of everything, but I was not expecting this. This trip was gonna be better than I expected. I was livin' it up on somebody else's money, and it felt real good.

"Ma'am, did you want me to see if we have another single room?"

"Oh no. That's ok. Thank you."

I went back up to my room, I mean suite, and jumped on the bed like a big kid and started screaming. It felt like I was living a dream. After I was finished screaming and jumping around in excitement, I called Ty.

"What's up, baby? How's your room?" he said, trying to act like he didn't know anything, so I played right along with him.

"Oh, it's all right. I should've gotten a larger room. It's just standard."

"Standard? You for real?"

"I'm just playin', boo. Thank you for the upgrade. It's very nice."

"I was about to say. I was about to call to that desk and cuss somebody out, all that money I spent."

"I just called to say thank you. Let me get settled in, and I'll call you a little later."

I rushed off the phone with Ty because I knew I needed to call Terrance to let him know that I made it. I tried calling his cell phone and the house, but I didn't get an answer. I figured he had probably gone back to sleep since we woke up extra early, so I left him a message. I was pretty hungry since the food on the plane was shitty. After seeing my room, I wished that Ty had upgraded my flight from coach to first class. That would've been very nice, but maybe I was being too greedy.

I saw a book with a list of restaurants and events going on in Atlanta sitting on the living room table, so I skimmed through it to see if anything interested me. There was so much to do, so much to choose from, but I felt kinda tired from my flight. I hadn't ever had jetlag before, but I guess there's a first time for everything. I decided to order some room service instead and just relax until later that evening. After my food arrived, I ate and fell asleep while watching television.

I was awakened by a noise that sounded like it was coming from near the door. I figured that it came from out in the hall, so I closed my eyes and tried to go back to sleep, but then I heard another noise. It was a toilet flushing, and I knew that I shouldn't be able to hear somebody else using the bathroom in the next suite, so I got up, and as soon as I walked past my bathroom, Ty came walking out.

"Shit, negro!" I said as I grabbed my chest. Ty stood there laughing so hard, he couldn't get his words out.

"You should've saw yo face, Kel. That was hilarious!"

"You almost gave me a heart attack, boy! What is wrong with you?" Then I thought about it. "What are you doing here?"

"When you told me you were coming to Atlanta, I realized I had some business to take care of over this way, so I decided to come during the same time you did, so we could spend some real quality time together, without you having to get up and leave me."

I knew there had to be a catch to Ty upgrading my room. He wanted it for his own pleasure.

"Why you look mad? You not happy to see me?"

"Would you have upgraded my room if you didn't come?"

"How you gon' ask me a stupid question like that? You know I would've still done it. Can I at least have a hug or somethin'?" I slowly slid across the floor and wrapped my arms around his shoulders. I was glad that I had someone to hang out with while I was in Atlanta, but I knew I still wasn't gonna be able to do some deep thinking with a clear head like I had planned. On a positive note, maybe by spending this time with Ty, I would be able to see if he was who I really wanted to be with.

It was what they called Downtown Atlanta Restaurant Week at the time, which meant during the whole week, selected restaurants had three-course meals for twenty-five dollars per person. Our first night there, Ty and I went to an Italian restaurant called Tringali's. They had the best cheese garlic bread I had ever tasted in my life. It was so good, I didn't even need to order an entrée, but I did anyway. After dinner, we went to the Sutra Lounge and did some dancing. We had so much fun, but what was gonna be interesting was being in Ty's presence during the entire night.

After arriving back at the hotel, as soon as we walked in the room, Ty began undressing me. I stopped him and reminded him that we didn't need to rush. We had the next few days together, without interruptions.

Just then, the hotel phone rang. Ty walked towards it, and I said, "No! It could be Terrance." I ran and picked it up, and as I suspected, it was Terrance.

"Sorry I didn't get your call earlier. I was knocked out."

"I figured that. That's why I left you a message."

"How's everything goin'?" he asked.

"Everything is so nice out here. It's busy."

I saw Ty walk in the bathroom. He never liked to hear my phone conversations with Terrance.

"I wish you could be here with me, Terrance. We would have so much fun."

"We'll have to make another trip out there together, then." I missed Terrance a little bit, even though I had been having so much fun with Ty. Maybe all Terrance and I needed was some time away together. Before I made a major decision about what I wanted to do, I needed to know was there any way to fix the damage with me and Terrance, because there was a lot of it.

I ended my conversation with Terrance, and Ty came in the room looking pissed the fuck off.

I looked at him and asked him if there was a problem, and he responded by raising his voice, saying, "I can't believe you up in my room talkin' to another nigga, talkin' about you wish he could be here with you. Bitch, what the fuck kind of shit is that?" I stopped him before he dug himself deeper in a hole. Ty had never called me out of my name, and it was not about to start.

"Bitch? Who the hell you callin' a bitch!"

"I'm just pissed the fuck off. After all this shit I den done for you, you still on that nigga's dick. You know how many women would love to be with me?"

"Well, go and get those other women and leave me the hell alone then, if it's that easy." Ty jumped at me like he was about to hit me. I tried to act like I wasn't scared, but truth was, I was scared as hell. I had never had a man hit me or even attempted to hit me, but I knew I wouldn't tolerate it. I could never understand how women stayed with a man who beat them every time they felt like it.

Ty backed up, gave me the evilest look he could've probably given, and walked out, slamming the door behind him. I didn't cry. I didn't do anything. I just stood there, still in shock. After a while, I soaked in the Jacuzzi and then went to bed. When I woke up later in the night, Ty was lying beside me with his arms around me. I looked at the table next to my bed and there was a vase full of red roses sitting there. I guess that was his way of saying he was sorry because he knew his ass had been trippin' earlier.

The next day was like nothing had happened. He never mentioned it and never even said he was sorry. He watched me as I got ready for the hair show. I was getting all jazzed up. I put on my baby-blue and white summer dress that tied around the neck and the back. There was a keyhole in the middle, exposing the middle section of my chest. I wore my white thong wedges, and of course, carried a matching baby-blue and white bag. Ty wouldn't go with me because he said he had a meeting that evening. I didn't really care. I didn't mind looking good all by my damn self.

The hair show ended up being a hit. Those stylists knew what the hell they were doing. Of course, most of the styles were styles that normal people wouldn't wear on any normal day, but the hard work and talent that was put into those styles was what was important. I thought about entering one year, but I knew I needed to learn how to do more exotic looking things before I took that step. After going to this hair show, I decided that I would be ready by next year to enter.

After I got back to the room, Ty wasn't back yet. He had told me that his meeting shouldn't be long, but I was gone a little over three hours, and he had left before me. I didn't take my clothes off, because I knew Ty would probably wanna go out somewhere when he got back. I fell asleep sitting in the leather reclining chair while I was watching TV. I woke up to Ty shaking me. He was sweating like he had been working out.

"Kel, get up. Get yo shit together. We gotta go." I moved slowly, but panicking at the same time.

"What's goin' on, Ty?"

"Just hurry up. Some of my clients ain't too happy with me." Ty was just grabbing shit, throwing it in bags. I went in the bathroom to grab my curling irons and makeup bag off the sink. I heard a loud noise coming from the living room and then heard voices. I was scared, so I stayed in the bathroom and crouched underneath the sink. The voices seemed like they were getting closer and closer.

"Mr. Wesley. You thought you could get over on us with that bullshit-ass product you had your boys to give us? I thought we was better than that," I could hear one of the men saying.

"I was set up, Bones. I gave my boys the right shit. They was pretty upset with me about a few things, so they must've replaced the good shit with some bullshit, but it will be taken care of," Ty said.

I could see the bottom half of two other men who were dressed in suits, holding guns. They didn't say anything. They seemed like they were Bone's bodyguards.

I still didn't understand what was going on until something that Bones said made it quite clear.

He said, "Ty, you know we go way back in the world of drug trafficking, and I've never had a problem with nothin' I ever got from you, but now this is a problem. When I buy over one million dollars worth of crack from you at one time and the shit is bad, that poses a problem for both me and you. I should kill yo ass right now for making me look bad . . ."

Ty tried to butt in by saying, "Bones . . ."

Bones raised his voice and said, "Nigga! I'm not done talkin'. I'll tell you when I want you to speak. The customer is always right. Now, like I was sayin', I should kill yo ass, but I still need my product, so you betta get me the good shit by tomorrow or yo ass is mine. Don't try to run either. Just get me the shit, and you won't have to worry about shit."

That right there explained a lot, like Ty's mansion, his nice-ass cars, his workers, all the nice gifts, and all the damn money. He was a drug dealer and not one of those wannabes either. He was a big-time drug dealer, dealing with millionaires. People were dropping millions of dollars at his feet in one whop. I saw Bones walk past the bathroom, and his men followed behind.

After the door closed, Ty said, "Kel. Come out, baby. Everything's all right."

I crawled from up under the bathroom sink and peeked around the corner before I came out. Ty was sittin' on the bed, shaking his head. "That's one of my biggest clients. Those boys don't know who they fuckin' with, messin' with one of my best clients."

"Somebody threatening to kill you, and all you worried about is losing them as one of your clients? Are you stupid? You are such a liar. How you gon' sit there and tell me that you own your own business and you distribute your product all across the country?" I thought about that shit after it came out of my mouth. Technically, Ty didn't lie, but he didn't come out and tell me he was a drug dealer either.

"Kel, would you have talked to me if I told you I was a drug lord?"

"Hell to the naw!"

"Exactly. I'm sick of dealing with the women that just go along with me bein' who I am just cuz they think they're gonna get somethin' out the deal. The gold-diggin' scallywags. I wanted an independent woman, like you, but as soon as I tell a woman like you what I really do, she won't give me a second look."

"Get a real fuckin' job, then maybe you won't have that problem."

"Then I also won't have all the nice things that I have because I can't get a good job because of my record. I'm comfortable with the way I live, and I plan on keepin' it that way." I really wasn't trying to hear any of the nonsense Ty was trying to tell me. I was still scared and paranoid as hell. There is no way I could live this type of life. That's when I decided I would be on a flight back to Chicago the next morning and never talk to Ty again.

Chapter 22

My feelings were very strong for Ty. Before I found out what he did for a living, I had actually considered leaving my good husband, who had a legit job, for Ty. I felt so stupid. Not because I was gonna leave Terrance, but because I was so naïve not to know that Ty was dealing drugs.. All the signs were right in front of me, but I guess I was blinded by love, just like Phelecia was. Ty had to stay in Atlanta to make sure all his business was taken care of and that there were no hard feelings between him and his client. He begged me to stay with him, but I told him that I didn't want to be subjected to that type of life. It wasn't healthy for me or for him, but he wasn't trying to hear that.

Ty went with me to the airport. I gave him a long hug and a kiss before I boarded the plane.

"See you later," I said. I had tears in my eyes because even though I hadn't told Ty I didn't want to see him anymore, I knew that I had every intention to avoid any contact with him whatsoever. It was gonna hurt so bad because he had become an important part of my life. He was now a constant and no longer a variable. I was just glad that I had found out the truth before I went running my mouth, telling Ty that while in Atlanta, I had taken a pregnancy test and found out that there was a possibility that I was pregnant with his child. That was the last thing he needed to know.

I hoped that one day, Ty would recognize that all the money in the world could never buy him happiness. Like the happiness that I was about to try and recover with my husband. I think that Ty had an idea that we wouldn't see each other again after he made it back to Chicago, because of the way he looked me in my eyes with sadness. We were complete opposites, and I guess the saying opposites attract was correct; however, opposites weren't always right for each other.

On the plane ride home, I thought about Mike. I thought about him because he had a good job, nice car, nice house, but I ended up dealing with someone like Ty, opposed to him. I believed Mike when he told me he loved me, and I believed that he could probably make me happy, but I decided that I was gonna give my marriage another chance. I don't know what went wrong from the beginning, but I wanted to fix it. The crazy thing was, was that Terrance didn't even realize anything was wrong with our marriage and had no idea what it had been going through during the past few months. He was ignorant to it all. Since it was Terrance's birthday, I didn't tell him I was coming home. I would just catch a cab home and surprise him. He really wanted me to be able to spend his birthday with him and now he would get his wish.

My cab pulled up in front of the house and my car was sitting in the driveway. Mike was outside watering his flowers, and stopped as soon as I stepped out of the cab. The cab driver got out to help me with my bags, but before he could grab anything, Mike was over there handling his business.

"You back so soon?" he asked.

"Yeah. Long story. Have you seen Terrance today?"

"Yeah, I saw him a little while ago. He parked in the garage." I went and unlocked the front door and looked around. The house looked empty. Maybe Terrance left without Mike seeing, I thought to myself. I went back outside to go pay the cab driver, but he was already pulling off.

"I took care of it," Mike said as he walked up to the house with all my bags.

After he brought them in, I told him thank you. He asked if I had thought about what we discussed, and I told him I had and that we would talk about it later. I hadn't talked to Terrance all day, not even to tell him happy birthday, and the sun was already going down, so that was the first thing on my list of priorities.

I walked Mike out and he went back to watering his flowers. When I walked in the house, I walked into the den, looking for the phone. That's when I saw an unwrapped box sitting on the couch. I opened the box, and it wasn't the gift that I had bought Terrance. It was the Rocawear outfit that I had picked up in the other store when Tif told me to look for something nicer. I felt like I was losing my mind. For a minute, I thought that maybe I had been so stressed out that I didn't remember going back getting that outfit. I found the phone and dialed Terrance's cell number as I walked up the stairs. When I got to the upstairs hallway, I heard a cell phone ringing. Terrance's voice mail popped on, and I no longer heard the ringing in the house. I figured he must've left his phone at home.

My bedroom door was slightly cracked. I walked in and to my surprise, found Tif in the doggy-style position, and Terrance was banging the shit out of her. They were so into it, they didn't even hear me come in. They were breathing and moaning too hard and loud to hear a thing. I guess that was what they called birthday pussy. I stood there thinking about all the times I had knowingly left them alone, thinking I could trust my girl. I thought about all the times Terrance was supposedly working late, and Tif was supposedly out on dates with her "man". I thought about how Tif was always trying to keep tabs on where I was, and when I was coming home. I thought about how Tif tried turning Bri against me. I thought about Phelecia's repast, when Terrance said he had work to do at home, and Tif didn't arrive until it was almost over. Then, I thought about the cum stains on my sheets in the guest room where Tif had been sleeping. They were the stains from my husband. I didn't know what to do, so I did the first thing that came to mind. I ran and jumped on Terrance's back and started beating him upside the head with the cordless phone. I startled the both of them. While Terrance turned over and tried to hold me down, Tif was hurrying trying to put her clothes on. I was screaming uncontrollably, not thinking about anything that came out of my mouth.

"You nasty-ass bitch! Everything I did for your ass, you do this to me."

As Tif was trying to pull her pants over her hips, she said, "You did this shit to yourself. You were just asking for somebody to take your man, cuz you're stupid as fuck. Don't you know how many women would love to have a man like Terrance? Well, guess what, he's mine now!"

"Yo ass must wanna die like your muthafuckin' daddy did, bitch!"

I was still wrestling with Terrance, trying to get up, and he said, "Calm down. You don't even have the right to be callin' nobody nasty or no shit like that. I gave you everything I could and treated you the best that I knew how. I try to come home and surprise you for lunch and see you in the window fuckin' another nigga' on my living room couch!"

I remembered that day. The day I ran into Reggie at the license branch, and he came home with me. After we fucked in the living room, I checked my messages, and Terrance had left a message saying that he was gonna come home for lunch, but he'd "probably just pick up a burger or something." I couldn't believe Terrance had known about Reggie this whole time. My whole world had just turned upside down in a matter of seconds, and I had never felt the pain I was feeling ever before in my life. I wouldn't even wish that amount of pain on my worst enemy.

I started crying like a baby and said, "Terrance, I love you."

"You don't love me, Kel. You love yourself and whoever else you been messing around with."

That hurt so bad for Terrance to think that I didn't love him. Tif stood there with her arms folded, looking down at me. I screamed, "Get out of my fuckin' house!" Terrance stood up next to Tif and I saw him grab her hand.

"She ain't going nowhere. You get the fuck out. She's the one who's been there for me when you should've been!" I couldn't stop crying. My head felt like it was about to explode. Just then, I ran in the bathroom and almost didn't make it to the toilet to throw up. I couldn't stand to be there any longer. I ran out the bathroom and pushed them both out the way and said, "Fuck both of y'all! This shit ain't right and y'all both know it!"

I ran down the stairs and grabbed my purse and keys out of the den. I was about to leave out, but then I went back in the den and grabbed the box with the outfit Tif had bought Terrance. I threw it out in the street. Mike was still outside. He ran behind me as I was running to my car.

"Just leave me alone, Mike. I can't take any more."

"What's wrong, Kel? Whatever it is can be fixed!"

"No, Mike. It can't. It should've been you. It would've been worth all of this if I had chosen you."

"It's not too late, Kel." I gave Mike a peck on his wet lips and got in my car. I went in reverse and drove over the clothes I threw in the street, and my tires shrieked as I put my car back in drive and flew down the street.

I didn't know where I was going. I felt like I was trying to drive long enough to leave the pain behind, but every minute that went by, I felt worse and worse. The sun had completely gone down and I was still driving. I finally decided to stop near my favorite picnicking spot at Whitebeach Park. I reached over on the passenger's seat and tried to grab my purse. Everything fell out, including Stacy's phone number. I looked at it and then threw it back in my purse. Then I saw a small torn piece of paper. I picked it up and noticed that it was the piece of paper on which I had written the phone number of the person who had hung up on me when I answered Terrance's phone a few weeks ago. I stared at it for a moment and quickly grabbed Stacy's number back out of my purse. The two numbers were identical. I remembered how many times the number was in Terrance's phone. It hit me. That's what Stacy wanted to talk to me about. She was having an affair with my husband, too. It was just pain on top of pain. Too much for me to handle.

I opened my glove box and pulled out two sheets of paper. I found a pen in the mess that had poured out of my purse onto the passenger seat. I began to write a letter. After I finished writing my letter, I opened my cell phone and slowly dialed Stacy's number.

"Hello," Stacy answered in her perky voice.

"Hello, Stacy?" I said, as if I didn't know if it was her or not.

"Who is this?"

"It's Kellie."

"Ooooh, girl, you sound bad. Are you all right?"

"I'm ready to talk, but I wanna talk in person."

"Oh, now you wanna talk!"

"Stacy, get over yourself and just meet me on the west side of Whitebeach Park."

Stacy hesitated and then said, "OK, but only because you sound like shit. Give me about fifteen minutes."

After I hung up the phone from Stacy, I got a call from Terrance's cell phone. I couldn't even bring myself to answer it. I didn't have shit to say to him, and he shouldn't have had shit to say to me. Terrance left a voice message, but I didn't check it. I waited about ten minutes for Stacy, then I folded the letter I wrote and scribbled Stacy's name on the outside of it. I rolled my window up until a crack was left, then I stuck the letter in there so that it would stick out, and rolled the window up as far as it would go. I put everything back in my purse, except for my Derringer, and reminisced about me and Terrance's days as a happy couple, the good times I had with Tasha, Bri, and even Tif, and I thought about my momma and everything she ever told me about life. Especially the part about not trusting women. I thought about the recent decisions that I had made and how things could've been different if my decisions were different. Then again, maybe they wouldn't have been different. Maybe Terrance would've still cheated with Tif and Stacy. I began crying harder and harder. My head, my chest, everything was throbbing. I just wanted the pain to instantly be gone. I took my gun that I had never used, the one that my cheating husband bought for me to protect myself, and put it up to my temple. I closed my eyes tightly, and then I heard something. I reopened my eyes and saw lights shining, coming my way. I tightly closed my eyes once more, and as my life flashed before my eyes, I pulled the trigger.

QIANA RAE

The End

www.ingramcontent.com/pod-product-compliance
Lightning Source LLC
Chambersburg PA
CBHW031313120626
46554CB00001BA/392